RUIN HER LIFE

NJ MOSS

First published in 2023 by Bloodhound Books.

www.bloodhoundbooks.com

Print ISBN: 978-1-5040-8670-7

For Patricia, without whom this book would not exist

1

ABBIE

Abbie walked into the classroom, her eyes aching from lack of sleep. Her body was aching too. She'd worked eleven hours in the bar the day before, and this morning, she'd worked another five in the shop.

She thought of her children, Becky and Chris. She was there to talk to Becky's teacher.

She made herself smile as Ms Lancaster rose from the desk. Abbie found herself resenting the other woman for how well-rested she looked.

Abbie reminded herself, as she often did, that it wasn't *their* fault – anybody she might aim her rage at – her husband had passed away.

It wasn't their fault all she wanted was to sleep and forget.

Ms Lancaster hadn't fired the cancer into Jack's lungs. The cigarettes had taken care of that.

"Hello, Abbie," Ms Lancaster said.

Abbie knew she was beyond tired when she almost snapped. Ms Lancaster was looking at her as though they were friends. That wouldn't be an issue if Abbie didn't want to tear her head off. Surely, Ms Lancaster knew why she was there.

There was no shame.

"I wanted to speak with you about something you said to my daughter."

"I see." Ms Lancaster sat and pulled her chair in.

She seemed to expect Abbie to do the same. When she didn't, Ms Lancaster sighed, as if she was disappointed by Abbie's lack of manners. Abbie felt thirteen, not her actual age of thirty-nine.

There was a danger in seeing things which weren't there: in imagining insults which didn't exist. Abbie had often felt it when dealing with teachers, doctors, anybody in *posh jobs*, as Jack had called them. Normally, she wilted under the pressure, going along with whatever they suggested.

But Ms Lancaster had suggested something truly warped, and her airy couldn't-care-less attitude was pissing Abbie off, honestly.

"It was a couple of days ago."

Ms Lancaster fiddled with her hair. She was wearing wooden bracelets, a few of them, and some kind of antique-looking necklace around her throat.

"Right..." The teacher nodded, as if still not getting the point. "I'm sorry, but could you elaborate?"

Abbie laughed, but really it was an expulsion of air. A valve releasing pressure. Was she pretending not to know?

"You told my fourteen-year-old daughter she should become a prostitute."

Ms Lancaster smirked. Bloody *smirked*. It was only for a moment, but Abbie saw right through her. The smirk disappeared, and a carefully crafted serious expression took its place. "I didn't quite phrase it like that."

Abbie had rehearsed this all morning at the shop, while stacking shelves, dealing with customers, trying to keep her service-worker smile fixed to her face. Of all the possible responses, she hadn't expected this. She'd hoped Becky was lying; it wouldn't be surprising.

"How did you phrase it, then?"

"Please. Don't raise your voice at me."

"How did you phrase it?" Abbie asked again.

Ms Lancaster groaned, and it was like she was saying, *This is so far beneath me, having to educate this stupid working-class woman.* And maybe that was in Abbie's head; maybe she had the proverbial chip on her shoulder. But she didn't think so.

"I simply explained to her that sex work is real work and she shouldn't be ashamed if she decided to pursue such a career."

Abbie was shaking, but she attempted to contain it. Jack would've put this right. He would've known how to handle it without causing more problems.

But Abbie couldn't think.

"I don't understand," she said. "You're admitting it?"

"Admitting it," Ms Lancaster repeated tightly. "That's quite a judgemental way of phrasing it."

"So you did say it, then. You told her she should become a whore."

"A sex worker," Ms Lancaster said.

"What?"

"Hooker, prostitute, *whore* especially... these are all degrading terms."

"I don't care. You told my daughter she should sell her body."

"That's not what I said. I explained that, if she *chose* to pursue that line of work, when she was an *adult*, she didn't need to feel ashamed–"

"What if I disagree?" Abbie's voice was rising. "What if I think she should be ashamed? What if I don't want my daughter even thinking about that sort of *work*, let alone doing it? What then?"

Ms Lancaster stood, this aristocrat with her oh-so fancy necklace, her look-at-me bracelets, with her hair tied up in an aren't-I-cute bun. "Please, I've already told you. Don't raise your voice at me."

"I'll raise my voice all I want." In her thoughts, Abbie heard Jack. *Your temper's going to get you killed.* "I just can't believe this. You shouldn't even be talking about stuff like this with my daughter. You have absolutely no right. No right at all."

Ms Lancaster smirked *again*. Abbie wanted to punch her in the face.

"Stop smirking at me."

"I'm sorry, but I can't continue this discussion if you're going to behave aggressively."

"You told my *daughter* she should *have sex with strangers* for money. She's fourteen. What's wrong with you? What sort of sick freak does that?"

"I think you'll find my position is extremely common, actually." At least the teacher was showing some emotion; her calm was cracking too. "The world's moved on, Abbie–"

"I haven't used your first name once. I've never used it. Why are you acting like we're friends?"

Maybe that was petty. Abbie didn't care.

"Fine..." And *again* with the smirk. "Miss Basset–"

"Mrs," Abbie cut in, thinking of Jack. "It's *Mrs* Basset."

Another of those mocking little smiles, and Abbie was really getting ready for an all-out screaming match.

"The days of denigrating and mocking that kind of work are over. Can you look me in the eye and say you want your daughter to grow up in a world where women don't support each other? I'd think you'd want to do the right thing and raise an empowered, non-judgemental woman. A feminist."

Abbie felt as though Ms Lancaster had just spoken another language. She didn't care about feminism, never had. Didn't care about politics in general, honestly. She and Jack had been too busy raising the kids together – and then she'd been too busy raising them alone – to give it much thought.

"This is about my daughter. What you said to her. You need to speak to her and tell her you were wrong to bring up that subject. You were wrong to say what you said. Even if you have personal views, all right, whatever. But you don't get to say stuff like that to *my* bloody daughter."

"Why do you care so much if your daughter pursues this kind of work?"

"That should be obvious. And if it isn't, it's because you're a bigger freak than I thought!"

Easy, little dove, she heard Jack say, in his teasing voice. She'd often joked that she hated that nickname, but she'd do anything to hear him say it again. He'd teased she would fly away, leave him, so he had to hold her tightly and cradle her wings to keep her there: with him, in bed, the heat of their bodies making everything okay.

Easy, little dove...

"If that's how you feel," Ms Lancaster said, oh-so civilised, "then I assume you think every feminist is a freak, to put it in your words?"

Abbie shook her head. "You told my daughter to have sex with men for money. I came in here thinking maybe Becky lied. Or she'd gotten it wrong somehow. But you're shameless."

"Ah, shame," Ms Lancaster said, her voice sharper. "So that's what this is about. Do you consider yourself a feminist?"

"Stop changing the subject." Abbie slammed her hand against the chair; she immediately regretted it as pain bit up her wrist, and she thought of work, of how necessary her hands were. "This isn't about f-f-*femininism.*"

Abbie cringed as she stumbled on the word. When Ms

Lancaster's eyes shone like it was the funniest thing in the world, Abbie felt like an insect.

"If you want," Ms Lancaster said, "the three of us can sit down, me, you, and Becky, and we can discuss the current thinking when it comes to sex work. I understand your concern..."

But she didn't; she said it flippantly, empty words, nothing but air. A way to move on to what she really wanted to say.

"In all honesty, however," Ms Lancaster went on, "I find your views troubling. I would really like it if–"

"Do you know what I would *like*?" Abbie screamed, all the pressure finally erupting. "To *kill* all feminists."

She spun and charged from the room, marching down the hallway, her fists at her sides, thinking of Jack, imagining his touch on her arm, squeezing gently.

Calm down, little dove...

But she couldn't.

She slammed her fist against the head teacher's office door, ignoring the other parents who were waiting, ignoring the receptionist. She slammed until her fist hurt.

TO TAKE A LIFE

This was what it felt like to take a life.

The killer reflected on that as the act was completed. This was the feeling; it would never be forgotten.

The killer could sense the breathing soul starting to become a corpse.

Was there meaning in the act?

There was blood and pain and silent screaming. There was panting breath loud in the ears and the need to say and explain a thousand things; there was the knowledge this could never be taken back.

There was the struggle and the chaos of it.

And there was time, fracturing, drawing up countless memories as if the old saying was reversed; the *killer's* life flashed before the eyes, not the killed.

All the choices, biting in a million different directions.

They all came here, to this pairing, connected in some perverse fashion by some depraved method in an apathetic world.

The killer saw it clearly. Far too late.

There was never a path out of this.

2

ABBIE

"She admitted it?" Jacqueline said, taking her glasses off and cleaning them with her floral dress. Jacqueline Wake was a good head teacher, understanding when Becky acted out, truly wanting the best for her.

"Yes, right to my face." Abbie purposefully made her voice low; she already felt like an idiot for screaming at Ms Lancaster. It couldn't help her, and of course she didn't want to kill all feminists. She didn't want to hurt anybody. She wanted her children to be okay. "I was sure I must've got it wrong. But she was smirking at me. She made me feel like dirt."

Jacqueline returned her glasses to her face. "I fear she may have gone too far this time."

"This time?"

Jacqueline sighed. "I've warned her before about this kind of behaviour, but it's never been this blatant. I'll have to speak with her and get her side of it–"

"But she'll just lie."

"I have to speak with her. But please understand, I *am* going to get to the bottom of this."

"I just don't get why Becky's English teacher would have to

talk about that. I get sex education, all that stuff, okay. But how does that even come up in conversation? It makes me feel ill."

Jacqueline frowned, the lines deepening in her kind elderly face. "Sophia has views of her own, which is fine. But she does have a habit of crossing the line at times."

"She needs to be fired."

"I understand how you feel, but I think a cooling off period would do us all some good. Are you happy to leave this with me for the time being?"

"She *can't* talk about that stuff with Becky. It's bad enough as it is, trying to keep her away from drugs and alcohol and boys. I try to be involved. I try to..."

This wasn't good; Abbie's voice cracked, a sob threatening.

"I'm sorry," she said.

"You don't have to apologise. You've been through a lot." Abbie knew Jacqueline was talking about Jack's passing a year previously. "Go home. Get some rest. I promise you I'm going to take this extremely seriously."

"Thank you." Abbie didn't feel like it was enough, but clearly it was the best she was going to get. "I shouted at Ms Lancaster, by the way. I said something I didn't mean."

"What did you say?"

"She was talking about feminism, making me feel really small, really thick. And then I shouted I wanted to kill all feminists. I was trying to hurt her, I guess. I just thought you should know upfront."

"I'm sure nobody would think you were being serious. I wouldn't give it any thought."

"I won't get into trouble?"

Jacqueline smiled softly. "You're not a student. It's unfortunate you lost your temper, but it's not the end of the world."

Abbie found herself able to return the smile. She'd been in

and out of this office several times this year: Becky was caught smoking on school grounds, had started a fight with another girl, had generally caused mayhem because it was easier than thinking about her dad.

She left the office and went out to the car.

Becky was leaning against it, the little girl who'd become – overnight, it seemed – a young woman with make-up on her face, her eyes borderline hateful, her school shirt rolled up at the belly to display her stomach.

Becky tried an innocent smile, and Abbie darted her hand out and grabbed her shirt, untying the knot and pulling it down.

"Wow, you're tough," Becky said.

"I'm on my last nerve today. Don't start."

"Am I in trouble?"

"That depends. Do you want to be a prostitute when you grow up? Is that your big dream?"

Becky softened a little; it was like her girl's face was pushing through the layers of make-up. But then a sneer replaced it. For the hundredth time that day – and this was the same every day – she wished Jack was there to help.

He'd be able to make her see sense. He wouldn't even have to say anything, or not much: a few words, that stare of his, and Becky would behave.

"I hope so," Becky said. "That would be amazing. Can you imagine how much money I could make?"

"In the car. Now."

Becky huffed and walked around to the passenger seat.

"If you want to act like a bratty little kid, sit in the back like one."

"Fine, I don't give a shit anyway."

Becky had never sworn at her before Jack's passing. But Abbie was forced to let it go, as she was with much these days.

Otherwise, they'd never stop fighting; there would never be any rest.

Was that an excuse?

Maybe Abbie wasn't good enough. Maybe it was her fault, how far Becky had slipped, both academically and personally.

Maybe Abbie was just a terrible mother.

3

SOPHIA

Sophia paced around her flat, her bracelets making a clicking noise as she wrung her hands; the meeting with Abbie Basset had not gone as planned.

Of course, when Becky's mother had called, Sophia had remembered the remark. Sophia had made it casually, as part of a wider conversation with Becky about women's rights, but she'd known there was going to be drama when Becky gave her that insufferable trouble-causing look.

Sophia had attempted to keep her calm and to maintain her position.

As she sat on the armchair – staring at her bookshelf; she didn't have a television – she wished she'd phrased it more convincingly. She wished she could've made Abbie see how dangerous her thinking was, and how unfair she was being, overstating the effect of Sophia's words.

Sophia had *not* suggested a teenage girl pursue sex work. That was a sick mischaracterisation. All she'd done was combat harmful stereotypes about the profession. There were women whose lives would implode if silent bystanders allowed Abbie's sexist and outdated views to proliferate.

Sophia picked up her glass of wine, took a long sip, her gaze lingering on the almost-empty bottle on the edge of the coffee table. The streetlights were glaring through her window; in the street below, Bristolians were laughing, partying, having fun, almost like they wanted to advertise it.

That was Abbie's fault: the bottle. Sophia had only planned on one drink that evening.

Sophia emptied the bottle into the glass – might as well – and took another sip. Apart from the issue about sex work, which Abbie had exaggerated to a ludicrous degree, Sophia couldn't stop thinking about the evil thing Abbie had said.

Kill all feminists.

The brutality of it made her shiver.

It took a vile individual to think such a thing, let alone to say it. Feminism was responsible for so many of the gains made in society, both present day and historically. Without the efforts of feminists, England's patriarchy would be even more oppressive, even more difficult to navigate, and even more dangerous for women than it currently was.

If somebody were to – Sophia swallowed an acidic mixture of wine and disgust – *kill* them all, as Abbie had suggested, a backslide would occur.

Women whose lives were too hectic to think about the cause, let alone to contribute, would allow men to take control, to *own* them.

Sophia finished her wine, then carried her glass and the bottle into the kitchen. She paused in the doorway, staring at the mess, all the dishes; she'd promised herself she would wash them that evening, but Abbie's deranged declaration had distracted her. Sophia was too drunk.

The head teacher, Jacqueline Wake, wanted to speak with her first thing Monday morning. Which meant Sophia had all weekend to think about what she might say, whose side she might take... and all of this while knowing Abbie had most likely twisted her position.

"Screw it."

It was nice to hear a voice, even if it was her own. Sophia was thirty-seven and, sometimes, she missed Clive, her ex-boyfriend. She even missed the arguments; at least there had been sound in the flat.

She grabbed another bottle of wine and returned to the living room with her glass.

Pouring, she thought about Jacqueline Wake.

Sophia found the name somewhat ironic, since it was so close to *woke*, and the head teacher was anything but; in fact, she was borderline comatose when it came to the topic of women's issues and social justice. She danced the dance when it was time, said all the right things, but Sophia always got the sense the mother of five – and grandmother of seven – looked down on her.

Sophia kept drinking, and then took out her phone and went to her audio recordings.

She clicked play and listened to the conversation with Abbie for the tenth or so time. Waiting for the worst part – Abbie's outburst – she sipped more wine, and more, until the glass was empty.

"Do you know what I would *like*? To *kill* all feminists."

The statement was so severe, and said with such vitriol, Sophia refused to believe it was the first time Abbie had thought about it. There was deep-rooted hatred there, some sort of masochistic rage, as if she didn't know she was hurting precisely *herself* with such sentiments.

Picking up her phone, Sophia went to YouTube and put on her favourite podcast. It was times like these she wished she had a television, but she'd told too many people about the bookshelf in its place; she'd look foolish if she suddenly purchased one.

"Change," Lyndsey La Rossa said, "doesn't begin with politics. It doesn't begin with demonstrations. It doesn't begin with legal reform. It begins with the individual person. You have to look inside and ask yourself, *What can I do to make this better?* There are too few of us who care to stand by and watch the world burn."

Sophia slumped in the chair, starting to really feel the effects of the alcohol. That was why she'd wanted to cut down, or ideally quit entirely for a little while; it was starting to lose its buzz. But the second bottle was doing the trick.

"Be extremely wary of those who say you're doing something wrong by trying to make the world a better place."

Sophia studied Lyndsey La Rossa, a self-assured woman, with flowing deep black hair and a fierce curve to her lips when she spoke. She was only in her twenties, but she'd already done more for race and gender equality than most people could dream of.

"They will use whatever tools they have, as has been the case all throughout history. Legal, social, even physical... they – by which I mean the unashamed agents of the patriarchy, the casual racists, the undesirables – will do *anything* to silence us. They sit stubbornly on the wrong side of history. Who's going to do something about it, if not us?"

Sophia kept drinking, thinking of the recording. She'd taken it as insurance.

There was a chance, she knew, of Abbie completely warping Sophia's words. And these were serious differences; advocating for the dignity of sex workers was not the same as foisting said work on a fourteen-year-old girl, as Abbie had stupidly suggested.

Sophia poured another glass, as Lyndsey spoke of change, of taking action, of how important they all were in the struggle.

"Kill all feminists," Sophia repeated, ignoring the slurring in her voice, struggling to focus as her vision wavered.

How could anybody let that thought into their head, even for a moment?

Sophia drank until she blacked out.

When she woke in a heap on the floor, she was famous.

4

SOPHIA

Sophia's TikTok videos normally garnered around four hundred views and ten or so likes. Once, she'd posted a rant which had hit one thousand views, and that had fixed a beaming smile to her face for days afterward. To think there were a thousand people out there, all eager to hear what she had to say. It caused a warm shimmer to move through her.

Sitting on her bed, she ignored the thudding in her skull, the dryness of her mouth. She'd planned on getting another glass of water, but she couldn't look away from the view counter.

One hundred thousand. And climbing. With nine thousand likes so far.

She didn't even remember making the video, though she didn't appear particularly drunk in it.

Sophia was stunned by how much effort her intoxicated self had applied.

The video began with her sitting on her sofa, which was far tidier than she remembered it being. She'd changed into a clean blouse; she had boss-bitch energy when she sat up, adjusting her hair, and there was dignity in her movements.

She felt proud the way she would for another person. She wondered, briefly, if she ought to always be blackout drunk.

"I want to do the right thing," Sophia said in the video. "I don't want to get anybody into trouble. But today I met a woman who made me realise why we still have a patriarchy, a pay gap, why we're living in constant fear every time we step out our front doors. I'm a teacher and one of the parents marched into my classroom, completely twisting something I'd said about the equality of sex workers..."

At least Sophia hadn't gone into the details. TikTok videos weren't long enough for her to fully explain all the nuances of it. She didn't want to risk other people misunderstanding her reasonable position.

"And when I say heated," Sophia went on in the video, "I mean this..."

Blacked-out Sophia had transferred the audio file to her laptop, since she was recording on her phone. She clicked play and Abbie Basset's voice filled the room.

"Do you know what I would *like*? To *kill* all feminists."

Sophia stared at the camera with the seriousness of Lyndsey La Rossa. For one sweet moment, they were the same.

"I didn't want to upload this. But I couldn't stop thinking about it. What sort of person says this? And more importantly, what should I do? It's very likely I'll have to speak with this woman again. But I don't know how I'm going to look her in the eye. And the truth is I'm scared. This woman is raising a daughter, and that's the sort of thing she says. So if I don't see you again..."

The video ended on a cliffhanger. Sophia went to the comments.

There were *some* asking how the recording had been acquired, pressing for more details, but most were vehemently on Sophia's side. Most were as disgusted as she had been. Most realised the dangers of Abbie's words.

Most wanted her to pay.

Sophia grinded her teeth, looking at the view counter, the likes.

If Jacqueline found out about this, Sophia's life would get far more difficult. But people were having enthusiastic and passionate conversations in the comments; she had provoked a gorgeous torrent of awareness, and perhaps the severity of Abbie's words would spur more people to become feminists.

She hadn't mentioned Abbie's name in the video. She hadn't mentioned Becky's. There was Abbie's voice, fine, but she sounded like any other woman born in the south-west.

The views kept going up.

The comments kept coming in.

More and more likes, more awareness, more ammunition for the cause: more world-changers.

Perhaps it was strange, thinking of her dad in that moment. If she hadn't done everything she could to get away from him – for good – she might puff herself up and prance around, bragging about what she'd achieved. She wasn't invisible anymore; she finally mattered, and he *would* care about her.

Sophia decided to keep the video up there for the time being. The internet was a big place. She highly doubted Abbie or Jacqueline would stumble upon it.

Sophia closed her eyes, ignoring the splitting knife of tension in her head, and decided on her plan.

She'd use the attention she was receiving to make more videos, not related to Abbie or the incident, and, once she'd expanded her platform, she'd delete the original video.

By then, she'd already have what she wanted.

5

ABBIE

Abbie dropped onto the armchair, closing her eyes, already feeling sleep trying to pull her down. She'd planned on watching some television this Thursday evening, almost a week since the standoff with Ms Lancaster; Abbie had a rare evening off.

But as she reclined in the chair, she thought it would be good to simply sit. Her muscles thanked her. Her sore body thanked her.

Jacqueline Wake had rung on Monday, explaining that she and Ms Lancaster had talked. "I promise nothing like that will ever happen again. If it does, there will be serious consequences."

Abbie would've preferred if they could go straight to the serious consequences part; she didn't trust Ms Lancaster to restrain herself. But there was only so much Abbie could do. Becky hadn't mentioned anything else.

Sleep was taking her when she heard it from upstairs, the *thud-thud-thud*.

She sat up, looking around for Jack; she wanted to ask him to go check on the noise. Her gaze came to rest on a photo of him instead, taken in Cornwall, where she and Jack were from.

The sound continued. Abbie's belly churned as she stood. She knew what it was; she'd thought Becky was out, staying at one of her friend's. Abbie had even rung Jules' mum to confirm.

Walking toward the bottom of the stairs, she quickly checked her phone, which she hadn't done for a couple of hours. Sure enough, there were a few missed calls, and a text.

Hey, Abbie. Just wanted to let you know Becky decided to leave early. I don't think she's feeling too great x

Abbie walked up the stairs, pausing outside the door. She could hear the moaning, the male grunting.

This was one of their rules: no boys in the house, no closed doors, and definitely no sex. Abbie felt sick.

She slammed her hand against the door; it seemed that was all she did lately. Beat up bloody doors.

Sheets rustled. Becky said something in a low voice. Then the male voice laughed, and that was it.

Abbie threw the door open violently, marching into the room. Clothes were strewn all over the floor. Becky was in bed, her quilt pulled up around her chin, a man at her side. The man was sitting up, a tribal tattoo on his shoulder, which meant he was at least eighteen.

"What do you think you're doing?" Abbie raged, walking across the room, standing at the foot of the bed. "You know the rules."

"*Mum...*"

"Have you been drinking?"

"Hey, relax."

Abbie glared at the man when he spoke, with his wispy facial hair, with that smirk on his lips.

"Don't tell me to relax, you pervert."

"Woah, Mum. *Woah.*" Becky sat up. "Freddie's sixteen."

"Don't see many sixteen-year-olds with tribal tattoos."

"He got it abroad, okay?"

Abbie kept staring at Freddie; he was still smirking, disrespecting her in her own home. "Is that true?"

He shrugged. "If you like."

"I need to speak with my daughter. Get out of my house."

Abbie hated the way Becky was looking at him: waiting for his response, thinking this whole thing was oh-so cool.

Freddie laughed quietly. "What if I don't feel like it?"

Careful, little dove, careful...

She heard Jack's voice as she grabbed the alarm clock – the one Becky had owned since she was twelve; it was a pink girl's item – and hurled it at his smug face. He ducked and it smashed against the wall behind him.

"Out of my house, now!"

The little prick didn't move. Instead, he reached over to the bedside table and took a cigarette, lit it, stared at her, grinned as he exhaled smoke.

Becky had an ill smile on her face; Abbie wondered if she'd been doing more than drinking. The room reeked of... of what she and this loser had been doing, this waste of space, this pathetic nothing who had no business touching her daughter.

"Nah, I don't feel like leaving," Freddie said.

Abbie looked between Becky and him, but Becky was staring at the floor, as though she wanted no part of this.

"Don't make me call the police."

Freddie made a *tsk* noise, as cigarette smoke filled the room. She wanted to ask him to put it out, but she knew he wouldn't. "Go ahead. I'm sure your neighbours would love that."

"You think I care about that?" Abbie said, even if the thought tired her. Purposeful or not, he'd hit on a sore point.

She wanted to be able to handle her home herself, to bring

order, not to have to rely on police or teachers and all the rest of it.

"Mum, please," Becky whispered.

"Please what? What are you doing with this person, Becky? Look at him. What sort of boyfriend – if that's what he is – talks to their girlfriend's mum like this? Imagine if your dad was here."

"Yeah, well, he's not," Freddie said.

Becky gasped. "Freddie!"

But he just kept smoking, staring at Abbie, challenging her. Finally, he said, "You just tried to physically assault me. You can't blame me for being angry."

Abbie had tried her best to let Chris' childhood continue after Jack's passing. She had no desire for him to be the man of the house. But at the same time, she couldn't let this stand. It was unacceptable.

"All right, Freddie," she said, and she left the room.

She was crying when Chris walked through the door. They were her usual quiet tears, the sobs stifled.

Chris had just been about to start kickboxing when she rang, his usual Thursday-night routine. After Jack's death, he'd offered to drop out of his electrical installation course at college and work full-time to help her, but Abbie had flatly told him no. She didn't want his future ruined; she could handle it.

But clearly, she couldn't handle this.

Chris knelt next to the armchair. He was tall, over six foot, with black hair cut into a skin fade, and he was wide, built like Jack's father, Chris' grandfather had been. "Are they still up there?"

She nodded, wiping her cheeks. "I'm sorry, Chris–"

"Mum." Chris stood, his fists clenched, his mouth tight in the way which reminded her of Jack so much it hurt. "Don't apologise."

Together, they went upstairs. Chris threw the door open and stared at Freddie. He was sitting up in bed, still smoking; around ten or so cigarette butts lay on the bedside table. Freddie was clothed now, at least, a vest and jogging bottoms, his feet crossed nonchalantly.

Freddie's eyes widened when he saw Chris.

"All right, tough guy?" Chris said.

Anybody else would've thought he was calm, but Abbie knew that slight tremor in his voice.

Freddie flinched. "Uh, yeah. You all right?"

"Not really, mate."

Becky gawped, seeming more sober, seeming to understand how badly she'd messed up.

"The thing is," Chris went on, "I don't really like it when people come into my mum's house and disrespect her to her face. So why don't we try this? You get out, you never come back. You never talk to Becky again. And if you've got a problem with any of that, I'll break your nose first. Then I'll break your arms, if you still want to play the big man. If you're stupid enough to keep going, I'll break your legs too. How does that sound?"

Freddie smirked, but it faltered when Chris stepped forward.

"You've got five seconds to get out."

Freddie looked at Becky, as if she was going to support him. But Becky was back to her floor-staring routine.

"Some parent you are," Freddie said. "Getting your son to–"

But he didn't get any further. Abbie cried out, wondering if she'd made a mistake ringing Chris.

Chris leapt at Freddie and dragged him out of bed. Freddie

sprawled on the floor, attempting to lash out. Chris ducked back and then, almost casually, punched him so hard in the face Freddie thumped against the wall.

"Told you about the nose," Chris growled, raising his fists.

Freddie ran at him, and Chris spun and kicked him in the belly, a move he'd learned when he was seven. Freddie keeled over and began to gasp, choking as he struggled to suck in enough air.

"Time to go."

Chris walked over and hauled Freddie over his shoulder, carrying him out the room.

"Don't hurt him anymore," Abbie said urgently.

"He's lucky I don't seriously hurt him."

Freddie began to struggle at the bottom of the stairs. Chris wasn't even breathing hard.

Chris dropped him on his back, staring down at him. "You must be high. Do you really want to do this?"

"I... please."

"Please? Please what?" Chris drove his knee into Freddie's belly, collapsing atop him, and finally the anger came: the fury which had been there all along. "I'll stamp your head into the concrete, you bastard. Please? *Please?* Mother*fucker!*"

Chris raised his hand, and Abbie screamed, "Chris!"

He paused, looking up the stairs; Abbie was stood halfway down them. She had tears in her eyes, and Abbie blamed them on herself.

"It's enough. Just get him out."

"You're lucky she's here." He stood, kicking Freddie in the leg. "Up. Out. Now."

Freddie dragged himself to his feet, limping for the door, his hands clutching his belly as his breathing wheezed loudly. Chris followed him and then closed the door loudly. Abbie heard the click of both locks, then Chris returned, leaning against the wall, finally breathing heavily. But not from exertion.

"I'm sorry." Abbie pressed herself against her son. "I shouldn't have made you do that."

"It's okay, Mum."

But Chris' voice cracked, fighting off tears. Abbie didn't fight hers; they flowed, stinging down her face. They only let each other go when Becky walked down the stairs. She was wearing her dressing gown, her hair tied up, her face looking so young it made Abbie sob harder.

"Mum, I'm sorry," she whispered. "I'm so sorry."

"Who was that, Becks?" Chris said.

"I don't even know," she said, wiping her cheeks. "I just... I got some booze and I went to a park and he was there and, we got talking. About Dad. About everything. I thought he was nice... I don't even know. I don't know."

"You can't ever treat Mum like that again. It makes me hate you. I don't want to hate you. You have to promise."

Becky shuddered. "I do. I will. I mean, I promise."

"What did you take?" Abbie asked, placing her hand on her daughter's shoulder, feeling love flow between them despite everything.

"He was smoking weed. I had a little. I'm not thinking straight. I just... I miss Dad. I miss him so much."

Suddenly, it was like the fight hadn't happened. They held each other, the three of them, for a long time. They held tightly like they never wanted to let go.

6

SOPHIA

Sophia could barely wait until class was finished to check her phone. It annoyed her, especially when Becky spent several minutes gathering her things, looking at Sophia with a knowing grin on her face.

A classic instigator, that one.

Perhaps Abbie had mentioned to her daughter about Jacqueline Wake's talk; truthfully, it had been more of a shout, with the older woman making Sophia feel tiny, cruel, and a dozen other things she most definitely was *not*.

Finally, Sophia was alone.

It was lunchtime; she was hungry. But this was more important.

She didn't let herself think about the future, the possibility of turning this into a career, into becoming a writer, a public figure, and perhaps a podcaster too, like Lyndsey La Rossa.

She didn't imagine TED Talks and packed theatres and lights shining down at her. No, she wouldn't go there, wouldn't entertain it.

For one thing, her dad would be able to find her. He'd tried to do it before, as if an apology could ever cure the things he'd done, or hadn't done. But if she became wildly successful, she'd be able to afford security.

The numbers were nowhere near as high as the initial video she'd posted, but she'd retained some viewers. Her latest video – an incisive commentary on the catcalling epidemic – had twenty-five thousand views; this was compared with the one and a half million her initial upload had received.

And the number was *still* going up on the original video.

The comments on the blackout upload were still coming in, many of them asking who the recorded voice belonged to. Jacqueline Wake didn't use TikTok, so there was small chance of her seeing the video; Sophia doubted the relic even knew how to use her smartphone. In fact, Sophia had never seen her mobile phone, and she wouldn't be surprised if it was a chunky block.

Sophia looked around the empty classroom, back at the phone; one was vivid, full of possibility, allowing her to pursue her true passion. The other was a classroom like any other.

She couldn't express herself there. She couldn't change anything, not with Wake-not-woke standing guard.

It was annoying, and frankly counterproductive, how many of the comments even on her newer videos mentioned the recorded voice. Some of them were trying to get a hashtag started.

#FightTheFeministKiller

It was a little wordy for Sophia's tastes, but that wasn't the main issue.

If this hashtag garnered more attention, if the views kept increasing, then there could be a problem. But she couldn't remove the original until it had given her its total effect, until it had created a new platform for her. Which it wasn't doing. The older video was still in circulation, clearly still appearing on people's feeds, or the views would have stagnated. That was unusual, as most videos on the platform faded as quickly as they appeared.

But Sophia's refused. It kept climbing. It kept *mattering*.

The phrase Abbie had so casually flung – which Sophia reasonably assumed was a representation of her world view, if not the literal translation of it – had sparked something.

People cared. People were defending feminism.

Which meant less harassment, less male-on-female violence, less catcalling, less discrimination in the workplace. Less bad things.

If she was able to financially support herself without this teaching job, she honestly believed she'd quit. She adored her work, within reason, but she never felt as though she could enact the change she so desperately needed to.

Why change twenty or so lives when she could touch a million?

Sophia paused in her comment-scrolling.

She read Abbie's name, and then she read it again.

Abbie Basset is the feminist killer.

Her name is Abbie Basset.

She lives in Bristol.

I know that voice. It's Abbie Basset.

Sophia read Abbie's full name so many times – at least thirty – it began to lose meaning, as though the letters had folded in upon themselves. Screaming between Sophia's ears: telling her she had to fix this somehow.

She'd researched what would happen if she was caught publishing the recording without Abbie's permission. She would certainly lose her job, and there was the possibility of criminal charges, though prosecution was rare from what she could find online. But even so, annoyingly, she needed this job.

There was a simple solution: delete her account, with all the videos.

It would hurt. But what other choice did she have?

She winced as some insufferable little prick laughed right outside her window. He sounded like he loved the sound of his own voice, like he was ready to conquer the world. She'd never say this aloud, but sometimes she despised the boys she was forced to teach. The shameless gall of so many of them.

Sophia was about to navigate to her account settings when she received a notification.

She stared.

Her heart was shimmering, new-date-like, with a novel excitement she hadn't felt in a long time. It was as though she'd accumulated all the pleasure from two bottles of wine and distilled it to a single moment.

Lyndsey La Rossa, her idol, had sent her a message.

I'M SORRY

What did you do when you'd killed a person?

What was the best step?

The killer had imagined unleashing anger countless times, as had most people at some point or another; it would be a tame individual who'd never had a murdering thought in their mind, if only fleetingly.

Road rage brought out the beast in everyone.

But the aftermath... what comes after ramming that lady off the road for texting? Where did you put the body?

It had only been half a minute, if that, but it felt far longer. Or perhaps only seconds had passed.

The killer stared down at the fleshy thing.

A noise upstairs.

Was there somebody else in the house?

Moving closer to the wall, the killer was driven by instinct, wanting to hide, to make it so this never happened.

The lifeless fleshy thing stared lethally, face full of judgement, threatening to make thinking impossible.

I'm sorry I'm sorry I'm sorry.

The killer wordlessly recited the words as if they held meaning.

7

SOPHIA

Sophia sat in the park, staring down at the message. She hadn't been able to stay in the classroom. She kept thinking about Wake-not-woke barging in there, somehow divining what she was doing. It was unfair, the way the head teacher was making Sophia feel, but there was nothing she could do for the time being.

Birds were chirping; the sun was shining. Nature was blah-blah-blahing and people were walking their dogs. But all that existed was the phone.

Absolutely LOVED your video, Sophia. Have you seen that this sexist woman's name has been leaked? LOL!

It was utterly surreal. Sophia felt as though her consciousness was drifting through her skull, phantom eyes aimed down at herself, this regular-looking woman on a regular-looking bench in a regular-looking park.

Lyndsey La Rossa wanted to speak with her! The only issue was the *LOL*, since there was nothing funny about Abbie's name becoming public.

It could mean repercussions for Sophia.

She only had half an hour before it was back to teaching *Of Mice and Men*. Her school had yet to realise how deranged it was, teaching the works of an outdated and misogynist figure like Steinbeck, and Sophia wasn't looking forward to it.

Typing out several messages, she finally settled on one.

This is an absolute honour for me. I've been a fan of yours for a LONG time. I'm so happy you enjoyed my video. But I have to admit, I'm a little worried about Abbie's name being out there. What if I get into trouble?

She walked around the park, knowing there would be no response. It was early morning on the East Coast, where Lyndsey lived. She probably had so much to do: more books to write, podcasts to prepare, speeches to craft, problems to solve, wars to wage.

It was after school, as Sophia was attempting to relax with a book and a glass of wine, when Lyndsey finally responded. Sophia had resisted the desire to check the comments, knowing Abbie's name was spreading, knowing it was getting out of control.

But she didn't want to delete the video until she got Lyndsey's opinion.

Sophia snatched her phone up when she saw Lyndsey's name on the notification window, replacing the most recent one; they had been coming in all day, people discussing the Abbie issue, her violent words, how something needed to be done.

But this was the only message she cared about.

Can I call you?

Sophia's belly tightened, a fist squeezing, and suddenly she knew she was still passed out on the floor. She hadn't made the video; none of this was happening.

But what if it was? What if one of her dreams – to talk with *the* Lyndsey La Rossa – was coming true?

Yes, she typed. *That would be great.*

8

SOPHIA

Sophia stared at her laptop, at the Zoom call, as the screen loaded. Her chest had become a crushing device; it was compressing her heart to the point of bursting, then releasing at the last second, before starting the whole thing over again.

Lyndsey appeared, looking self-assured and beautiful as usual. Her black hair cascaded down to her shoulders. When she smiled, Sophia knew everything would be okay, somehow; the smile was aimed at her, just as Sophia had often imagined.

Already, this was the most thrilling experience of Sophia's life.

"Thanks for agreeing to speak with me," Lyndsey said, in her gorgeous hybrid accent: part her native Brazil and part American.

"Oh... yeah, definitely," Sophia replied lamely, already feeling like she was failing somehow.

She needed to get her act together.

"I'm not sure if you listen to my podcast?"

Sophia had mentioned being a fan in her message. She fleetingly wondered if Lyndsey had even read it. "Yes, I do. All the time. Sometimes multiple times an episode." She was almost stuttering in a rush to get the words out. "I mean... I'm not a crazy superfan or anything. But yes, it's great. *You're* great."

This had to stop; she wasn't behaving in the self-assured fashion she'd envisioned. She'd imagined this so many times, but never like this, never in a way that made her feel small, how Wake-not-woke made her feel.

Lyndsey smiled tightly; clearly, the compliments were tiring her. Sophia promised herself she'd do better.

"That means a lot," Lyndsey said. "So you know I often cover viral videos. Wherever I can, I like to interview the creators, if I believe they can offer something to the show. Your video isn't as popular as many of our others, but I believe your subject matter warrants it."

Sophia swallowed; her throat was getting tight. This was far too close to, well, something she *actually wanted to do*.

"You want to interview me?" she whispered, her head flooding. With possibilities. With consequences. With the perfect unfairness that it had to be *this* video which had struck her idol's attention.

"Is that so surprising? The video was a real eye-opener. Of course, we all know women like this exist. They make our jobs so much more difficult, don't they?"

Our jobs, Lyndsey had said, as though she and Sophia were the same. Which they were. Sophia had just never expected Lyndsey to see it.

"Yes," Sophia whispered. "They do."

"I can't imagine thinking such an evil thought, let alone *saying* it. Do you have the rest of the recording?"

"No, just that clip. I deleted the rest."

This part was true; she'd deleted it two nights previously, fearing what would happen if somehow somebody found it, and, just as Abbie had, utterly twisted what Sophia had intended to say about sex work.

"That's a shame. But it's not a deal breaker."

"But…"

Sophia bit down as Lyndsey's smile twitched, then turned down, and suddenly the world was crashing. Sophia desperately wanted to get it back.

"But what?" Lyndsey said.

"I'll lose my job." Sophia made herself say it, though disappointing Lyndsey was the last thing she wanted. "And I think it's illegal, uploading recordings taken in secret."

"Hmm." Lyndsey wasn't listening anymore; she typed, looking over her computer screen, nodding at somebody else. "I'm not sure that's true, Sophia. Did you call a lawyer?"

Sophia shook her head. "I just… well, I googled a little. To be fair, there was conflicting information."

"I'm sure it's not," Lyndsey said firmly. "Perhaps there might be some civil issues. But I'm certain it's not a crime. Anyway…" She waved her hand; this wasn't important. "I like to get my show arranged in plenty of time, so I'll give you until tomorrow to decide. End of day, my time. Does that sound good?"

"I'm not–"

Sure, Sophia had been about to say, but then Lyndsey cut in fluidly.

"Great," Lyndsey said. "Message me on TikTok. I'll make a note to check tomorrow. Speak soon."

"I just–"

The call ended, and Sophia was left staring, thinking of all the things she could've done better.

9

ABBIE

Abbie lay in bed, staring at the ceiling, trying to sleep... and knowing that trying was the last way it was going to happen. Jack had often joked about that, as she'd rolled from one side to the other.

Are you trying to knock me out of bed?

And then she'd tell him she thought he was asleep; he'd tickle her. *How could I sleep with a rhino like you next to me?*

They'd laugh together, maybe hold each other, talk about the kids. Sometimes, they had quiet sex.

Whatever it was – even if he didn't wake – it was better than lying there alone. And yet she knew *this*, however painful, was preferable to lying next to anybody except for Jack.

People said she'd move on with time. She'd find another man. But Abbie wasn't sure about that.

She thought of Cornwall, of finding Jack, of how they'd saved each other. She'd felt like half a person before she met him; he'd often said he felt the same.

Nobody thought they would work. They were both too wild, too passionate, too alike to ever make a good couple. And, of course, there was the *scandal*.

But they had worked; Chris was testament to that. And so was Becky, even if her grief was causing her to seek comfort in places she shouldn't.

Still, the drama the other night seemed to have triggered something in Becky. She was doing better; she was making an effort with the chores, coming home on time.

Perhaps things would keep getting better.

Abbie rolled over, her hand moving across the bed. She'd promised herself she'd stop tracing the outline of where Jack had been. No good could come of it; the passage of her fingers across the sheets only reminded her of the emptiness. Even so, she raised her hand. She imagined touching his shoulder, trailing her nails down his bare skin.

"I can't sleep," she whispered, her voice seeming to carry further with nobody beside her to catch it. "Jack, are you awake?"

She blinked; more tears. For Christ's sake.

Sitting up, she grabbed her phone, intending to mindlessly scroll.

She had four missed calls, all from a number she didn't recognise.

There was no need to panic. There was no need to think about *before*, about Cornwall, how she often did when something like this happened.

Who is this?

She sent the text quickly.

It was almost midnight, but her phone immediately started to ring. It was the same number.

Abbie answered. Already, her body was primed for a fight. She hated that about herself sometimes: how easily she could fall into a pit of anger, only realising how deep until she'd climbed out.

"Hello?" she said.

"Hi."

Abbie would know the voice anywhere. There was so much bitterness laced into that single word.

"Caroline. How did you get my number?"

"Janine," Caroline said. "You *do* remember your own sister, don't you?"

"I spoke to her last week." Abbie grabbed a fistful of quilt tightly, hoping she could keep her anger there. "She shouldn't have given it to you."

"Wine works wonders, darling. But you'd know that, wouldn't you?"

There it was again: the implication Abbie had gotten Jack drunk. That was the only way he'd choose Abbie over Caroline.

"What do you want?" Abbie sighed. "I've apologised a thousand times. I don't know what else I can do."

Caroline and Jack hadn't had any kids together, but it still didn't justify the decision Abbie had made.

At the time, it hadn't felt like a choice; it had felt as though some unseen force was dragging her to Jack, and he to her, but she'd known he had a girlfriend. She'd heard whispers he was going to propose to Caroline. And she'd made the choice – she could see, almost two decades later, it *was* a choice – to act on her impulses anyway.

It didn't help that the three of them had gone to school together.

She wished Caroline would move on. It was sad, dwelling on the past, though Abbie wouldn't phrase it like that to Caroline. Abbie had, after all, stolen her boyfriend. Almost two decades previously, and Jack and Caroline had only been together for a year, versus Abbie and Jack's nineteen.

No, these were excuses. Abbie had hurt Caroline. So had Jack.

But time was supposed to heal, wasn't it?

"Caroline?" Abbie said, when the other woman didn't reply.

"Do *not* snap at me, slut."

Abbie's hand clenched tighter and tighter. She was conscious of keeping her voice low; both her children, *Jack's* children were asleep.

"Have you been drinking?" she asked.

"I've been thinking about Jack. I've been crying for his loss. *That's* what I've been doing."

Abbie wanted to say, *"You have no right, you pathetic loser. You never knew the man who died. You knew the person he was before we fell in love and had kids. You were nothing to him."*

Instead, she waited.

"He was such a good man, wasn't he?" Caroline coughed back a theatrical sob. "I know he made a mistake, but–"

"He didn't make a mistake," Abbie cut in, despite knowing better. "We fell in love. We had two beautiful children. What we did was wrong. He should have broken up with you first. But it was not a mistake, choosing me."

Her voice was still low, but it was threatening to rise.

"So high and mighty," Caroline said, and Abbie could imagine her sitting there, glass in hand, twisting her hair around and around her manicured finger. "You won't be soon, *Abs*."

Shamefully, Abbie felt herself weaken. She'd been on the heavier side as a girl. *Abs* had come to mean her lack of abs, a surprisingly clever dig at her weight; Abbie had long suspected a parent of coming up with the nickname.

"Are we done?" she asked.

"You're done," Caroline said. "There's no forgiving what you said."

"And what did I say?"

"Pfft."

"I'm hanging up now."

42

"Do you want to know what started *my* journey into feminism?"

Abbie was caught off guard. "What does that have to do with anything?"

"It was you," Caroline went on. "It was what you did to me. You stole my life because you didn't respect me... as a woman. You've always been like that, ever since school. You've never looked out for your own."

Abbie forced herself to let go of the sheet; Chris was awake in the next room, walking into the hall, probably to use the toilet. Abbie had to be quiet.

"You're drunk. I've got no idea what you're talking about. But for the record, I don't consider all other women *my own* or anything like that. I've never wanted to be in any group. And maybe I've not always behaved like a saint, but I've said sorry about a hundred times. Anyway, it's nothing to do with whatever you're bloody talking about."

"Yeah, we'll see." Caroline laughed grimly. "Try killing us, you deranged bitch. See what happens."

Abbie hung up, and then there was a knock at the door.

"Yes?" she said, aware she'd failed; toward the end, her voice had risen to a near yell.

"Are you all right?" Chris asked.

"Yeah."

"Can I come in?"

"Sure."

Chris walked in, wearing a vest and shorts, his hair messy. He always looked like a toddler, despite his size, when his hair was like that. "Was it her?" When Abbie nodded, he said, "I thought she didn't have your number anymore."

"Apparently Aunt Janine got drunk and gave it to her."

"Well, that was pretty shitty."

"Yep. But don't swear."

"Fair enough. What was she saying?"

"I don't even know. Something about…"

Abbie trailed off, a thought striking her, striking her with something like violence. It couldn't be true, could it?

"Mum?" Chris walked around the side of the bed. "What's wrong?"

"It's probably nothing," Abbie replied, but it was too much of a coincidence.

How would Caroline know? Were she and Ms Lancaster friends?

"What is it?" Chris sat on the edge of the bed.

Abbie heard the tightness in his voice. It was a complicated emotion, but she could read it; he'd always been so much easier for her to understand, ever since he was little, so much more straightforward than Becky. Chris would do whatever Abbie needed him to, but that didn't mean he wanted to; that didn't mean he was happy about his childhood's end.

"Like I said, it's probably nothing," she said, using her Mum voice. "Now go to bed. I've got work in the morning."

Chris left, and Abbie sensed he was grateful she was handling this on her own, whatever it was.

She repeated the words in her mind.

It's probably nothing.

10

SOPHIA

Sophia was drinking wine again; she was getting as much down her as she could, because it made thinking about the whirlpool easier. That was how she'd started to think of it, as more creators began to use the hashtag she'd accidentally spawned.

She should have been happy, of course. And to some extent, she was. More people were fighting for the cause. Sophia was responsible for raising the masses, stirring a movement; she was a leader.

Sighing, sipping, she stared down at her phone.

A few videos which had used *#FightTheFeministKiller* had far more views than hers. This made sense; they were larger creators. But she was losing control. This was *her* chance, and people were taking it from her.

She walked into the kitchen, wishing she'd somehow created this video without using Abbie's voice. It wasn't fair she had to constrain herself because what she'd done happened to be a fireable offence.

How much did she care about her job, really?

Standing in the kitchen, she stared down at the dishes, suddenly disgusted with herself. There she was, gulping wine, her head hazy, her nerves sharp enough to cut, and she was living like a pig.

"Right."

As usual, she sadly welcomed the sound of her own voice.

She rolled her sleeves up and attacked the kitchen; cleaning it as she hadn't since her moving-in inspection. It was one in the morning.

Technically – she reflected as she scrubbed the grime from the draining board – she had almost twenty-four hours to make her decision. But surely Lyndsey La Rossa wouldn't want to wait, not when there were so many other options.

Abbie's name was all over the internet, in the comments section of every video using the hashtag.

It was quarter to two when Sophia finished the kitchen. The floor needed a clean, but she would leave that until tomorrow. She felt oddly satisfied, looking at the shiny draining board, the pristine surfaces. Plus, the cleaning had sobered her up.

All throughout history – she ruminated as she returned to the living room – women had faced choices. Warriors and activists and protestors and queens and slaves and all the great range of womanhood, had decided...

What would they do? How would they fight? *Would* they fight?

The consequences for Sophia's historical sisters had been severe, far greater than losing their job and perhaps paying a fine. It was time for Sophia to stop making excuses. It was time for her to take control.

Despite her conviction, she composed the message several times. But they all came out too messy, clouding the essential fact of what she was trying to say.

All she had to say, when it came down to it, was this.

I'll do it.

She just hoped Lyndsey hadn't already chosen somebody else. She hoped it wasn't too late.

11

ABBIE

"Mum, wake up."

She opened her eyes to Chris staring at her, his features twisted so much she thought Becky must've died. She became convinced of it almost instantly, especially when he didn't laugh or smile it away. Chris could be like that sometimes, grimness turning to his usual boyish breeziness.

But not this time.

Abbie sat up. "Is Becky all right?"

Chris shook his head, and that only made it worse.

She remembered rushing around, gathering the children, first when Jack was diagnosed and then when it was time to say goodbye. There was no reality in which she and Chris could sit at Becky's hospital bed; there was no world where Becky had a funeral.

Abbie refused to accept that.

"Mum, no... I mean, she is. It's not that."

"Jesus. Then what could it possibly be?"

Chris sat on the bed. Abbie already knew the answer to the question. The previous night, when Caroline had randomly brought feminism into the conversation, the statement Abbie had made in anger, the statement she didn't mean...

"People have been messaging me." He ran a hand through his hair, looking so much like Jack, she almost hated him for a moment, resented the reminder. And then hated herself for such a deranged thought. "All about you. Calling you... I can't even say it, Mum."

"Show me."

"My phone's in my room."

"Get it."

"Mum..." Chris looked four and forty in the same grimace, like he was going to save her and needed saving himself. "I don't think you want to see it. Honestly."

"I have to."

He stared at her for a long time, as if waiting for her to back down. But Abbie couldn't; she'd only imagine more and more comments until her mind was poisoned completely.

Chris left, shifting his shoulders the way he did before a kickboxing match.

They were some of Abbie's most special memories, even if they'd terrified her at the time: staring into the ring as her baby got ready to go to war. But Jack's passion had been so sweet, so sincere, so supportive. So *him*.

Chris returned, handing her his mobile. Then he stepped away, as if he didn't want to be anywhere near it.

"Which messages?" she asked, looking at his conversations.

"All of them. The ones you can see, anyway. These are message requests."

"Requests?"

"I'm not friends with them, so they won't see I've read them."

"Why does that matter?"

Chris smacked one hand against the other. "They're losers, Mum. If they've seen I've read them, they'll send more."

Abbie began cycling through the messages.

Kill all feminists? Your mum's a pathetic waste of space. She better hope she never sees me. I'd happily stamp on her face.

Your mother is a joke.

She deserves exactly what SHE wants to do. She deserves to DIE.

I'd love to rape her until she became a corpse.

Abbie threw the phone onto the bed.

She pictured Ms Lancaster's oh-so sophisticated face, imagined the sound of her pretentious wooden jewellery rattling as she set up the recording device: a phone, a secret mic, whatever it was. Then Abbie thought about grabbing the phone-mic-whatever-it-was and driving it through Ms Lancaster's forehead.

"Mum, what's happening?"

"Something bad."

Becky had found the video on her phone, apparently already aware of her teacher's TikTok account.

They'd watched it several times, Abbie wanting to hurt Ms Lancaster more with each viewing, each time she took in her self-satisfied smirk, the way she talked as if she was better than everybody, everywhere.

Abbie's name was all over the comments.

Worst of all, Ms Lancaster had purposefully only included the worst part: the outburst, the part Abbie had regretted instantly.

"It must've been Caroline," Chris said, laying his fists against the kitchen table. "She's a bitter loser. I bet she spends all her time watching that stuff. I bet she was so happy when she heard your voice. She leaked your name. I know it. *Bitch*."

Becky's gaze flitted to Chris, then to Abbie, as if waiting for her to reprimand him. But Abbie was too tired; she had work soon, hours during which this would only get worse. She'd made the mistake of reading the comments under the video, and they were worse than the messages in Chris' inbox.

Becky sighed, looking achingly young without any make-up on: like the child she was pretending not to be. "Why did you have to say that?"

"What. The. *Hell*?" Chris glared. "She was angry, Becks. She didn't mean it. Do you seriously believe Mum wants to kill anybody?"

"I'm not saying that. But why did you have to *say* it?"

"There's lots of things you've done that I could point out, Becks–"

"Enough." Abbie didn't want Chris to start listing off all Becky's supposed sins. "I think you're probably right, Chris. I bet it was Caroline. She sounded proud enough on the phone. But it's done now. It's out there."

"Yeah." Chris was nodding, just like Jack had when there was a problem around the house; it was his 'I'm getting excited to buy DIY supplies' nod. Except Chris wanted to fix his own mother; Abbie, once again, was relying on her son when she should have been leading the way. "What are we going to do? *That's* the question. I'd say start with the police."

"The police?" Becky and Abbie gasped at the same time, then shared a look which melted years away.

"This must be illegal," Chris said. "She didn't get your permission. She can't go around... sl-sl..."

"Slandering?" Becky said.

"Yeah, exactly. She can't. It's not fair. Call the police, Mum."

"I haven't got time for that now. Neither have you. College, school, work. Then we'll sort this out."

"Sort it out." Becky picked at her sleeve. "I don't see how. It's the internet. It's out there. Whatever happens now... well, it's just what happens. It's out of our hands. And school? That means I'll have to see *her*."

"Yeah, right," Chris said. "She'll call in sick."

Becky folded her arms tightly. "We've already lost."

Chris shook his head. "You make me sick sometimes."

Nobody said anything, not even Abbie, and that just made it worse.

Abbie knew she should've stuck up for her daughter. But – and shame tore her up at this thought – she agreed with Chris. Abbie might've been shocked when Chris suggested the police, but that didn't mean she was ready to take this without defending herself.

She was tired. She didn't want any part of this.

But Sophia, and probably Caroline, had *dragged* her into it.

Fine then. All right.

She'd fight, just like Jack would have.

12

CHRIS

The buzzer went off, but Chris kept beating on the heavy bag. The muscles in his wrists and his forearms were burning. He could feel his knuckles pressing through the glove with each strike, his legs pulsing as he swung them around in vicious arcs.

It was better than being at college; he rarely skipped class, but he thought it was justified after all that crap with the video, *#FightTheFeministKiller*, Mum's voice on the internet.

The messages.

The bag whined as it rocked on the hinges.

Heavy music blasted in his ears. His mind was a mess, his technique clumsy as he did something his coach always warned against: let his aggression overrule his training.

In the end, he was almost roaring with each strike, instead of the controlled *tsk* of air which would regulate the flow of his oxygen and keep him energised.

He turned when he saw somebody waving.

It was Graham, the manager at the gym, an older man with a bald head, teardrop tattoos on his face, and a tragic habit of sometimes slurring his words. That was why Chris wasn't pursuing kickboxing as a career; Dad had told him to commit to something which didn't involve repeated brain damage.

Taking off his headphones, Chris tried to smile. But Graham wasn't smiling. He looked like an awkward boy, his hands clasped in front of him.

"Is something wrong?" Chris asked.

"I'm sorry, mate. I feel like an arse."

"What is it?"

Graham looked around the combat gym, mostly empty this early in the morning. There were a couple of pro fighters and one amateur which Chris recognised, the pros lightly sparring and the amateur practising on the speed bag.

Finally, Graham turned back to Chris. "You know I wouldn't do this."

It was like Graham wanted Chris to guess. And then he did. For a terrifying second, Chris felt his animal nature rising, like a geyser bursting up inside of him, roaring at him to hurt Graham for bringing this to him when he'd recently read so much evil stuff about his mum.

But it wasn't Graham's fault.

"The gym fees," Chris said. "Mum didn't pay them?"

"I'm sorry."

A flicker in Graham's expression, right when Chris said 'Mum'. It was like the manager was judging him for allowing his mother to handle his finances: judging him for not stepping up, sorting it himself. If Chris had told him that Mum had forbidden it, that would only make it worse, more embarrassing.

"How far behind are we?"

"Just a month. I expect she forgot. It's not like we're going to push you out the bloody door. I reckon your old man's ghost would level me out if we tried that."

"I bet he would. I'll get you the money. You have my word."

"That's good enough for me." Graham paused. "Shouldn't you be at college?"

Chris turned away, shaking his head, shame touching him. "Nah, there's a teacher strike on or something."

Chris walked beneath the underpass. He often walked home this way, despite the neighbourhood's reputation; despite the shouting, the mayhem, the drugs, the violence. Sometimes, Chris wondered if he was looking for a fight, and that was why he never found one. Even if he walked past a group of lads, they left him alone.

Maybe it was how he carried himself. Maybe he ought to buy a walking stick to bait them in.

When he rounded the corner, his first instinct was to smile.

It was Jimmy.

It was the kid who distracted the teacher so Chris could sneak out the window and escape detention. He and Jimmy had ridden their bikes down the steepest hills they could find, laughing with the wind in their faces.

He looked worse than the last time Chris had seen him, five months earlier: his cheeks were gaunt, his eyes pits, his hair greasy. But worse was his walk, as if wanting to seem confident, a fake smile on his face Chris recognised from school.

Chris wanted to cry, and he wanted to hurt Jimmy until he snapped out of this drug crap.

"Chris," he said, acting like his appearance was normal, acting like it wasn't strange he was hanging around an underpass alone. "You all right?"

Chris kept his distance. "Yeah. You all right?"

"Yeah, on the straight and narrow. You know how it is." He

laughed loudly, and the laughter turned to a hacking cough. "Listen, not to be cheeky–"

"I don't have any money. And if I did, I wouldn't give it to you."

"No need to be a dick."

"Just makes me sad, is all."

"What does?"

Chris couldn't say it, so he gestured vaguely at his old friend.

"We can't all be angels. I just wanted to say a friendly hello."

"You were going to ask for money."

"Well..."

"I don't have any. That's a problem right now, in fact."

Jimmy shifted on the spot. "We all got problems. Listen... it ain't a big deal, but you don't talk about that school stuff to anyone, do you?"

This seemingly came from nowhere, but Jimmy looked eager. Like he'd been waiting to make sure of this. Chris remembered the conversations: the revelations. How relieved Jimmy had seemed as he shared his most private thoughts.

"I know we're not close anymore, but I wouldn't do that. Listen, I'm happy for you to walk with me if you want."

Jimmy smiled briefly, then his face became serious. "Fair enough. Let's walk."

Chris hadn't expected Jimmy to take him up on the offer. The more they walked, the clearer it became. It was in Jimmy's body language, his twitching. Chris was almost sure he could smell something, past the piss and the old stink of the underpass: fear, nervousness.

Dad's childhood hadn't been great, so he'd never had much of a formal education, but he was clever; he'd taught Chris to watch people, to be patient, to look for signs.

And the signs were right there. Jimmy was about to pull something.

When they rounded the final corner, it became clear.

Two men stepped out.

"I'm sorry," Jimmy said.

Chris looked at the tallest, a redhead with pale skin, showing the pink line of a scar on his upper lip. "I already told him I don't have any money."

The man grunted. "What's in the bag?"

"My gym stuff."

"Give it here, then."

Chris thought about Dad at the end, how wasted he'd become. He thought about Caroline, who never left Mum alone, always popped up ready to cause some drama. He thought about Becky's teacher and the secret recording she'd made. He thought about his gym fees.

He thought about crying alone at night, knees drawn to his chest, face pushed against the pillow so nobody would hear.

He said, "No."

The other man coughed out a harsh laugh. He was wearing a brand-new tracksuit, shiny white trainers, and standing a couple of feet behind the first; it was clear he was the leader of this sad little gang. "That's not really an option."

"If you want this bag..." Chris' heart was pounding, and he almost liked it; it was giving away control, accepting that whatever happened in the ring, happened. It was so much easier than everything else. "You can take it."

The leader looked at the redhead. "After you, dear fellow."

Chris stepped back, passing Jimmy, and placed his bag on the ground behind him. The use of *dear fellow* jarred him. The leader spoke like he was in a play.

The redhead seemed a little awkward. The bulky man was probably used to his appearance being enough.

When the redhead made to reach for his pocket, the leader said, "What next, my friend? An axe? If you require a weapon to handle this child, you're useless to me."

Chris was grinning now; he didn't try to fight it. This was war. This was the peace nothing else brought. The only reason he hadn't pursued kickboxing was because he'd promised Dad. Otherwise, he would live for this.

"Get an axe," Chris said, sounding drunk, even to himself. "Get a knife. Get a gun, prick."

The moment the man stepped forward Chris knew he'd never trained in fighting. He had the gym muscles. He had the look.

But he didn't have the stance. And he'd clearly never taken a kick to the head.

The man took the shot terribly, turning his head *toward* Chris' shin in panic. Chris felt the impact, the violent thud, and for a second, he knew he'd made a mistake; he'd killed the man. But then he collapsed and started to wheeze, lying on his back.

Chris spun and grabbed Jimmy, hauled him right off his feet, slammed him against the wall. But then Jimmy started to cry, and he was that little kid again, riding his bike bravely down the hill.

Chris couldn't do it; he let him drop, then turned to the leader.

"Are we done?"

"That was impressive."

"Means a lot coming from you, loser."

The man grinned. "You're a brave man, flinging those words at me."

Chris picked up his bag. "I'm leaving."

He walked past the leader, then backed away, keeping him in sight, until he was out of view.

He didn't care if it made him look scared. He wasn't going to turn his back on these lowlives.

"If you're ever in need of employment," the man shouted after him, "reach out to Jimmy. You could earn a sizeable sum standing around looking tough. You could make more if you actually had to fight."

Chris kept walking, ignoring the niggle of temptation.

SOMETHING BAD

The footsteps were taking a long time. Or it could have been the time-twisting effect at work again. It could be the adrenaline, or the cold fact of the dead body on the floor.

There were a few places to hide. Behind the fridge, under the table; there was a spot under the stairs, a small nook.

And then what?

What if the person walking down the stairs turned, saw the killer?

This was never meant to be a spree.

Moving to the place under the stairs, the killer ignored the dust and the thick air. Shuffling backward, there was little space, but some shadow in which to hide.

The killer hoped the person on the creaking stairs offered a chance to get out of there without being spotted.

Otherwise, something bad would happen.

Again.

13

ABBIE

Abbie sat in the small breakroom at the back of the shop, her tuna sandwich untouched on the plate in front of her. She'd made the mistake of scrolling through more comments, discovering afresh how much people hated her.

The problem is, she said it so flippantly, the way these sexists always do. She gave no THOUGHT to how her words could make others feel.

To this comment, there was a reply: *But she didn't release the audio herself. She was clearly being recorded in secret.*

And then, in reply to this one, a long string of counterarguments:

So you think it's acceptable to fantasise about murdering women... as long as it's in private? I guess you think Ted Bundy would've been a great guy if he only THOUGHT about killing women.

LOL, what a defence. I guess it's cool if I kick a puppy in the head as long as nobody sees it.

I cried when I heard this. I was raped at eleven and feminism saved me. This woman is pure evil.

There's no excuse. But keep making them, hon. You're just telling on yourself.

More and more, and it was making Abbie's head hurt.

She was tempted to ring Caroline, to explain to the interfering witch how much trouble she'd caused. But Caroline was only part of the problem; anybody could've recognised Abbie's voice in the video Sophia uploaded.

Instead, Abbie rang Jacqueline Wake.

"Yes, hello?" Jacqueline said, after the receptionist had put Abbie through.

"Hi, sorry if you're tired of hearing from me." Abbie tried for a laugh, but it came out sounding strange. "It's Abbie, by the way."

"I know." The warmth in the head teacher's voice sounded far more genuine. "What's this about? I'm a little up against it today."

"I'm sorry. It's important. I... Well, it's a bit of a weird one." Abbie was sure she could hear Jacqueline's nails impatiently tapping against the desk, so she pressed on. "Ms Lancaster recorded our conversation from last week. The one where I lost my temper. She uploaded it to her TikTok account. Or part of it. The part where I say 'kill all feminists'."

"Wait a second. Say that again. All of it. Sorry, Abbie... no, hang on a second."

Abbie paused, thinking the last part was for her, but then she heard somebody reply in the background; the head teacher wasn't alone.

"Abbie?"

She repeated herself, explaining about the video, the recording.

"You're telling me one of my teachers *secretly recorded* a parent and *put it on the internet*?" Jacqueline's voice was trembling. "I have to make sure I've heard that correctly."

"That's what happened. I can send you the video."

"Yes, do that. Email it to me. Make it simple. A link I can click, no fuss."

"I'll do that."

"Perhaps this explains why Sophia's been behaving so strangely lately. And perhaps it also explains her absence today. Say what you want about her, but she's usually punctual, at the very least."

"Somebody recognised my voice from the video," Abbie said. "It's all over the internet. Chris has been getting nasty stuff sent to his Facebook. I'm sure it would be the same for me if I had social media."

"This is unacceptable. It's illegal—"

"I'm not sure that's right," Abbie said. "I did some research online. You can record somebody in secret."

"And upload it? Defame them?"

"I don't know."

"She'll never teach again. I know *that* much. Mark my words. She will *never* teach again. Have you contacted the police, to check?"

"No, I wasn't sure—"

"Be sure," Jacqueline cut in. "I won't stand for this. She had no right to do that. What was she thinking?"

"I don't know. But I didn't mean it. I don't even know a bloody thing about feminism. I've been too busy."

"Quite right, dear, quite right. I'm disgusted. Absolutely sick to my stomach."

"There's a hashtag," Abbie said.

"A what?"

"It's this thing, like a category, I guess. Everybody who uses it is talking about me. It's called 'fight the feminist killer'. That's what I am." Abbie chewed the inside of her cheek, a bad habit, one she'd thought she'd left behind. "Can you imagine that? Me walking the streets, machete in hand, killing a bunch of people when I don't have a clue what they even stand for, really. I've never been interested in politics or anything like that."

"How are you feeling about it all?"

Abbie sat back, wondering how she could put it into words. There was a tightness to her muscles, each one, and a ball of violence in her gut. And yet there was a scratching of something else too, almost like guilt, telling her she never should've said that.

You've got a temper, little dove, but I wouldn't have it any other way...

"I don't know," Abbie said after a pause. "I wish none of this was happening."

"Are you in work today?"

"Yes. I'm not missing work." Abbie's voice was crisp; she was thinking about Chris' kickboxing in particular, knowing she was a couple of days late on the payment, hoping Chris wouldn't have found out. "She wins then, doesn't she?"

"She won't win," Jacqueline said sharply. "This is my fault. I let her push it too far too many times. Her politics I could handle, fine. Her little comments. Always on the edge of the line. But bringing up prostitution to a student? That should've been a sign."

"It would've been too late anyway," Abbie said. "And you had no idea she'd go this far."

"It makes me wonder what I've said in her presence. It makes me wonder if she's recorded *me*. That's no way to live. It's pure Bolshevism."

"Pure what?"

"It doesn't matter. Ring if you need me. I'm here for you. You don't deserve this. And I want you to hear me: I *know* you didn't mean it, all right? I know that."

"Thank you. Speak soon."

Abbie stared down at her damp-looking sandwich, and then

at the dirty walls, and then at the grimy shelving units. She decided she'd clean this room the next time she had a free couple of hours, maybe during a rainy day when the shop was quiet.

She'd do some good. She'd focus on something else.

But it was difficult not to think about all those comments, the hate, the raging on the internet.

At least it wasn't happening in real life. They were messages, that was all: comments she could easily ignore. She didn't *have* to look.

And yet, she picked up her phone. She scrolled.

She read about what a terrible person she was, telling herself it wasn't true.

14

SOPHIA

It was three in the afternoon, the point at which Sophia would normally be getting ready for her post-lesson routine. She'd review all her materials for the following day, arrange her plans, ensure everything would run as smoothly as possible for the children.

It was strange, but the closer she got to the interview with Lyndsey La Rossa – there was only half an hour to go – the more she missed the kids, the books, and the more she thought she might've made the worst mistake of her life.

She leaned against the kitchen counter, staring out the window at the grimy rain-spattered street below.

The cause was what mattered, she reminded herself, all the good she could do. She was being weak, allowing her mood to become far too volatile.

Her path was *the* path; there was no turning back.

The video was out there, the views exploding ever since Lyndsey had posted a reaction video of her watching Sophia's original video, launching into a speech at the end.

A speech like the ones Sophia had heard on her show many times, but with something vital and new.

"I'll be interviewing Sophia on my next podcast. She has something valuable to offer the world. She is unashamedly standing up against the bigotry they would love for us to never see. But she saw it. And she had the bravery to do something about it."

But Sophia didn't feel brave.

A bottle of wine was screaming at her from the rack. *Drink me drink me drink me*, but so far – somehow – she had resisted. It gave her a bad feeling, drinking when the sun was up, and yet she couldn't deny the urge.

Perhaps it was a shortcut to articulate speech. Perhaps it blotted the endless roaring doubt in her mind, allowing her to be who she was supposed to be: the woman from the TikTok video, anxiety diffused.

But she was also conscious of needing to be... well, conscious. She wanted to say things she chose, not notions suddenly flown into her mind on alcoholic wings.

She grabbed her phone, turning from the window, walking around her flat – and reflecting, as she did so, that she spent an inordinate amount of time pacing the small confines of her existence.

But it wouldn't be small forever. Not if she took this chance.

She wasn't sure why she did it. She'd dumped Clive, not the other way around, and it had all happened almost a year previously.

"Hello?" he said, answering the phone. "Who is this?"

Sophia sat on the armchair, suddenly certain there were tears in her eyes. This was precisely the sort of behaviour she was fighting to eradicate: the way men twisted a woman's mind, made them seek value in the reflection of their gaze, instead of within, where it mattered.

She should have hung up. But some perverse impulse forced her to speech.

"So you deleted my number."

"Soph?" Clive said, his voice getting low.

"Who else would it be? You'd *know* it was me if you hadn't deleted my number."

"I kept getting drunk and almost ringing you. But you made it clear you wanted nothing to do with me. You didn't want to be friends. What did you expect me to do?"

"I don't know," she said, sighing. "I honestly have no idea."

"Is everything all right?"

"I've got an interview with Lyndsey La Rossa."

"The feminist lady?"

There was so much derision in his tone. It was one of the reasons she'd ended things: his unwillingness to at least *pretend* he didn't find one of her foundational beliefs ridiculous. And then he'd proposed, acting shocked when Sophia told him she needed time. She wasn't sure about children, about a family.

"Not sure?" he'd said. *"You're thirty-six. How much time do you think we've got?"*

That had been *it*, the end. She wouldn't let him speak to her like that.

So why was she ringing him? Why was she leaving him in silence on the other end of the phone?

"Soph?" he said, drawing her to the present.

"Yes?"

"I said, that's great. I'm happy for you. I know how crazy you are about her. What's the interview about?"

Unfair shame touched her; she couldn't tell him the truth. "About feminism. Go on. Laugh."

"I'm not going to laugh at you."

"I didn't mean to snap," she said, and suddenly her voice was all twisted up. There was a sob in there, too much emotion. "I never meant to snap at you."

"I understand."

It was the way he said it, the implication. He was always using excuses she never sought for herself, as if he knew her mind better than she did. "This isn't about my dad."

Sophia's father – and this wasn't a big deal; it was hardly ever worth mentioning – had been a drug addict and had neglected her terribly. He'd left her for days without food at times, and he'd brought all kinds of immoral people into their home. There had thankfully never been any physical abuse, but the emotional scars were deep, cutting at her heart, even in her thirties... she hoped they would fade soon.

"I never said it was. Not everything is a fight."

"Some things are, though. And that's what you never understood."

"I fought for us. I wanted to marry you."

"And when I said I needed time–"

"You don't *have* time."

"Janet Jackson had a baby at fifty. I'm not even forty yet. Your comment isn't only ignorant, it's sexist."

"Here we go."

"It's the truth," she said. "There are plenty of women who have babies later in life. All I wanted was a little time to make my decision, and you made it sound like I was evil for it. You made it sound like I was broken or... or *wrong*, somehow. Poisoned down to my bones."

He sighed in that particularly obnoxious way. "I've got a girlfriend. I wish you the best, but please don't ring me again."

"You do?" she said, annoyingly curious.

"Yeah. It's going great. I don't think she'd like me talking to my ex."

"She sounds possessive."

"She is. And I'm possessive over her. We like it that way."

He hung up, and then it happened.

Sophia began to cry, softly at first, but then jagged sobs that turned into gulps, like she was drowning. She wanted Clive to be here, but not the man he'd shown himself to be.

He'd wanted, needed somebody beneath him, somebody to whom he could measure himself and always come out on top.

Sophia refused to be that woman. She refused to subjugate herself.

Perhaps, one day, she'd find a man. She'd decide to have a child.

But it would be *her* choice. And, even if Clive's misogynistic mischaracterisation was correct – which it wasn't – she would adopt, find a child and love them with all her heart. She didn't have to do something, *be* something, simply because a man instructed her to.

When it was time for the interview, she was steady. She was prepared; she was no longer thinking about having a drink.

She'd do this. And do it well.

15

SOPHIA

Sophia stared at the laptop screen, studying herself in the little corner window. She was wearing a blazer, with emphasised shoulders, and she had one button undone on her shirt; it was casual, a tiny bit sexy, but nothing over the top.

She wondered if it *was* too much, actually, and was about to button it when Lyndsey La Rossa appeared on the screen.

Suddenly, Sophia wanted to melt into her chair.

Lyndsey was a real badass conquer-the-world woman, making Sophia look like a kid in fancy dress.

She cautioned herself against this sort of thinking; it would hardly help make this big moment as special as it deserved to be.

"Don't look so scared. This is exciting."

Sophia remembered university, hanging back in the seminars, her tongue and lips refusing to give voice to the eloquence in her mind.

She sat up straighter. "I'm ready."

Lyndsey clapped her hands loudly, causing her ruffled sleeves to shift around. "That's what I like to hear. Did you take a look at the questions?"

"Yes." Lyndsey had sent them over in the early hours. "I've got good answers for each one, I think."

"You think?"

Sophia leaned forward, stared – no, *glared* – at the camera. "I've got excellent answers for each question."

"Then let's get right into it. Are you ready to start?"

Before Sophia could say anything, a countdown appeared on the screen of the recording software. Sophia took slow breaths, just as she had as a girl, when Dad and all his apparently impressive friends were causing mayhem next door.

Not that any of that mattered; her dad was a pig, big deal. Just like most men. Or maybe not most: a lot, anyway.

Lyndsey introduced Sophia, and then interlaced her fingers. Sophia knew the look well. She'd never expected that unique combination of expectance and prejudgement to be aimed at her.

"The question everybody is dying to know is... why did you record Abbie Basset?"

Sophia cringed when Lyndsey used Abbie's full name. It was yet more evidence of what Sophia had done: thrust Abbie into the harsh brightness of the public light, to deal with whatever consequences might come.

"I was scared," Sophia said, remembering the answer she'd rehearsed. "Abbie had made sexist comments in the past, and she has a reputation for... shall we say, less than friendly behaviour toward the staff? She's said some truly vicious things to me, and honestly, I wanted a defence in case things went bad."

"Went bad. I hope you don't mean violently?"

When Sophia made a *tsk* noise, Lyndsey's lip twitched, as if she wanted to beam but was holding herself back for the sake of the camera. Sophia had never felt so special. "This is a woman who proudly declared she'd love to kill us all. This is – and I'm sorry to put it so bluntly – a nasty person. An agent of the patriarchy, you might say."

"I see your point. If she's willing to kill somebody for their political beliefs, who knows what she'll do to you?"

"Exactly, that's it exactly."

"We'd also like to know," Lyndsey said, with the sun shining from across the room, a patch of it on her face, then her neck as she shifted, a tigress ready for a fight. "Why did you only upload part of the audio?"

"I wanted to protect her privacy," Sophia said. "Despite everything, I never wished her any harm. I thought – naively, I now see – I could keep her identity secret. It was never my intention for anybody to know who she was. The shorter the clip, the less chance of it happening. I'm shocked anybody recognised her."

"So what *did* you want to do?"

"I wanted to start a conversation, to illuminate an important issue." Sophia was gifted with another glorious grin. "The issue of patriarchally brainwashed women is a serious one, in my view. I try to withhold judgement, to tell myself I can never know exactly what they're going through. But is there an excuse, for example, for a woman fighting against her own right to choose?"

"No," Lyndsey said firmly. "Any woman on the so-called pro-life side of the aisle sickens me. But like you, I try to remind myself of how they may have reached that point. Brainwashing is, indeed, a big part of it. These men know exactly what they're doing."

"Would they willingly rob themselves of their brood mares?" Sophia was getting into this, not quite a full-fledged tigress, but a cub, swiftly growing. "Childbirth has been used as a patriarchal enslaving tool for as long as there have been men and women."

"That's not to say we find the idea of motherhood in anyway *bad*..."

"No," Sophia agreed vehemently. "But it comes back to choice. And I don't see why any man – and, by extension, any woman whose words have been twisted by a man – should be allowed to decide for us."

Lyndsey nodded in that special slow manner, as though taking on Sophia's profound words gently, lest she shatter them. "What do you say to those who claim *you're* in the wrong for recording somebody without their knowledge?"

"I would say they don't know Abbie. They don't know how intimidating she can be. She has a temper unlike any I'd ever seen before I met her. She's a thoroughly horrible person." Sophia was thinking of the various run-ins they'd had, culminating in Abbie's utter malformation of Sophia's reasonable position. "She looks down on people as a matter of course. Let me ask you this. If you were a teacher, alone in a classroom with a volatile person, would you take measures to defend yourself?"

"Are you asking if I'd have any issue outing somebody with genocidal intentions?"

"Yes."

"She wants to kill us all. All we want is to fight for equality. There's no question as to who's on the right side of history here."

"Exactly. I don't wish Abbie any harm. I hope everybody remembers that."

Lyndsey scowled, and Sophia wished she could take it back. Sophia was making herself appear weak.

"But she does deserve what she gets," Sophia quickly said, before Lyndsey could speak again. Her palms were soaked; she could feel the sweat seeping through her trousers as she clung desperately onto her thighs.

Lyndsey said nothing, and Sophia wondered if it was intentional: making her say the words, so Lynsey didn't have to.

"Let's move onto the topic you were discussing when Abbie Basset had her outburst."

Again, Sophia cringed. It made no difference. Abbie's name was out there. But Lyndsey kept using it.

"Why was she in your classroom at all that day?"

"I'd made an offhand comment about shame."

"Shame?"

"I merely offered the opinion – quite reasonable, in my view – that we ought not to shame and degrade sex workers. Some women choose certain kinds of work, and I don't think they deserve any hate for that, no more than a baker or a barber or whatever, whoever." Sophia's pace picked up. "It would be like me walking into the Little Pint and..."

She stopped, realising what she'd done.

She'd given the name of the bar where Abbie worked: something Sophia only knew because Becky loved talking about it in class, her voice obnoxiously loud.

"And?" Lyndsey prompted.

"And screaming at Abbie," Sophia finished weakly. "All for the crime of choosing a specific kind of work. Sex workers deserve our respect the same as any other woman. Even Abbie."

"Excuse me." Lyndsey adjusted her sleeve. "But it's difficult for me to respect anybody who wants to kill me. Well, thank you, Sophia. I'm sure we'll be talking again very soon."

That was... it?

"Thank you," she said, and then the recording ended. "I thought your interviews were normally longer."

With the recording done, Lyndsey sat back. "I'm test-running a new segment, shorter, punchier. I was honoured to have you as my first guest."

"Oh." Sophia beamed, though part of her wished she'd had more time to properly explain herself. "How did I do?"

"Oh, fine, fine. We'll see how it plays on the show. I meant what I said. I'd love to have you on again."

"If it does well," Sophia said, trying to sound jokey.

But Lyndsey nodded unironically. "Yes, if it does well. Thank you again. Speak soon."

Once the call was over, Sophia almost ran into the bathroom. She sat on the toilet seat, pathetically grateful for the coolness of it.

Grabbing her phone, she went to her TikTok. She deleted the video, then deleted *all* her videos, then her entire account. She would appear on Lyndsey's show. That was enough of a chance. She didn't need to leave the evidence online.

Sitting back, she thought about what she'd said.

Little Pint.

The name of Abbie's workplace. The bar. The one Becky went on and on and *on* about, sharing the most inane stories, like the time her mother had accidentally served a customer a pint of milk because the music had been too loud for her to hear properly. *"Can you imagine? Mum's crazy sometimes..."*

16

ABBIE

The paranoia hurt. Abbie tried to remind herself – with each customer – there was little chance anybody in her regular life had watched Ms Lancaster's TikTok video. There was almost zero chance, and yet she couldn't stop herself from wondering.

She began to question the tiniest of facial twitches, a tightness of the mouth, a raised eyebrow which could've been judgement or could've been nothing. It was worse when younger people came into the shop, those more likely to have seen the video... and those more likely to agree with Ms Lancaster's assessment.

Abbie was evil. An enforcer of the... what was it called? The system men used to keep women down, whatever it was.

That was her. A frontline soldier in a war she didn't understand.

She spent the day too self-conscious to behave as she normally did. She found herself listening to her voice, wondering if she sounded regular, constantly questioning it. And even if she knew the questioning was probably the thing upsetting her the most, she couldn't stop.

Nobody knows, little dove...

It was difficult even for Jack's voice to make a difference.

Toward the end of the day, when the shop was quiet, Abbie leaned against the counter and closed her eyes. She thought of Jack, not lying in the hospital bed, his strong muscles turned to saggy skin and tragic bone, but as he'd been before his diagnosis.

She thought of him in the garden, grinning over at her as he flipped burgers on the barbeque. The love heart on his shoulder shifted as he moved, Chris' and Becky's name on either side of it, with Abbie's in the centre. She'd loved tracing that heart after they made love, a confirmation of her life, the future they were working toward, the present they were basking in.

Still – she reflected as she opened her eyes; she couldn't stand there like a weirdo for too long – there were some positives.

Jacqueline must've spoken to Ms Lancaster, because the teacher had deleted her TikTok account entirely. There were still other videos out there, referencing it, and Abbie's name was floating around on the internet.

But it was progress.

Perhaps this wouldn't be as bad as her anxious mind was trying to convince her.

It was almost time for her shift to end. The shop would be open until eleven, but one of her colleagues would be taking over soon. Abbie had the evening free to herself, which was a luxury she would normally try to enjoy. But she knew it would be more difficult that evening.

The bell above the door rang. Abbie repressed a curse. It was the bane of workers everywhere, a true lottery: what sort of customer would this be? Somebody who was content to quickly buy their things, or somebody who wanted to pass the time of day?

Usually, Abbie liked a chat, but not when she had somewhere else to be.

Caroline stood in the doorway.

Abbie blinked, as if to erase the woman. She *was* Caroline, wasn't she?

The last time Abbie had seen her was three and a half years previously, on a visit to Cornwall. They'd passed each other in the street and, luckily, Caroline hadn't spotted her; this may have had *something* to do with Abbie hiding behind a wheelie bin, but she couldn't be sure.

Caroline had changed. Her shoulder-length brown hair was dyed bright pink, shaved on one side, and she had tattoos of stars on the bald section. She'd had a boob job, taking them from probably a B cup to a D or an E. Her lips were fuller, and her cheeks had a shiny, mannequin-like quality.

She was wearing leggings and an extremely tight top, as if to draw attention to certain parts of herself.

"What's the matter?" Caroline walked over. "You're not happy to see me?"

17

CAROLINE

Abbie stared at Caroline from beneath a dirty messy fringe. She'd lost weight since her most recent Facebook profile photo, her collarbone pressing through her loose-fitting shirt, snagging it. Her cheekbones, annoyingly, had a nice cut to them, but otherwise she looked like a skeleton, too bony to be of interest to anyone.

Caroline thought about the moment she'd caught Abbie and Jack.

She and Jack had reconnected at work, after a few brief encounters in school. Caroline was working on the admin side of the fabrication plant, Jack as a manager. They'd struck up an office romance, and it had quickly developed into a relationship.

And then one day, when she'd walked into work...

She bit down, pushing the memory away; it always made her tremor. It always reminded her of what Abbie had stolen. The life she was supposed to have.

And worse, Abbie behaved as though Caroline was in the wrong for daring to bring it up from time to time.

"Who told you I work here?" Abbie said, then she sighed. "Janine."

"Your sister isn't too happy about you running away from your problems. Everybody thinks it was a very cowardly thing to do, in fact, *Abs*."

The nickname had a different meaning than it had in school. Previously, it had been a dig at Abbie's substantial size. But Caroline wondered if it was worth using anymore; Abbie was on the opposite end of the spectrum.

She might actually *have* abs.

"I'm going to be having words with her." Abbie leaned against the counter with that insufferable arrogance.

It made Caroline think of walking through the plant, following the noises to Jack's office. She hadn't wanted to believe the rumours; her friends had spotted Jack and Abbie together. But she couldn't mistake the noises, Jack's moaning, and then a woman's over-the-top screaming, like she *wanted* Caroline to find out.

"What do you want?"

"I just wanted to say hello." Caroline wondered if she should tell her: shatter her life, her precious memories, the fiction she'd created. She could do it. She had an atom bomb in her pocket. "And to let you know I'll be living in Bristol for the foreseeable. I thought it would be lovely if we could at least try and be friends."

"I don't want to be your friend."

"I thought you might say that."

Abbie sighed, stood up, folded her arms. It was bothersome: how at ease she appeared, how unshaken. "Have you got a job in Bristol?"

"I'm self-employed. I can work anywhere I choose."

"Doing what?" Abbie said suspiciously.

"Online modelling. I've built my own business. I'm doing very well."

Abbie shrugged. She didn't seem impressed. It was

annoying. "Good for you. But honestly, I've got nothing to say to you."

"Well, I've got something to say to *you*." Caroline laid her fists on the counter, leaning toward the boyfriend-stealing bitch. "You're going to regret what you did. You're going to *really* regret it. Maybe I was too nervous, too kind back then, letting you off the hook so easily. But not anymore. I've done a lot of reflecting these past few years. I've done a lot of growing. And I've decided something."

"Oh yeah, what's that?"

Caroline bared her new teeth: white, straight, Hollywood-like. "I'm going to ruin your life."

Abbie stared, masking her emotions; it was infuriating. "Try, Caroline. I'd love to see that."

"You will." Caroline turned. "I'm quite rich now, by the way, one of the most popular webcam workers in the UK."

"Webcam workers," Abbie said derisively.

"You should look me up. Some weeks, I make three or four thousand, all for sitting in a warm room and entertaining my fans. Have fun trying to pay your rent working in this hovel, slut."

Caroline left, walking onto the street, her adrenaline rushing just as it had back then: when Jack had emerged from the office in his trousers, still shirtless, with Abbie's fingernail marks down his chest.

He hadn't said sorry. He hadn't told her it was a mistake.

He'd frowned, saying, "We need to talk..."

And then Abbie had appeared in the doorway, wearing his shirt, the same shirt Caroline had worn after she and Jack made love. Abbie's expression had been unhinged, her lips shaped into a sadist's grin.

"*Tell her,*" Abbie had said, a strange sort of desperation in her voice. *"You never loved her. You were never going to propose to her. You want me. Just me. Forever. Go on, Jack."*

Jack had spun on her. *"Abbie, don't be cruel."*

"She bullied me for years in school. You think I care about her feelings? Tell her we've been sneaking around behind her back. Tell her we've been laughing about it. Tell her we call her pathetic, a real sad act, for thinking you'd ever want to spend the rest of your life with her."

Caroline's throat had tightened, choking off any response she might've made. Her shoulders had dropped, her gaze doing the same, and she'd waited.

As Jack had snapped at Abbie to stay in the office, as the door had slammed, as Caroline's vision of the future cracked and splintered, she'd waited for the end to come.

18

BECKY

Becky swung back and forth, kicking her legs, gripping the metal links so hard they dug into her hands.

Her head was a mess, but that was nothing new; she had become somewhat used to it, and even missed it when she felt those unusual moments of peace. Ms Lancaster hadn't been in that day, and Becky had acted like a real clown in class, making the substitute teacher's job difficult.

She'd felt weirdly proud of it as it was happening. But with a little reflection, she wished she'd just gotten on with her work. It wasn't worth it.

But it was necessary, so maybe it *was* worth it; most of her classmates had watched Ms Lancaster's video. It was becoming a scandal in school. Becky's friends were supporting her, but she'd already noticed a change in some of her other classmates. Becky had to put in the work, show she wasn't letting this situation get to her.

It was like she had this mist around her, poisonous, and nobody wanted to get near it. Except for her mates, and already they were behaving a *tiny* bit different. Or maybe Becky was overthinking.

At least Ms Lancaster had taken down her TikTok account, but that didn't matter when half the school had downloaded the video.

A lot of her classmates were mocking Ms Lancaster, making fun of her classic up-her-own-arse attitude. But there were others, especially the posher kids, who were taking Mum's words seriously. They didn't care if Mum hadn't meant it; she'd always had a temper, but she was good when it mattered. She always did the right thing in the end.

Becky kept swinging, looking across the park as a man entered. She dragged her feet across the ground, stopping herself, when she saw who it was.

Freddie, the boy who'd given her weed, the boy Chris had beaten up. He was wearing a baggy jumper, hiding his tattoos, but she was sure it was him.

She thought about running, but then it was too late.

He spotted her, swaggering over.

Becky looked around the park; it was empty, the traffic quiet beyond the fence, nobody walking their dog on the green.

She suddenly felt like an idiot for ever going there alone.

"All right, sweetheart," Freddie said, taking a joint from behind his ear, grinning.

"Hey, Freddie," she said quietly.

"You got anything you want to say to me?" He came to stand right over her, and Becky couldn't believe she'd ever had sex with him; she could hardly believe she'd ever had sex at *all* sometimes. He shook the railing of the swing, jostling her around. "I'm talking to you."

She flinched, wishing he wasn't so close. She could stand up then, at least. "Don't be mean."

"You could've warned me about your psycho brother." He lit the joint, inhaled deeply, then offered it to her. When she shook her head, he laughed darkly. "A good girl now, is it? Suit yourself."

"I didn't know Mum would ring Chris."

Becky hadn't thought about that situation at all. Freddie had appeared, said some nice things, and then she was high; she couldn't think about anything, and basically just did everything he'd suggested.

"Chris, such a tough guy. Attacking a half-naked bloke. Not even giving me a chance to defend myself."

Becky almost laughed, but she stopped herself. Freddie would never be a match for Chris if it came to a fight.

"Something funny?" Clearly, Becky hadn't hid it as well as she hoped. "Well?"

She leaned back on the swing, as far as she could get before the momentum tried to push her right up against him. "N-no."

"I saw something funny earlier," Freddie went on. "Kaitlin sent it to me. You know Kaitlin, don't you? Howell?"

Becky nodded; she was in the year above.

"Apparently, your mum's getting pretty famous. Her name's all over the internet. She wants to kill all dykes or some shit." Freddie inhaled more, the smoke reeking as he exhaled. "Don't matter to me. But if she's going to be famous one day, might be I've got an idea."

"How do you know Kaitlin?" Becky asked. Anything would be better than talking about *this*.

"I was leaving when she was in year seven."

Becky did the maths. Or tried to. She knew it meant Freddie was older than he'd claimed. "I thought you were sixteen?"

"Oh yeah, sure, course you thought that."

"I did." Becky shut her eyes for a moment, trying to force the tears away. "How old are you?"

Freddie's laugh got even lower. "Open your eyes. You look like a retard."

The word made her inch back even more. She stared at him, trying not to cry, finding it difficult to believe this man had ever been... it was too sick to think. *Intimate* with her. She wished Dad was here for the millionth time that day.

"What do you want?" she whispered, as he continued to stare.

"We're going to make a little video."

"No," she said. "Don't even think about it. You'll have to kill me so Chris never finds out. You'll have to kill me, you understand?"

"Shut up." He grabbed both her shoulders, squeezing so hard she thought her bones would crack. "Raise your voice at me again and I'll screw your ass until you bleed. *Got it?*"

He shook her, and Becky nodded, unable to talk as the tears finally burst free.

"Good whore," Freddie said, backing off and looking around. "Made me drop my joint."

Becky told herself to leap to her feet, to run away, but then he'd recovered his joint and he was looming over her again. The chances kept coming and then going, her thoughts too slow to force her body to action.

"Anyway, I'm not talking about that sort of video. You were a terrible fuck anyway."

Perversely, some part of Becky wanted to prove him wrong. Maybe it was the popular girl part, the piece of her always seeking validation. She hated herself for it.

"What is it your mum said? About feminism, right?"

Becky pawed at her cheeks. "Yes."

"What exactly? You're so ugly when you cry."

"She said she wanted to kill them all. But she didn't mean–"

"Shut up," he said. "All right, what you're going to do is take my phone and record a selfie video. You're going to talk about how against feminism your mum is. Say she's always talking about killing them. Say you're making the video because you can't live with the guilt. Got it?"

Becky thought of where that could lead; she pictured her mum's face, wrinkled with ruin, the hurt of another betrayal. Becky had been trying to do better since Chris and Freddie's fight.

"Please don't make me," she whispered.

"All right then."

Freddie dragged her from the swing. She screamed as the metal links scraped against her hands, and then she was on the ground. He drove his knee into her back, the force crushing her chest, killing any further noise she might make.

One, two, three...

Each strike was aimed at the same point in her side, right below her ribcage. She'd never felt anything like it.

There was hardly any pain, just the desperate need to breathe. Worst was the casual way he did it, like she was an animal who needed discipline.

Her vision hissed with embers, making it difficult to see as Freddie hauled her up and forced her back onto the swing.

"Right," he said. "Are we going to have any more problems?"

The pain arrived as Becky regained control of her breath. Her bones felt like they might shatter. Something felt disjointed, like it didn't belong in her belly.

"I need a hospital," she whimpered, her words hoarse, difficult to push past the tightness in her chest.

"Shut. Up. Are you ready?"

He took out his phone, looked around the park, then aimed it at her.

"Actually, I'll record. I'm one hell of a cameraman. Keep crying. Those ugly tears are perfect."

"What are you going to do with it?"

"Whatever I want. Hurry up."

Once it was done, Becky walked home, flinching at every noise. Her hands were wrapped across her middle, but she wasn't sure which was more painful: protecting herself or not. Even the breeze blowing against her school sweater hurt.

Freddie had taken nothing else from her. But Becky would have preferred that.

She would've done anything he wanted, even things which would make her scrub her skin raw in the shower for hours afterward, if he hadn't forced her to record that video.

NO WAY OUT

The killer nestled deeper into the nook, knowing this couldn't end well.

The footsteps were moving closer to the corpse.

The screaming would start soon, and all the killer wanted to say was, *I didn't mean it. I'm sorry. I didn't want it to end like this.*

But no words could fix what had already happened.

There was no way out of this, not when the footsteps rounded the corner. Not when the person stared down at the corpse.

A shuddering breath escaped them.

Soon, the killer would have to act.

It was a mistake hiding there.

The killer should've run when there was still a chance. Now there was a choice, an ugly vicious unfair one.

Kill again as an act of self-preservation or take the consequences.

19

CHRIS

C hris stared at the police officers, thinking it was a little unlucky they were both women. This was the sort of comment that'd have Mum telling him women could be just as tough as men. And Chris agreed, mostly, though he also felt confident that, if he were a criminal, he could make short work of these two if it came right down to it.

But emotionally, in terms of their backbone, Mum was right. Mum was proof.

"And she's deleted the audio, you say?" PC Kent said, before blowing on her tea. She had short hair, a hard face, a nose that looked like it had been broken at least once.

"Yeah, but not before half the world learned it was Mum's bloody name."

Mum looked sharply at him, making Chris feel like a little kid. He was still amped up from the fight, from seeing Jimmy... and from the offer of easy money.

"I'm sorry," Mum said, turning back to the officers. "Yes, she's deleted it. But my son's right. Somebody commented with my name, and then it spread everywhere."

"Somebody?" PC Fester said.

She was as ridiculous as her name. At least her colleague had worked to put on a bit of muscle and, if the nose was any indication, had trained in some form of martial arts. Or maybe rugby. *Something.*

PC Fester was at most five and a half foot tall. Her frame was laughably weak. Chris couldn't imagine her going toe-to-toe with the goon he'd fought in the underpass. He couldn't imagine her going toe-to-toe with anybody.

"Not Ms Lancaster?" PC Fester asked.

"No," Mum said. "But it was on her video."

"In the video, did Ms Lancaster name you?"

"No."

The officers exchanged a glance. Chris' foot was tapping against the floor. It seemed simple: knock down Ms Lancaster's door, drag her into the street, and make her apologise. Make her beg for Mum's forgiveness.

"She recorded Mum against her will," Chris said. "Then she uploaded it. It's illegal."

PC Fester stared. Chris could tell she hated him. She was looking at him the way so many of his teachers had in secondary, like his very existence was a stain.

"It's a grey area, practically speaking," PC Fester said. Even her voice was weak. "It's true that it's illegal to publish audio without consent, unless it can be argued it was done for the public good. Journalists, for example."

"Ms Lancaster isn't a fucking journalist–"

"Chris!" Mum sprang to her feet, glaring down at him, and he knew he'd gone too far. "You will *not* swear at a police officer. I didn't raise you to be that stupid and mean."

Chris ducked his head. "I'm sorry, Mum."

"Don't apologise to me."

Chris ungritted his teeth. "I'm sorry, PC *Fester*."

The officer caught the emphasis. Mum probably did too.

But they silently agreed to let it pass.

Mum sat, brushing down her trousers. It was eleven o'clock; the officers had arrived four or so hours after the call, since they had planned to be in the area for another matter anyway. Chris had rang the non-emergency number; Mum had still been unsure.

Outside, the night was dark, and Chris knew Mum preferred it to the light. She didn't want the neighbours spotting the police car, though they surely had.

Becky was upstairs, moping, refusing to help defend Mum.

"She may not be a journalist," PC Fester went on. "But that argument is immaterial now, anyway."

"It's what?"

"It doesn't matter," PC Fester said. "Since she deleted the video."

"But Mum's name–"

"Is out there, yes, and connected to a statement she supposedly made. A rather nasty statement."

PC Kent turned quickly to her colleague, a warning in her eyes. Chris saw it; he felt certain Mum did too. They always noticed when a posh person's veneer slipped, and Fester was clearly the posher of the two, more similar to Ms Lancaster than she was to Mum.

With a grimace, PC Kent turned back to them. "The point is, frankly speaking, it would be extremely difficult for us to prosecute a case like this. Especially since there have been no negative repercussions... unless something's happened which you haven't mentioned?"

"No," Mum said.

"Yes," Chris corrected. "Me and my sister, Becky, we're getting all sorts of crap sent to our Facebook accounts. And people are saying evil stuff about Mum online. They're saying they're going to kill her."

PC Kent's grimace got tighter. She was all but saying she had more important things to handle, and it was undoubtedly true. Fights in underpasses for one, or drug-addicted zombies who were once happy smiling carefree kids zooming down hills on their bikes.

"Have any specific threats of violence been made?"

"What do you mean, specific?" Mum asked.

"Has anybody given you reason to believe they know where you live, or that they're going to visit you at work, for example?"

Mum flinched, as though hiding something. "No, nothing like that."

"Listen." PC Kent glared at her colleague again, as though warning her not to say anything else, then rested her elbows on her knees; she looked at Chris, then Mum. "I want to help you, but this case seems far more civil, than legal."

"Meaning, what? Sue her?" Mum said.

PC Kent shrugged. "I'm not saying you should or shouldn't do anything. But it's an option to consider."

"It's not an option for me. I don't have that sort of money."

"So you're... what?" Chris said. "Going to do nothing?"

"We're going to keep a line of communication open between us," PC Kent replied. "Hopefully, this is the worst of it. Some nasty comments online. The video taken down. But if the situation progresses, we'll respond accordingly."

Chris wanted to flip the table, but suddenly it was all polite British goodbyes, even a little small talk about whether or not it would rain the next day.

"You shouldn't have called them," Mum said, once they were gone. She dropped onto the sofa. "I knew there would be nothing they could do."

"It's bullshit." Chris paced up and down in front of her. "Why should she get away with it?"

"Maybe PC Kent was right. Maybe the worst of it is over."

"They could've sent a bloody man."

"What does that have to do with anything?"

"Come on, Mum. You heard Auntie Fester. She agrees with Ms Lancaster. *Ooh, a rather nasty statement.*"

Mum shrugged. "She's allowed her opinion. If PC Fester had been a man, maybe he would've thought it was nasty too. Jesus, Chris, *I* think it's a nasty thing to say. It's not like I bloody well meant it. And PC Kent seemed sensible and honest to me. I'm sure if there was something to be done, she would've done it."

"I'm not. And I don't know why you are, honestly. You seemed up for a fight last night."

"Jacqueline has told me Ms Lancaster's career is over, at least at her school. She's taken the video down. I consider that two–nil to us."

"No, Mum. The messages make it about five hundred to two."

They turned when Becky walked into the room. She had her mopey face on, pouting, as if she wanted to make it all about her. Chris was finding it more and more difficult to love his little sister lately. It hurt to think about it, made him wonder what Dad would say.

But what sort of daughter was she, hiding upstairs instead of defending her own mother?

"Come here, sweetheart," Mum said, standing.

Becky walked over and fell into a hug; she did it just as she had as a toddler, tragically grateful for the contact. Suddenly Chris wished there was two of him so he could punch himself in the face as hard as he could. Becky was just a kid, when it came right down to it, even if she wanted to act older.

He sat, energy draining out of him, wishing he could just be a kid too.

20

SOPHIA

Sophia was ignoring her social media accounts, ignoring her texts, everything. There must've been messages, both cruel and kind, but she wouldn't look. She didn't want to know. Her heart wouldn't stop thudding.

She felt primed, ready to burst into action, but she'd done everything she needed to. It was time to wait; Lyndsey's podcast would be uploaded in a few days.

Turning over, she thrust her face into the pillow, wondering if sleep would ever come.

Then a harsh cutting noise. Somebody was sawing through the door.

She sat up, shaking her head; sleep had been closer than she'd realised. The flat's buzzer. She rarely heard that sound. She wasn't expecting a delivery.

"Hello?" she said over the intercom, wondering if somebody had hit it by mistake.

"Is this Sophia?" It was a woman's voice, the accent heavy West Country.

"Yes, why? Who are you? What do you want?"

The woman laughed disarmingly. "I'm a friend, don't worry. I'd like to have a chat."

"A friend..." Sophia's heart was getting even quicker, so fast it pained her.

"My name's Caroline," the woman said. "Abbie stole my man from me, basically ruined my life, and now I think she's going to try and ruin yours. There was a police car at her house earlier."

"How did you get my address? It's unlisted."

She'd made sure of that with every new property, so that her dad would never find her.

"Nothing's unlisted if you have enough money. I was telling the truth. Abbie's gone to the police. She's going to try and get you arrested. Maybe she'll succeed. But I've got something to make her stop. I've got something that means you'll never have to worry about Abbie ruining your new career. That's what you're after, isn't it? On your Twitter you describe yourself as a proud feminist and an agent of change. Have you checked your Twitter lately? You've got twenty thousand new followers."

The words came out in a rush, making it difficult for Sophia to keep up.

"Twenty thousand," Sophia repeated.

"And it's going up every minute. Are you going to let me in? It's freezing out here."

"No, I'm not. I have no idea who you are."

"I told you–"

"I'm not inviting a stranger into my house."

"Trust me, you'll want to see this. I've been saving it for a rainy day. It will make you bulletproof."

"What is it?"

"To put it bluntly, it's blackmail." Caroline laughed in an off-putting fashion. "If we show Abbie you've got this, she'll never ring the police again. She won't interfere with whatever else you've got planned. I assume you *have* something else planned?"

"That's none of your business."

"Fine. If you won't let me up, can we meet tomorrow? A public place? You want to see this, trust me."

"What is it, exactly?"

"That would be telling. There's a café on the corner. Looks like a proper hipster place. I bet you love it. We could meet there."

Sophia ignored her subtly mocking tone. "No, not there."

The staff at Ulysses knew about her TikTok account. There was a chance they'd watched the video. And yet she was curious about Caroline's offer.

Blackmail. Bulletproof.

One word was grotesque; the other was a shield.

"You name the place, then. I'll give you my number. You can text me. We'll meet wherever you want."

"And you won't tell me what it is before we meet?"

"Nope."

A suspicious part of Sophia wondered if Wake-not-woke was somehow behind this; the head teacher had been ringing Sophia all day, but she'd ignored her. "Fine, let me get my phone."

Sophia walked into Caffè Nero, her head ducked. Nobody had recognised her, which... *obviously* they hadn't. It wasn't as though she was flooding the front pages of the tabloids. She hadn't been on the news. Lyndsey's podcast wasn't even out yet.

But Sophia couldn't help it. Even if she wasn't a celebrity – yet – there was the chance somebody she knew would spot her, come over, start talking about the video.

She'd done the right thing, recording it, uploading it; she'd helped the cause. And yet she couldn't stop the sweat from sliding endlessly down her forehead.

"Sophia?" A woman stood, with a stylish Viking-style haircut, artful tattoos on her exposed arms, and pretty stars on the bald section of her head. She was wearing a dignified shirt and chino trousers. "Sorry for freaking you out last night."

Sophia smiled tightly. "I hope you understand why I couldn't let you in."

"It's all right." Caroline gestured at the table. "Take a seat, if you like. I haven't ordered yet. What's your poison?"

Once Caroline had brought the lattes over – leaving Sophia to look around the café, scanning it, in the meantime – they met eyes. Caroline smiled with far more ease than Sophia. Or perhaps Caroline was just a better actor.

"How did you find me?" Sophia asked.

"Money. And I'm internet-savvy. It's just a question of putting the two together."

Sophia guessed this meant a private detective of some sort. She pressed on. "You mentioned something about Abbie stealing your boyfriend."

"Yes, she did. And she was shameless about it. Cruel. She basically laughed at me when I found out. She called me names. And then she forced Jack to move from his hometown. We couldn't even be friends, apparently."

"That's awful," Sophia said, finding it difficult to summon any emotion beyond acute self-awareness.

She had to focus; she should've anticipated this. If she was going to do Lyndsey La Rossa's job one day – have her own podcast, speaking engagements, all the rest of it – she needed to make herself iron. Immovable.

"Anyway..." Caroline picked up her coffee, blew on it, took a short sip. "That's not why I wanted to meet. I wanted you to know, I've got something which will make Abbie far less of a problem for you."

"Really?" Sophia asked, feeling dirty, and yet curious all the same.

"It's this." Caroline reached into her bright-green handbag and took out her phone. "You might want to play it under the table. It's on mute. But things would get awkward if somebody saw it... before we want them to."

Sophia did as the other woman said, clicked play on the video; it was already queued up.

"I'm not saying we *have* to release it," Caroline said. "But it doesn't hurt to have an insurance policy. All we have to do is let Abbie know it's an option. Get it?"

Sophia locked the phone screen, looking up, sickness churning in her belly. "Yeah, I get it."

21

BECKY

"I heard my mum talking about it," Mila said, using her classic stuck-up tone of voice. Which was the one she used most of the time, really. "She said it's *dangerous* to think like that. That's kind of, I don't know, a little concerning, isn't it, Becks?"

"No." Becky was sitting up in bed, staring down at her phone, at Mila's annoying grin; her supposed friend was taking way too much pleasure from this. "Your mum's an ugly moron, so why would I care what she thinks?"

Mila's face dropped, and Becky felt a sick shiver of victory run through her. She didn't want to put Mila down, or her mum, or anybody.

But sometimes she had no choice. Sometimes the Milas of the world forced her.

"My mum's not ugly," Mila muttered, toying with her blonde hair.

"Well, mine's not dangerous."

"*I* don't think her opinions are dangerous," Mila said. "But my mum said they could be."

"Could be," Becky repeated. "You didn't mention the *could* a second ago."

She was doing her best not to think about what Freddie had made her do. It had been a few days since the horror in the park; her ribs were turning purple, fading, but the pain was still there. The memory was almost the worst part. But the truly evil part was the video, the things he'd made her say, as he aimed the camera at her.

She'd run as soon as it was over, his chuckling chasing her. It was all a big joke to Freddie.

Mila shrugged, then started tapping on her phone, as if to subtly remind Becky she had a phone *and* an iPad.

Becky sat back, letting Mila text, thinking of Mum. She'd been doing okay since the video went viral, mostly because Ms Lancaster hadn't returned to school... and she'd stopped going online.

"It's like it never happened," she said the previous night, an old-Mum smile on her face; the smiles which had come so easily before Dad died. "No internet, no problems. Just delete any messages which come through. And *don't* tell me about them. Easy."

But it wouldn't be easy if the video surfaced.

Mila began to talk about a boy she fancied. Becky did her best to join in, but she couldn't stop thinking about recordings. Everywhere, all the time. She'd started wishing she was born ages ago, like the fifties or something, maybe even before.

It would have to be before, actually, because she wanted no microphones.

"When were microphones invented?" Becky asked.

"I don't know. Are you doing homework or something?"

A time before recordings... then a person could say something by mistake, apologise, and move on. There wouldn't be this horrible feeling whenever she thought about Freddie's video. Ms Lancaster would never have been able to twist Mum's words against her.

And what if there were more out there? What if one of the boys she'd had sex with had recorded her?

What if Ms Lancaster had been recording Becky, secretly gathering some of the harsher stuff she'd said in class, to use against her when she was grown up?

It wasn't fair. She hated it. People shouldn't have to worry about that all the time.

"I have to go," she said.

Mila made to protest, but Becky couldn't take it anymore. She couldn't pretend she was interested in Mila and Aaron and the look he'd given her in art class. She had to do something about Freddie.

She only had one option; she went to find Chris.

It was nine, Mum working at Little Pint, leaving Chris free to claim the living room. He was sprawled on the recliner, laptop open, with the TV on playing cage fighting, but it was on mute.

The only noise came from Chris' laptop.

It was Ms Lancaster's voice, then an American's; Becky didn't recognise her.

"What's this?" Becky walked up behind the chair.

Chris looked up at her, his eyes red. At first, Becky thought he'd been crying, but then she saw the rage. His hands gripped the laptop tightly, from both ends, like he was getting ready to fold it in half.

"Sophia did an interview with some American feminist."

"Sophia? First names, is it? So you've been getting close?" Becky tried to force the banter past the feeling of everything closing in. Trapping her. Trapping *Mum*, really, and it was selfish for Becky to make this about herself.

"I'd rather shoot myself in the head," Chris said. "But I

looked her up. She's been trying to get famous for years. You just have to look at her Twitter to see that. And here's her chance. She's going to stamp on Mum's face, use her as a stepping stone."

Becky looked at the screen, at the publication date. "This was uploaded yesterday. Have you told Mum about it yet?"

"No. She seems like she's dealing with it so well, even after the police basically said they'd do nothing. But this... I'll have to tell her soon."

Becky understood why he said that; the video interview was nearing a million views.

"But maybe this will be the end of it," Chris went on. "I don't want to stress her out. If it ends here, she never has to know. She doesn't have to worry. Stuff like this, it blows over. As long as nothing else happens, I reckon we could be okay."

Becky looked at a photo of Dad, a portrait taken on holiday, with a British sea sitting steel-coloured behind him. Becky wasn't even sure where it was, but she liked the look of his eyes: capable, not willing to back down from something he believed in.

But when she turned back to Chris, she couldn't make herself tell him about Freddie, about the video. She couldn't be like Dad.

"How many times have you watched this?" Becky asked.

"A few," Chris replied. "It's bad. She even gives away the name of the bar. Little Pint. Just says it right in the video."

"And you *still* haven't told Mum?"

Chris stared up at her, teeth gritted. Becky almost took a step away. Chris had never been violent with her. She couldn't imagine a world where he hurt her with anything other than insults.

But right then, she wasn't sure. There was something new in his face. Like a locked part of him was rattling.

"What if it blows over? What if there's nothing to worry about? I don't want to stress her out for no reason."

He resumed the interview, then picked up his phone. Becky watched, annoyed he hadn't told her about it sooner, but she also glanced at Chris' phone from time to time. He was looking for work, which Mum had told him not to do.

"Wait a second," Becky said after a couple of minutes. "I thought you had training tonight?"

"Nah, that place is overpriced. I'm going to find somewhere else. Listen to this bit. The bit where she basically says Mum is Hitler."

"You've been going to that gym since you were twelve."

"This is the bit." Chris gestured at the screen. "Where she says Mum has a *reputation*. It's slander. I was looking it up online. Mum could sue for this."

"With what money?"

"She could sue," Chris said, staring at Ms Lancaster with that unhinged look. "And she'd win, no doubt about it. She'd win."

22

ABBIE

Abbie pulled the pint, listening to the old talking point from the new customer. "How can a pint be little? A pint's a pint, ain't it?"

"That's what I keep telling them." Abbie raised her voice over the music, offering her best smile. "But they don't listen to me."

"Well, they should, darling." The man winked, then left, walking over to his friends. They were the sort of blokes she could imagine Jack with, making them all laugh, and doing it so casually it sometimes made other men jealous.

She wiped down the bar, knowing it was better to look busy, even on a quiet evening. Or to *be* busy, since that meant she didn't have to think too obsessively about the run-in with Caroline a few days previously, or Ms Lancaster's little trick.

Or Jack.

Or hoping Becky didn't spiral. And Chris stayed on the right path.

She closed her eyes for a moment; she'd been doing this fairly often the past few days, centring herself. She'd focus on the present, whatever task happened to be in front of her.

The music got louder as people began to dance.

Little Pint was known locally as a 'pre-drink bar', not quite a pub, not quite a club. A place just quiet enough – before nine – to hear each other speak, but not *so* quiet it put people off. Not that Abbie cared about any of that; she was just happy for the steady and flexible work.

Her phone vibrated from her pocket several times during the next hour, but she didn't have a chance to check it. When she did, she quickly excused herself and went to the bathroom. It was Graham, one of Chris' coaches and the manager at the gym.

"Hello?" Abbie said, standing in the stall. "I haven't got long. I'm at work. Is Chris okay?"

She had visions of Chris lying on his back, skull fractured, eyes glassy.

"That's why I wanted to talk," Graham said. "Chris, is he... is he done with kickboxing? It's fine if he is. He's got the skills. He can take care of himself now. But I was wondering if it was something personal–"

"I don't understand."

"He quit a couple of days ago. I assumed you knew. I'm sorry."

"He quit? Why?"

"I'm not sure. I told him it was all right, you paying a little later."

A pulsing had started, a tight band across her forehead. "He wasn't supposed to know about that."

"I didn't mean–"

"I had to beg him not to work when his dad died. He thought it was his job to support me, not the other way around."

"Abbie, I'm sorry–"

"It's fine. I'll talk to him."

"Abbie–"

"It's *fine*."

She hung up, leaning against the stall. But she could only give herself a few moments.

Once she'd returned to the bar – mind full of all the ways Chris' boisterous nature could ruin his life if he didn't have a clear purpose – she tried to lose herself in work. She could normally make the time go quicker by staying focused, but she couldn't stop thinking about Chris.

His pride, his goodness, his temper, his boyish belief he could fix things if he only shouted loud enough.

Toward the end of her shift, her co-worker told her the boss wanted to see her. Keith rarely visited Little Pint unless he had to; he had fifteen bars and shops all over Bristol.

Abbie went to his office, the music getting quieter beneath her. She brushed down her hair before knocking on the door.

"Hello?" he called.

"It's Abbie. You wanted to see me?"

"Ah, yes. Come in."

Keith was a nice enough man, as far as bosses went, but his hard-edged face made for an intimidating grimace. He was wearing it now, as his chunky fingers drummed against the desk. His eyes were surprisingly kind, bright, and he had a full head of brown hair despite his fifty years.

"You want a coffee or anything?"

Abbie shook her head.

"Right. I wanted to talk to you about this in person. I got a strange email this morning."

"Okay..."

"Some Bristol feminist society, hang on..."

Abbie kept herself composed on the outside, but panic flashed across her mind; this was Ms Lancaster, dragging her back in.

Keith handed her his phone. "Have a read of that. It'll be easier that way."

Abbie looked down at the email, not letting herself focus on the words at first. But Keith was staring at her expectantly.

Dear Keith Murray,

It has come to our attention you have an extremist sexist under your employment, a woman by the name of Abbie Basset. She has admitted to wanting to kill all feminists. Read that again, Mr Murray.

KILL.

Here are some other words if you'd like some context: murder, annihilate, execute, eradicate...

It should go without saying that such sentiments stand in complete opposition to the betterment of women's lives, and, indeed, to society as a whole. There are countless people in Bristol who would be disgusted to know the Feminist Killer has served their drinks, especially the student clientele on whom Little Pint relies for much of its revenue.

Many students are, I'm sure you know, proud feminists.

It is not our place to tell you who to employ.

But we would like to inform you that South West Feminists will make no secret of Abbie's sickening views. All local feminist bodies will be informed, and we will do our best – as we always will – to ensure the worthwhile goals of feminism are, at every turn, protected.

With respect,

South West Feminists

This stuff wouldn't stay on the internet, where it belonged. She felt like an infection had started. It was spreading to her regular life: to Keith's tough stare.

"I don't know what to say," she muttered. "One of Becky's

teachers secretly recorded me. In the heat of the moment, I said I wanted to kill all feminists. She provoked me. I didn't mean it. I don't know how they knew I work here, though. Maybe it's online somewhere. Maybe one of the kids mentioned it to someone."

Keith was looking at her impatiently, but it was difficult to judge, since he often looked that way. "All right. Well."

"I'm not sure what I can do about it," Abbie said, thinking of Chris' gym fees, thinking of rent, of water, of food, of life. "I *don't* want to kill all feminists. I've got nothing against the students who come here. Obviously. I know some of them by name."

Keith sat back. "Let's just calm down, shall we? I'm not firing you."

I am calm, Abbie was about to say, but then she realised she was standing over Keith. The idea that Abbie would attack a man twice her size, would attack her *boss* was absurd. But so was the idea she was planning on a feminist-focused killing spree, and plenty of people were willing to believe that.

"Sorry," she said quietly. "I know it's not your fault. I'm just sick of this. I didn't *mean* it."

Keith looked at her for a few seconds; she could tell he was thinking of her as a poor widow. Which she was, perhaps, technically speaking. But she didn't want to be pitied. But she also needed his pity; the necessity tore her up, made her want to quit right then just to force him to stop looking at her like that.

"I'm sure nothing will come of it," he finally said. "Maybe they'll email a few colleges, whatever. Maybe one or two people will care. But most people have got more important things to worry about."

I hope so. Abbie pushed that sentiment away. "I know you're right. As if anybody's going to boycott their favourite bar because of a silly argument."

"Exactly," Keith said, though he didn't sound sure. Abbie had the feeling he was saying whatever he needed to stop her from snapping again. "How about we do our best to forget this nasty business? Unless it becomes a nuisance..."

He left it unfinished, but she knew where it would lead.

If it became a nuisance, she would have to go.

Little Pint had a brand, it was popular.

Abbie was just the woman who poured the drinks.

As Abbie left the office, she got another text.

Hey, friend. It's Caroline. It was LOVELY to catch up the other day. I was wondering if you're free tomorrow at all? Sophia and I would LOVE to see you x

Abbie didn't have the patience for a texting back and forth.

Hovering near the door, she rang Caroline.

"Hello?" Caroline answered, her voice artificially sweet.

"What do you want?"

"Charming. I simply wanted to–"

"I'm not recording you. Cut the sickly-sweet act. What is this? Why are you hanging around with Ms Lancaster?"

"*Ms* Lancaster. You're so precious. Do you remember in school, how scared you were of the teachers? Do you remember that time–"

"I remember school. I remember being scared of teachers. I remember being bullied and being fat."

"We want to see you."

"Why?"

"We've got something to show you. It will only take a couple of minutes."

"I don't want–"

"It would be a shame if Becky and Chris had to find out before you."

"Find out *what*?"

Caroline sniggered. "I can't tell you over the phone. And it'll be easier if I show you, anyway."

"And if I say no, you show this whatever-it-is to Becky and Chris?"

"I didn't say that. I said it would be a shame if they found out first."

"That's the same as saying it. You're not as clever as you think you are. Why does Ms–Sophia have to be there?"

Abbie cringed, realising she'd corrected herself just as she had in school, when Caroline and the other kids teased her about something.

"This concerns her too," Caroline said. "What time works for you?"

"I'm not working until eleven." Abbie had to go; even if this was a bluff or a trick, she couldn't risk it. Whatever it was, she had to see it first. And if it was nothing, it was just another reason to hate Caroline. "I can meet between half eight and eleven."

"Excellent. Shall we go for coffee? Nothing expensive, of course... or it can be my treat."

"I'd rather drink a cupful of poison than let you pay for me."

"Something cheap and cheerful it is then. I'll text you a few options. See you tomorrow."

Abbie wanted sleep – no surprise there – but she had one last thing to take care of.

Returning home, she went straight to Chris' room, knocking on the door.

"Yeah?" Chris called, sounding alert despite the late hour.

"I got a call from Graham today..."

"Oh." Chris walked loudly across the room, pulling the door

open, wearing the PJs that didn't quite fit him anymore; they'd been a present from his dad. "I guess he was moaning about me quitting the gym?"

"Not moaning, but–"

Chris raised his hand. "Let me save you the hassle. This isn't about the gym fees. I'm not having a crisis. I've been thinking about it for a while, and I've decided I want to focus on my college work. If I'm not going to try and go pro, there's no point getting kicked in the head for the sake of it, you know?"

The ever-present tightness in Abbie's chest loosened just a little. "Really?"

Chris laid his hand on her shoulder. "Really. And please, try to relax. Just a little."

"All right, I'll try." Abbie gave his hand a squeeze. "And *you* try to get some sleep, okay? And let me know if you change your mind. I was going to pay the–"

Chris pressed her shoulder. "You're too hard on yourself, Mum. But yeah, if I want to start again, I'll let you know. Deal?"

"Deal."

23

CHRIS

C hris stopped smiling the moment the door closed. Returning to bed, he grabbed his laptop and read Jimmy's last message.

U got to be careful with this bloke mate. If u say ur gonna work for him then back out it ain't good.

Chris gritted his teeth, thinking of where this *#FightTheFeministKiller* situation could lead.

But there was something holding him back: maybe the phantom pressure of where Mum's hand had been pressing into his, or perhaps it was the photo of Dad... it was behind him, but Chris could feel it drilling holes into the back of his head, Dad's eyes glaring, roaring at him not to do this.

Do you think I'm scared? Chris wrote.

Not saying that mate. Just saying be careful. U want me to put u in touch?

What's the work exactly?

Think of a bouncer. Except there ain't no police around when things get really bad. Just u.

Chris turned, looked at Dad; he was standing outside the garage where he used to work, toddler Chris on his shoulders.

Chris imagined all the things he'd say, too many to pick a single one, but all with the same basic message.

Chris could do better. He wasn't the same as Jimmy, or many of his other friends who'd fallen down druggy or criminal holes.

Mate? Jimmy sent. *I can text my contact right now.*

Hold off a little while, Chris replied. *I need to think some stuff through.*

Alright mate.

Chris climbed from his bed and walked to the window, peering out at the street.

There was a figure standing in the shadows of the opposite house, a small man in a large overcoat that fit him unnaturally. It was difficult to make out his features, but Chris thought he saw the figure smiling. Leaning closer to the glass, Chris saw the man's balding head, hair peeled across it, showing his scalp when he walked into the light of the lamppost and down the road.

Maybe it was paranoia. Chris prepared himself anyway. It could've been nothing, it was true.

But it also could've been somebody who'd heard about this fallout and decided to follow them.

He wanted to hurt Mum, freak them out by lurking ghoul-like outside the house.

If that was the case – if he was there to cause problems – he'd regret it. Chris would make sure of that.

24

ABBIE

As Abbie walked into the chain café, she imagined the reassuring pressure of a knife in her back pocket. She'd never carried one – and, realistically, she wouldn't – but the thought brought her some perverse comfort. At least, then, she'd know she had some way to retaliate if Caroline proved to be more deranged than she clearly was.

What could she have? What had made her sound so gleeful on the phone?

Caroline rose from the corner. The place wasn't busy, a few people scattered around the tables, plenty of room for Caroline to turn the path into her runway and strut over.

She looked like a cartoon character come to life; if Abbie didn't want her to disappear, she'd pity her. All of it looked so forced: the shaved head, the look-at-me tits. It was all so desperate.

Caroline paused, reaching into her Gucci bag. She did it with an exaggerated gesture, as if keen to draw attention to the label. Abbie ignored the schoolyard feeling which touched her, making her feel poor, somehow lesser because she couldn't afford a fancy bag.

"Cigarette?" Caroline said, taking out the packet.

"I don't smoke."

"Maybe you should have–"

Abbie could see it coming; it was the nasty crumpling of Caroline's features, the tightening as if she was experiencing pleasure. She was about to say something about Jack, about smoking. *Maybe you should have been more careful with Jack and smoking...*

"Jack never smoked." Abbie stepped right up to the bitch. "You would've known that if he hadn't dumped you."

Caroline beamed. "That was uncalled for."

"You're sick. You live to get a rise out of people."

"If you say so. *I'm* going for a cigarette."

"What about this thing you want to show me? Or is that as fake as your tits?"

"You say that like I should be ashamed. I paid handsomely for these lovelies, and – if I do say so myself – the surgeon did excellent work. I'll show you what I have after... maybe you'd like a little chat with your *Ms* Lancaster first?"

Caroline walked away, opening the door loudly. Wind whipped in, hissing, and then the door closed and the place seemed oddly quiet.

Abbie spotted Ms Lancaster – Sophia – as she emerged from the bathroom. She was wearing a long hippie jacket, with slits up the sides, and dozens of pins all over it. Her hair was held up with a wooden clasp.

Her face was incredibly punchable as she tried to force her lips into a smile, but then they trembled, and she just stared at Abbie.

Abbie walked over to the table, keeping her hands purposefully at her sides, telling herself to be calm.

"Abbie." Sophia bowed her a head a little. "It's... uh, nice to see you."

"Is it? I'm surprised to hear that. I thought I was a crazy feminist-killing lunatic."

"That doesn't mean we can't be civil," Sophia murmured, sitting and clasping her hands together.

Abbie sat opposite, hating how maternal she suddenly felt toward Sophia; the woman reminded her too much of Becky, fiddling with her jewellery, her cheeks flushed, her gaze unable to settle.

Abbie switched off that aspect of herself.

"Did you tell anyone where I work?" Abbie said, thinking of the previous night. "Little Pint, I mean. Did you mention it in one of your TikToks before you deleted your account?"

Sophia kept looking down at the table.

"Thanks for that, by the way," Abbie forced herself to say. "I know you didn't have to delete your account. It means a lot."

"Hmm." Sophia picked at the table. "She wasn't supposed to..."

"What?" Abbie said, thinking about what kind of shame it took to secretly record somebody and then not even look them in the eye. "Who wasn't? Supposed to what?"

"Caroline. She wasn't supposed to leave us alone together."

"Scared, are you?"

Sophia looked up. Abbie kept expecting her to laugh, to say it had all been some unfunny joke. There wasn't the same conviction as in the classroom, when it all started.

"I don't know," she said after a pause.

"You could answer my question, at least."

"I... I'm not sure."

"You're not sure if you told anybody my work address?"

"What are we talking about, kids?" Caroline walked around the table, sitting next to Sophia; immediately, the teacher sat up straighter, her chin raised, seeming far more poised. She was a bloody coward. "I hope I haven't interrupted anything."

"Sophia was about to tell me if she'd spread the name of my work around."

Caroline looked at Sophia, then turned back to Abbie. "You don't know about the interview."

"The interview?"

"Have you ever heard of Lyndsey La Rossa?" Caroline asked.

"No. Should I have?"

"Probably," Sophia said, oh-so confident with her new bestie at her side. "She's one of the most important feminist icons of the last half century."

"I've been too busy raising my family, grieving my husband, and generally living my life to care about that." Abbie sneered at the teacher – or ex-teacher if Jacqueline had her way – and hoped the words hurt. Sophia was childless, alone, tragic. *Pathetic.* "So no, sorry, I haven't had time to sit around dreaming about all the problems I supposedly have just because I've got a hole instead of a pole."

"So vulgar," Sophia said, shaking her head slowly. "And such a perverted mischaracterisation of the feminist cause. Lyndsey has three children."

"Tell her how many views." Caroline was toying with her dyed hair. "I saw you checking earlier."

Sophia's lip trembled, just for a moment, less than. There was a human in there somewhere, Abbie was sure of it. "One million and seven hundred thousand."

"For an interview about me? That's ridiculous."

"There's nothing ridiculous about what you said." Caroline's grin was wolfish. "To *kill* all feminists?"

"I'm so sick of this." Abbie gripped the table, sitting back, ignoring the stares of the other patrons. "I said something in anger. It's not like I sat there for an hour crafting this bloody statement, where I'd thought through all the pros and cons or whatever. Isn't a person allowed to get angry anymore?"

"There's a difference between getting angry and–"

Abbie pointed her finger at Caroline. "Just shut up. This has nothing to do with you."

"But she's right," Sophia said. "Getting angry is one thing. Proclaiming you want to commit genocide because you happen to disagree with somebody's political viewpoint – a viewpoint which aims to make *your* life better – is just wrong. It speaks to internalised misogyny to the most extreme degree."

"Exactly." Caroline nodded. "That couldn't be more true."

There she was, the empty-headed nothing at Sophia's side, the leech, the life-stealing nobody. Caroline deserved worse than Sophia; at least the teacher could speak, read, do something, help the kids understand literature.

"You're nothing but a whore," Abbie said, knowing this was death if she was being recorded. But not caring.

"Charming." Caroline blew on her fingernails, pretending the words didn't hurt. "But you're proving Sophia's point with that sort of language."

"It's true. You can brag about the money you make. You can strut around with your sad hair and your pathetic fake tits. But deep down, you know you're nothing but a prostitute. You sell your body for perverts online. I bet you've sold it in real life too. I bet, for the right price, you'd let anybody do anything to you."

Abbie stopped, breathing heavily. Her voice had risen, but luckily not enough to cause a scene.

"If you're recording me," she went on, "have fun with that clip."

"We're not," Sophia said. "But we should be. There are so many problems with everything you just said. To reduce Caroline's business down to such... such *barbaric* terms. And then to act as though sex work–"

"Not this again. I really will take your head off. I noticed you kept that part out of your little video. You know, when you admitted to telling a fourteen-year-old girl she should become a hooker?"

"Tsk. That's not how I phrased it at all... and it's not even a close approximation of what I said."

It was circles, always, going around and around. Abbie would never get her to admit it again.

"So during this interview, did you mention Little Pint?"

"I may have, once, by accident."

"Right." So that explained the email; Abbie tried not to think about what else might come. "You're going to have to contact this lady and tell her to remove the video. You did the right thing with your TikTok account. Do the same here."

Sophia began shaking her head before Abbie was even done talking.

"I'll sue if I have to," Abbie said, keeping her voice steady, hoping they couldn't see how much she didn't want to do that: the money, the drama, the stress of it all. "I've been researching it. I don't have the money, but there are non-profits I can apply to." She was thinking of what Chris had mentioned that morning, as they'd eaten breakfast. "You've slandered me."

Sophia looked at Caroline. It was a bizarre sight, this seemingly well-put-together teacher staring at this weirdo for guidance.

"That's what we're here to discuss," Caroline said. "We thought you might mention going to the police, or suing, or something like that. So we wanted to make a deal."

"That's easy. Delete the interview. Stop slandering me. Leave me alone."

"No. The deal is this... whatever happens, you won't go down the legal route. You won't get the police involved. You won't sue. You can fight back in other ways, if you want. You can do interviews. But no police. No lawyers."

"Why would I agree to that?"

"Because otherwise..." Caroline reached into her Gucci bag, producing her phone with a flourish she must've practised. "I release what I have."

THE SCREAMING

The screaming finally came, followed by a frantic voice.

"No, no, no. Oh my God. No. *No.* Who did this? *Who did this?*"

The killer was paralysed, locked into position, knowing that it was going to be necessary to move soon.

A *thump* as the person collapsed next to the corpse. The voice was torn with agony.

"You're okay. Everything's going to be okay. I'm here. Don't worry."

But there was plenty of reason to worry.

And nothing was okay.

25

CAROLINE

C aroline waited for the warmth to come, the release she'd expected every time she thought about showing it to Abbie: the grand *it*, the wrecking ball, the obliterator that would make it impossible for the other woman to ever look down on her again.

But annoyingly, there was something else. Maybe it was the way Sophia fidgeted at her side, throwing bad vibes out there, as if Caroline should feel guilty for what they were doing.

Or it could've been Abbie's blank expression as she stared down at the phone.

Abbie kept staring, far longer than Sophia had. Her eye was twitching, but that was the only sign she was fully comprehending what she was watching.

Caroline remembered lying in bed with Jack, before Abbie had stolen him away; she could still feel his chest against her fingertips, hair tickling her palm, as she stroked him tenderly and they talked sleepily of the future.

Of marriage. Of kids. Of a regular life.

Caroline's life was far from regular, and that was a good thing. A *great* thing. She was more successful working for herself than she ever would've been had she stayed tied to a man. But that didn't remove the pain, even if Abbie enjoyed belittling it, making it seem small simply because it had happened years previously.

Finally, Abbie looked up.

"Y-you faked this," she said, voice raspy. "This isn't... it can't be... it's not r-r-real."

She bit down, as if forcing away tears. Caroline thought of how Abbie had tugged on Jack's sleeve anytime they encountered each other in public; and the move, taking him away from his friends, his family, and using Caroline as an excuse.

Even if Caroline couldn't take the pleasure in this she wanted, she still had her plan. Or the vague notion of a plan: a direction to aim for. A way to craft the future she deserved, if she could take any opportunity which presented itself.

Which she would. Ruthlessly.

"It's simple," Caroline said. "Go to the police, try to sue, and I post this video on my website."

Abbie blinked, and tears slid down her cheeks. "That can never happen."

"So it sounds like we understand each other."

"It's not an unreasonable request," Sophia said, her tone wheedling, a bully trying to be friends with her victim. It was a pathetic impulse; Sophia needed to choose a path and stick to it. "I honestly have no ill will toward you, except for your frankly sickening views. But you, personally, I don't wish you any harm. Leave the police out of it and that video will never..."

Sophia trailed off when Abbie stared coldly at her. "You're just as bad as her." She gestured at Caroline. "Worse, because I think you know how wrong this is. I think you can see it, on some level. But you're doing it anyway."

"There was a story when I was in university," Sophia said. "About Millicent Fawcett. Have you heard of her?"

Abbie kept staring.

"It's not true, but we used to say that Millicent, a suffragist, a women's rights campaigner, would torture puppies in her basement."

"What a hilarious joke," Abbie said dryly. "It's strange, isn't it? You can joke about torturing puppies, but I can't say something in anger."

"The point is," Sophia went on, and Caroline was a little proud; there was fire in her voice. "Sometimes it's necessary for good people to do immoral things. It's naïve to expect the road to equality to be paved with roses and smiles and chocolate and... and just happy things. I have a chance to truly make the world a better place. It's not a chance many people will ever get. I can't let you stand in the way of that."

"So you'll blackmail me. You're not a good person, not if you're willing to do that."

Caroline gestured at the phone. "Are you done with that?"

Abbie gazed down at it for a few moments.

"Don't be stupid. I've obviously made copies. And that's my second phone, without anything important on it. You can steal it if you want. Maybe it will help you pay rent after you lose your job for being a sexist bully."

Abbie slid the phone across the table, then stood quickly. "No police. No lawyers."

Abbie turned and almost ran from the café, slamming the door so hard Caroline expected the glass to shatter.

"That was horrible," Sophia said quietly.

Caroline pushed down her natural instinct; this weakness, in somebody who'd done something so bold, was unacceptable.

But she needed Sophia. For the time being.

"But what you said is true. Sometimes, good people have to do bad things. And it's not like we lied. As long as she keeps her word, we'll keep ours."

Unless a better option presented itself.

26

ABBIE

Abbie walked quickly, then broke into a jog, then a sprint. She darted into the alleyway and keeled over.

Vomit burned up her throat, splatted onto the concrete. She couldn't stand; the world was tipping sideways, and then, somehow, she was sitting in the puke.

She stared at the graffiti on the opposite wall, the misshapen words, and willed them to stay still.

But as she cried, the letters became the shapes from the video. She saw it all in vivid detail; she saw the impossibility of it, and yet she knew it had been genuine. Jack had looked the same, right down to his tattoos.

Abbie tried to think of a reason why he'd do that, anything which would make sense, but there was nothing.

It had been violent, aggressive, almost homicidal in its intensity.

His memory ripped her right down the middle, then halved again, and again, until all the grief turned to hate and she wanted to throttle the naïve bitch who'd taken the name *little dove* as though it meant something.

She wanted to throttle *herself*.

She stayed like that for far too long. It was like she was paralysed: just as she had been after Jack's death, she and her children sitting in the hospital, almost comatose, as they attempted to process what had just happened. What had just ended.

But there was no processing this.

Abbie had to get to the shop. It was time for work.

Standing, she looked at the vomit on the back of her legs, a big blotch. That was her marriage. The sick. And the trousers were her idea of what her marriage had been: the lie.

Caroline had just puked all over her marriage.

"Are you all right, love?"

She looked up, realising she was on the ground again; she was crying, her whole body shaking, as she relived the video. The man was wearing a football T-shirt and seemed friendly enough; a group of men stood a few feet away, clearly his friends.

Abbie climbed to her feet. "I'm fine. Thank you."

Without waiting for a reply, she walked the other way, deeper into the alley, finding someplace she could break down in peace.

When she finally gathered herself – drawing together the broken shards of the woman she'd been before, the woman she hated for her naivety, the woman she wished she could become again – she began the walk back to her car. She'd parked outside the city, on a residential street, to avoid parking costs.

The street was quiet, the world murky and depressing.

As she approached her car, she heard footsteps behind her.

For a truly mad second, she thought it was Jack coming to explain.

She spun.

A man stood a few feet away, small but wearing a large dirty overcoat. He looked somehow shrunken, perhaps in his sixties, a small head with thin hair smeared across it. His cheeks were red with broken capillaries, and he weaved on the spot, his lips moist.

"H-help me," the man said, taking a few stumbling steps toward her.

Abbie moved closer to her car. There was nobody around; this man was clearly weak. He could barely stand. His eyes were glassy, as if he was hardly seeing her.

But it could be an act. She'd just learned how good people could be at pretending.

"I haven't got any money."

The man blinked. "I wanted to be g-good. I wanted to be a g-g-good man."

He was almost crying. Abbie was tempted to offer him some comfort, whatever she could, a few small words of solace that would bring him out of his private pain.

But then the man suddenly lashed out, slamming his hand down on a nearby car.

The alarm began to blare, and the man ranted, waving his hand.

"I wasn't always this way! I wasn't always this way! I wasn't always this way!"

Abbie screamed when he darted at her.

She'd never opened her car quicker.

Starting the engine, she sped down the street, tyres squealing. In the rear-view, she saw the man in the overcoat slump to the ground.

And she thought she heard something too.

She might've imagined it.

But as his ranting receded, her car carrying her away from the madman, she thought she heard her name.

27

BECKY

Becky preferred walking on her own most of the time, but ever since the scene with Freddie in the park, she hated the final stretch from the bus, down the path, and finally onto their estate. She flinched at every noise, just as she had during the walk home that night, and her ribs still hurt a bit.

She was getting crap from the girls in school, since she refused to change publicly during PE, but the teachers were understanding.

We're here if you need to talk...

No teacher could ever understand how insane that sounded. As if Becky was going to share what she'd done, what had been done to her, what might happen... with a teacher, a stranger, basically. It was bizarre for them to even suggest it. But that left her in a difficult position, because she couldn't tell Mum or Chris, and definitely not her friends.

When Becky turned the corner, she didn't try to run. There was no point.

Freddie was leaning against the wall, smoking a cigarette, a newspaper tucked up beneath his arm. "Hello, darling."

"All right, Freddie," she said.

"Yeah, all good, all good. I thought I saw you walking down here the other day."

"I always walk..." She stopped, but it was too late. "This way."

Freddie had caught the pause. He tilted his head, like a predator noticing a new weakness in its prey. "Mind if I walk with you?"

"No, yeah. I mean, Chris might be home, but it's fine."

Freddie sneered. "Why would I care about that?"

Becky didn't state the obvious. Freddie was terrified of Chris. If Freddie hadn't forced her to make that video, she could've told her older brother... and then what?

Chris wouldn't be able to stop himself this time. He'd beat Freddie so badly he'd end up in prison, leaving Freddie to do whatever he wanted. Chris would have to kill him, then, ruining his life for this pathetic bully.

They walked side by side down the narrow lane. On one side there was a wall; on the other, there was a metal fence that looked into the rear section of several shops.

"Picked up the local paper this morning," Freddie said, waiting until they'd passed the elderly man and his determined-looking dog.

"Ah, cool."

"Yeah, it is cool. Very cool." He stopped, making Becky do the same without even thinking; her ribs throbbed, as if getting her ready for another round. "I don't normally read it. Bunch of lies, ain't it?"

"Yeah."

"But a mate pointed something out to me. Want to see?"

Becky nodded, though all she wanted was to get away from this person, this *man* who'd given her drugs and taken her to bed. And she knew, of course she did, that she was a person too; she could've chosen not to take the joint, to bring him home. But then, she was a kid, wasn't she? Was she still allowed to call herself a kid?

Sometimes, she wasn't sure.

Freddie was waving the paper in front of her face.

It was a small column, without photos.

"Read it," Freddie said. "If you can read."

Local Teacher Goes Viral by Secretly Recording Parent

Becky skimmed the article, which told her nothing she didn't already know. She'd never been great at reading, another reason it was simpler to misbehave in Ms Lancaster's classes than actually try.

Not that Ms Lancaster had a class anymore; she still hadn't returned to school.

"Do you get it?" Freddie beamed as he flicked his cigarette to the ground. "I reckon it's starting. I was watching some stuff about it last night. This is it."

"What?" Becky whispered.

"If one of the bigger papers picks this story up, it could go national. Or even *inter*national. Do you know what that means, hot stuff?"

As he smirked, Becky could almost believe he was the same boy she'd met in the park that first time: the one who'd listened, who'd held her, who'd told her he'd take care of her. But it was the same with all boys, all men; they said and did anything to get what they wanted from a girl.

Dad had been the only different one, standing by Mum, always defending her, never wavering.

"Yeah."

"Imagine that. Your mum famous in America."

"That's crazy."

Becky made to walk on, but Freddie shook his head. That was it, and Becky snapped back into place, an obedient pet.

She hated herself. She hated him. She hated the ground and the sky and the wall and the chewing gum and the sound of a forklift beeping as it reversed on the other side of the metal fence.

"I wish you were older," Freddie said in a musing tone, casually taking a pack of cigarettes from his pocket. "If you were eighteen, we could make a sex tape. But I'd come across looking like the bad guy then, wouldn't I?"

Freddie lit his cigarette. "Are you deaf?"

Becky had assumed he didn't need an answer. "I think so. I'm fourteen. You're..."

He winked. "You're obsessed. Age is just a number."

She shrugged, her throat tightening. Mum was going to be livid about the article. She hadn't even learned about the interview yet, as far as Becky knew; it was one thing after the other.

"I'd like to know," Becky said, somehow, though it was difficult to force the words out.

"I'm twenty-one. Happy now?"

"Twenty... one."

He glared at her. "Is there a problem?"

Freddie was by far the oldest boy – *man* – she'd ever slept with. If Freddie had been even a little nice, had treated her halfway like a human being, she'd probably brag about this to her so-called friends. They'd all be jealous.

But her feelings, the deep roots at the base of her, were telling her this was wrong. There was a girl in school they all teased; she'd had the same boyfriend since primary, and that was hilarious, apparently.

But as Becky processed Freddie's age, she couldn't remember why it was funny. She couldn't remember what was better about this, what she did: with Freddie, with the demanding boys, with the expectation she'd somehow put in porn-star performances at fourteen.

Suddenly, Freddie's hands were on her. She was up against the wall.

His cigarette flew from his mouth, ash spitting over Becky's cheeks, burning her skin.

"I asked you a question."

She gasped, as he crushed her in powerful hands. "What? What?"

"Do you have a problem with that?"

"No," she said quickly. "Definitely not. It's sexy."

Freddie loosened his grip, his glassy eyes glinting. "Sexy, is it? Not as sexy as you were the other week. Proper bouncing, weren't you?"

Becky felt unwell. "Yes."

"Just your age." Freddie sighed darkly. "You'd make such a good slut for the camera. I can tell just by looking at you. You were made to be treated like a good whore, weren't you?"

His voice was getting husky in a way Becky didn't like. It reminded her of the park, before she'd stupidly brought him home.

He kept saying disgusting things, about how she was made to do what he wanted, how it was her only purpose.

"Maybe it's good your daddy died," he whispered, kissing her just below the ear, his lips cold. "Now I can be your daddy–"

Everything was a reflex: her knee driving straight into his balls, her nails raking down his face, then his arms as he defended himself.

And her footsteps when she realised what she'd done.

Running down the lane, struggling to draw in enough air through her constricting throat, she ducked her head; it was like she thought she could dodge his voice, dodge his words.

"You're done!" he roared. "You hear me? You're *dead*."

Becky sprinted the rest of the way home, running harder than she had since before Dad died; she'd quit hockey shortly after.

There was no doubt in her mind. She'd made a mistake.

But also, what Freddie had said was wrong. She knew some people were into that weird fetish stuff, but not Becky, never. She didn't want to mix her dad with any of that.

Dad was Dad, full stop, nothing else to add.

He was good and honourable and always did the right thing.

28

SOPHIA

Sophia sat in her living room, swiping on her phone, going through the photos Caroline had sent her. The whirlpool was getting out of control. It was spinning chaotically, reminding her of the years she tried to stifle: huddling in her room, staring at the flecks of damp on the walls, her dad yelling, *"Another line, another line..."*

And nothing Sophia could do about it. Until university, and then after – running, hiding, ignoring him.

Four local south-west newspapers were running the story, all repeating the same basic information: the recording, Abbie's evil words, the viral TikTok, the interview with Lyndsey.

Lyndsey had messaged her with the same images and a congratulatory note.

It won't be long until it's in the nationals. Then you can really get to work on your platform.

Sophia flinched when her phone rang, Jacqueline Wake-not-woke's name appearing on the screen. She sent it to voicemail, the way she did every time the head teacher tried to contact her. The most recent voicemail had informed Sophia she was on extended leave, which was likely to become permanent when Jacqueline completed the process of firing her.

Sophia could've gone to the union, or spoken to Jacqueline on the phone, but there was no point. What she'd done was, by the school's standards, wrong.

It didn't matter that she was working for a greater purpose.

After another sip of wine – it helped settle her buzzing mind – she thought about Abbie's face as she'd stared at the phone earlier that day. She tried to feel triumphant, telling herself Abbie deserved it. She did, on one level, but there was part of Sophia which wanted it all to stop.

The whirlpool was going around and around, dragging so many people in.

But that was the *point*.

After sipping wine and reading – or trying to read – for about an hour, her mobile rang. An unknown number.

She never normally answered these, but Lyndsey had mentioned she should answer any calls, just in case a *gorgeous opportunity* presented itself.

"Hi, is this Sophia Lancaster?" The man sounded skittish, like one of her boys. Not *her* boys, not anymore. Those days were over. "Of Lyndsey La Rossa fame?"

Sophia smiled, a reflex she enjoyed. It was so much better than frowning. This was a piece of her dream, being attached to the one and only Lyndsey La Rossa. "Yes, speaking."

"I hope you don't mind the call. My name's Sebastian Newport. I was wondering if I could ask you a few questions."

"Are you a journalist?" she asked.

"Guilty." He laughed, a little titter, and told her who he was with. Sophia's hand tightened on the phone. It was a national newspaper, and not the tacky kind. Sophia had held a subscription with them for years. "Truth is, Sophia... can I call you Sophia?"

"Absolutely."

"The truth is, I wanted to get your side of the story first, before some of my less virtuous colleagues muddled things up."

"Oh, I'm certain you're in this for entirely noble reasons."

"This is going to be a huge story if I have anything to do with it," Sebastian said. "You just need to ask yourself... do you want to set the narrative, or do you want Abbie to?"

"I think you'll find my interview with Lyndsey already has two million views."

"*Almost*, yeah, but I get your point. This isn't the internet, though. This is mainstream. This is the big leagues. This is how you get on the telly. This is how you *really* get your name out there."

"That's funny. I heard print was dead."

"Tell that to supermarkets all over England. We're not dead. We're just getting started."

Sophia paused, wondering what the right thing was. But really, the *right thing* wasn't the concern. She needed to fashion a springboard from which she could launch into a new career, far more lucrative and worthwhile than teaching; she'd ruined that, and she would have to accept it.

"Hello?" he said.

"I'm here."

"I guess you're deciding whether to tell me to mind my own business, eh?"

"Something like that. Have you spoken to Abbie yet?"

"No. I've tried, but she's not answering. I'm tempted to make a trip up there, but I'd rather see if the story has any traction first. I'm into multi-story issues these days."

"I suppose it's easier than thinking of new ideas."

"Not thinking of ideas. I'm reporting on facts. I just prefer if those facts have some lifespan to them."

"What do you want to know?" Sophia asked. "I explained everything in the interview with Lyndsey."

"I've got a list of questions."

"Okay." She sighed, staring at her bookshelf. She thought of *The Great Gatsby*, the unbroken unopened books in his library, the grand façade of it all. "Let's get started."

29

CHRIS

Chris wrapped his hands around Ms Lancaster's neck. He'd never hurt a woman before, physically at least; there had been times with ex-girlfriends when he'd behaved less than honourably, not at all how Dad would have. He'd shouted and cheated and caused havoc, but that was over. He was growing, learning.

Except he was squeezing her neck so hard her cheeks were bulging. Her eyes watered and protruded and then her hands were on his face, and she was stroking him, whispering, "It's okay, Chris, it's all going to be okay..."

Reality flitted; Ms Lancaster was bent over in front of him, looking over her shoulder, and Chris wanted it. That was the worst part. He hated and he wanted her. "Go on, you sexist pig, harder, deeper..."

He sat up, panting, blinking away sleep.

Sunlight filtered in through his window, resting on the glass display cabinet on the wall. It contained his grandfather's watch, an antique-looking thing that triggered a memory: Dad earnestly sitting Chris down, explaining that this was the only valuable thing the Basset family had ever held on to.

"And now it's yours," Dad had said. *"I want you to give it to your kid one day. I think my old man would get a kick out of that."*

Chris had been young, but he knew this moment was important. His dad's voice never wavered, never choked up, but it had then, and Chris wondered if he would cry.

"I promise I'll take care of it, Daddy," Chris had solemnly said.

Dad's smile had been better than any gift. He hugged Chris tightly. *"I know you will. I love you."*

Despite the warmth of the memory, the sour dream of Ms Lancaster clung to him, forcing him to his feet, across the hall and into the bathroom.

Showering angrily, he scrubbed away the last moments of the dream. He wanted nothing to do with her, and especially not in *that* way. The first part... had it been a murder? It was already fading. He thought it had been.

She'd killed him, or perhaps it was the other way around.

It didn't matter. Chris would never kill anybody.

After the shower, he changed into the shorts and T-shirt he'd carried through with him.

Becky was waiting for him in the hallway. Chris could hear Mum in her room, where she'd been since the previous night. It was odd, her not coming down to say hello, or to cook Becky's dinner; Chris had cooked it. Something was wrong, but it wasn't hard to guess what; the Ms Lancaster stuff was finally getting to her.

Becky stepped forward, hair a state, eyes sleepless pits. Her school uniform looked baggy on her, as though she'd shrunk overnight. "Have you seen the article?"

"Are you dim?" Chris snapped. "We talked about it last night."

"Not that one, dickhead." Becky showed him her phone; it

was a national newspaper's website, one of the fancy ones Dad had never read. It was the sort that talked about climate change and the Tories and all that boring stuff, not the kind with naked women on page three. "Do you see it?"

Chris looked at the most recent online story. There was a photo of Mum on one side and one of Ms Lancaster on the other.

'Kill All Feminists,' Says Mother of Two… But Was This Teacher Right to Record Her?

Chris read the article, the quotes from Ms Lancaster; there were none from Mum.

'I admit it's a big step to take,' says Sophia Lancaster, 37, a secondary school teacher of English working in the Bristol area. 'But I also found it necessary. Abbie has demonstrated, on several occasions, absolutely abhorrent behaviour toward me and several members of staff.'

Chris read on, clenching his teeth, as the reporter recounted Ms Lancaster's viral video, the deletion of her account, then the interview with that feminist twat, Lyndsey La Tosser.

Jacqueline Wake, 69, head teacher at the school where Sophia Lancaster is employed, had this to say: 'I am taking Sophia's actions extremely seriously. It is completely inappropriate and immoral for a member of staff to secretly record a parent during a private discussion.' When asked to comment on Abbie's sexist remarks concerning feminism, Mrs Wake responded, 'I have no comment except to say that Abbie Basset is a lovely person going through a difficult time, and she wouldn't hurt a fly.'

Chris took the phone from Becky, scrolling to a section where the reporter had quoted 'esteemed feminist icon and wildly successful podcaster, Lyndsey La Rossa'.

'I believe Sophia was entirely within her rights to record Miss Basset's destructive and — frankly — genocidal statement. Let's be clear about what she said: to kill all feminists. If Abbie Basset has to suffer some discomfort as a result of her damaging diatribe, then that's too bad. It's nothing compared with the suffering of women all over the world: women for whom feminism is their only chance at an unchained life.'

"It's skewed," Chris said, his hand trembling. "Have you read it, Becks?"

"Yeah," she muttered. "You're going to break my phone."

He almost threw it at the wall; he wanted to snap that nobody cared about her stupid bloody phone. But she had her mopey face on. Chris didn't have it in him.

He handed it back to her. "Did you see how skewed it was?"

"At least Mrs Wake backed Mum up."

"Yeah," Chris muttered. "A few lines. We need to talk to Mum about this."

Becky looked at the closed bedroom door, biting her lip.

"What?" Chris said, reading his little sister.

"I don't know. She was weird last night, when I came in, before you got home. She was just sitting in the living room staring at the wall. It was like after Dad died."

"Either way, she needs to know about this. The interview was one thing. She never goes online. But this is going to spill into the real world. Is it just the website, or do you reckon it's in print too?"

Becky shrugged.

"Can I get a bloody reaction out of you, Becks? This is serious."

She stared, as if she had more important things to worry about.

Chris marched to Mum and Dad's room... *Mum's* room, he reminded himself, was always reminding himself.

He pounded on the door in time with the thundering in his chest. He felt like he'd just drank three doses of a pre-workout energy drink. Ready to fight but with nothing to aim his fists at.

"What?" Mum called, sounding as though she'd been crying.

"Mum, it's gotten worse."

"What has?"

Chris closed his eyes, warned himself to breathe slowly, be patient. "The Ms Lancaster stuff. She's in a national newspaper."

"That explains the phone calls."

"The... they tried to contact you? I'm coming in."

"Just wait–"

Chris pushed the door open, walking in with his hand over his eyes. "I can't see anything, all right? But we need to talk."

Mum rustled around, then said, "It's fine, you can open your eyes."

Open your eyes. The words replayed in his mind. They seemed significant; it was what Mum and Becky needed to do, really look at the situation, realise they needed to take action.

Mum was sitting on the crumpled quilt, wearing her uniform from the shop. But it didn't look clean and ironed, as Mum's clothes always did; she'd always taught them that, no matter how much clothes cost, keeping them presentable was important. Chris wondered if they were from the previous day.

"What?" she said, sounding like Becky, petulant, nothing like Mum at all.

Chris tugged at his T-shirt. "There's an article in a fancy-pants *national* newspaper about you. Calling you a sexist. Telling the whole world what you said, a few fucking words in anger."

"Don't swear, Chris," she murmured, but there was no life in her at all.

"What's the matter with you?" Chris walked to the edge of the bed. "Don't you care? This is bad. Things are going to spin out of control."

"And what do you suggest I do, exactly?"

"I don't know!" he shouted. "Let's sue them. We can contact one of those charities I mentioned. You know, the non-profits. They might take it on... what's it called?"

"Pro bono," Becky said quietly from beside him.

"Exactly." Chris reached over, softly touched her shoulder; he wanted her to know, even if he was short-tempered with her at times, he still loved her. "Thanks, Becks."

"I only know because some of the dickheads in school called it *pro boner*. Don't act like I'm a genius."

He let his hand fall.

"Don't swear," he said a moment later, when Mum remained silent. He turned back to her. "We can try the police again–"

"No." Mum looked hard at him, like she was on the edge of tears. "You won't do that. You'll stay out of it. You'll let me handle it."

"But you're not handling–"

"I said *no*, Chris. Why won't you ever fucking listen to me?"

Becky gasped. Chris stepped back. He couldn't remember Mum speaking to him like this, ever.

"I'm just trying to help," he whispered.

"No police. No lawyers." Mum looked at the digital clock. "I need to shower. I'm going to be late for work."

She stood, moving as if to run away from this conversation: as if the article didn't matter. Chris walked into her path, his arms spread. "You can't ignore this."

"Move, Chris," she said.

"No."

Mum stepped back, more tears glistening in her eyes, then one slid down her cheek. "Just... move."

"Mum."

He made to hug her, but she stepped even further away.

"No police," she said. "No lawyers. That's what I want. Please move."

"Why?"

"Because I've got work–"

"Why can't we fight back? I thought that's what you wanted."

She looked to one side then the other, as if debating running around him, but there was nowhere to go. Chris felt like a bully, physically blocking his own mother. He felt pathetic. But she wasn't taking it seriously.

Mum rubbed the tear from her cheek. "What I want is to get ready for work so we don't lose our home."

"What would Dad do? He wouldn't take this–"

"Your dad would do what he always did. Whatever he wanted. Move. *Now.*"

She screamed the last word, and Chris stepped aside. Mum's words made no sense.

"What does that mean?" he yelled after her, the reaction delayed as his mind tried to untangle it. "Dad was the best man I knew, any of us knew. Don't..." He trailed off, looking at Becky. "What did she mean? I don't get it."

Becky shook her head, looking like she was going to cry too.

149

30

ABBIE

After her shower, Abbie pulled back the quilt and gathered up the shredded photos. There were pieces of Jack in each of them: half a forehead, the corner of his smile, a tattooed arm. She almost put them in the bin, but then quickly shoved them in a drawer; maybe she'd glue them back together one day, and maybe she'd do the same to his memory too.

Downstairs, she sat at the table. Becky was picking at her toast. Chris stood across the kitchen divider, angrily buttering his.

"I shouldn't have said that about Dad," Abbie said.

"Why did you?" Chris grunted, staring stubbornly down at his task like he wanted to murder the butter.

"It's silly," she said; she *lied*. She'd never lied to her children before, not about something this big. "I was thinking about an argument we had, going over and over it last night. Sometimes, I wish he was here to defend himself, to explain things to me. And when I realise he's not, I just get..."

She pushed the sob away. It was becoming ridiculous, how close to tears she'd been ever since the confrontation with Caroline and Sophia.

Chris walked around the divider, leaned down, and hugged her.

"I get it," he said, squeezing her supportively. "He wasn't perfect. But he always tried to do the right thing."

"Of course he did." Abbie made herself lie again. "I just forget that sometimes."

Chris returned to the kitchen, then brought his plate to the table. Becky was still picking at her food, but Abbie didn't have it in her to... to what? To *parent*? Was she really going to allow this to make her useless to her own children?

Suddenly, she was disgusted. What a joke.

"Eat your food, Becky. You need your energy for school."

Becky smirked, then began to eat.

"Why don't you want to get help?" Chris asked softly, as though he thought she was going to shout at him again.

"Because..." She paused, thinking, wondering what possible reason she could have. "It will take too long. Court cases take months, years, sometimes longer, don't they?"

"I think so," Chris said.

"They do." Becky spoke through a mouthful of toast. "We learned about one in school. An American one. I can't remember what the case was about, though."

"By then, the damage will already be done," Abbie said, wondering if this was true. It *sounded* true. "If we're going to fight back, we need to do it another way. Not with the police, since they clearly don't want to help. And not with lawyers, since that will take too long."

"How, then?" Chris asked.

"I don't know. I'm still hoping this will blow over."

"It's in a national paper, Mum..."

"And tomorrow something else will be. And the next day, something else. The world moves quickly. It's not like it was when I was a kid."

Chris looked doubtful – she couldn't blame him – then shrugged and took a bite from his toast.

31

CAROLINE

Caroline pushed her breasts together, pouting at the camera. "Hey, Ryan, baby. Ooh, thank you."

Raging_Ryan881 was one of her most loyal viewers. He was also a moderator for her livestream, which meant he watched the comments and made sure nobody got too pushy.

Caroline had a policy of respect, decency, and goodwill on her channel.

She spit on her breasts when Ryan tipped her again: the specific amount for her to make her tits shine with saliva.

Massaging her breasts, more tips came in. They were getting her closer to the goal of full anal penetration with a nine-inch dildo.

There was a device inserted in her vagina, a small vibrator, which was linked to the livestream. Every time somebody tipped, it shivered inside of her, the tremor getting more exaggerated the higher the tip.

She felt little, physically, as it hummed and whirred. She'd been streaming for three hours; it was difficult to keep up any real sensation for that long. But she was able to moan and find some enjoyment in it.

The sweetest was the little burst of warmth in her mind each time she received a new tip, a new viewer; that session, she'd made around a thousand pounds, and six thousand viewers were watching her.

She spit on her breasts again when Ryan tipped the same amount, and again, and again.

"Ooh, baby," she said.

He sent her a tipped message, paying extra so it displayed on the screen.

I can hardly type. You're so beautiful. You're an angel.

Ryan gave the best compliments, making her smile feel genuine.

A moment later, somebody tipped to have their name written on Caroline's body. "Oh, God, you drive me crazy."

There were already five names on her body: upper chest, belly, neck, and both her arms. She found a space on her breasts and clumsily wrote the name, then went back to massaging herself, making her lips as pouty as possible, which was an art.

She went on with her work for half an hour, getting closer to the final show. She'd already practised with the dildo in private, and she knew it was going to hurt. But the platform was competitive; she needed to make things more extreme, stay relevant, beat the competition.

She was getting rich, and she wanted it to stay that way.

Then another tip came in, this one as a private message. Viewers could choose whether their messages appeared for everybody to see, or just for Caroline.

Caroline almost paused when she saw the name, though her professionalism kept her hands in motion.

Jack_Basset_1985 had sent her a private message.

I miss you so much.

The words sent a shattering feeling through her, as if the

young woman within was trying to break through the surface. But still, her hand kept going, even if the sensation between her legs couldn't be more distant.

She heard her own moans as though they came from somebody else. The public comments, the ones everybody could see, were telling her how beautiful and sexy and funny and kind she was.

Then another comment came from Jack. Jack Basset, born in 1985. *Her* Jack... the man she should've forgotten a long time ago, and *did* for a while, until–

You were my one true love.

Caroline opened her mouth and began to moan even louder, shifting her body like she was gripped in the most intense orgasm of her life.

It was a perverse feeling, as she split into two; there was the cam girl, all bouncy tits and forced pleasure sounds, and then there was Caroline, Jack's lover, the broken-hearted woman who was still trying to piece herself back together.

Another private tip came in as her 'orgasm' culminated with melodramatic cries of lust. She sounded like an amateur even to herself; she wished she could do better, put in her regular next-level effort, but there was too much clashing in her mind.

She was thinking of how badly she'd wanted to be with Jack in school, the boy one year above, the rugby player with the sandy blond hair and the easy smile. She remembered how awful it had been for her at home, with all that stuff, the arguments between Mum and Dad, Dad leaving, not caring. It was a cliché, but it didn't stop the pain.

Sitting in a park, Caroline had sat gripping the swing links so hard they'd made impressions in her hands which lasted an hour. But then Jack had walked by with a group of his friends.

And fine, he hadn't told her he loved her right *there*. He

hadn't done anything more than tell his friends to go ahead, and then he'd come and sat with her, saying little. But what he said had mattered.

"Life's hard, but it'll get easier. I promise you that."

Perhaps her crush had gotten a little out of hand in school, what with her brief... not *stalking*, but her brief phase of being a tiny bit too enthusiastic.

She'd started attending after-school dance classes, for example, because the studio had a window which looked out on the playing fields, letting her watch Jack as he rallied his team, as he casually shrugged off the other players, as he showed her with every gesture what an incredible life partner he was going to make.

And maybe Jack's position as manager had *something* to do with her decision to apply for the fabrication plant.

She recalled his face as she'd walked into his office, the slight narrowing of the eyes. That had been one of the worst moments of her life: the knowledge he didn't recognise her. But then he had, after a pause, and a smile had reshaped his kissable lips.

"Ah, Caroline, nice to see you again."

I'm not dead. But I need your help.

Caroline quickly typed a response. She was only supposed to respond if the tipper had paid enough, which Jack hadn't. No, not Jack. Whoever this was. Probably Abbie, the sick freak.

But would Abbie play games like this?

Who are you?

In the comments, people were asking what she was doing, why she had stopped.

What's wrong, angel?

Is everything okay?

What's the holdup?

This is getting so boring.

Jesus, slut, do something...

I can't keep spending money to talk, Jack_Basset_1985 replied. *Text me if you want to speak properly.*

Caroline hurriedly scrawled down the attached number, and then sat back, struggling to breathe. She could feel the ink of the men's names seeping into her skin, certain it was invading her blood, her body, but she was a professional.

She hadn't worked this hard – and endured several surgeries – to quit because some cruel lunatic wanted to upset her.

"Ooh, aren't you an impatient bunch?" she said, pursing her lips, pushing her breasts together, forcing her mind to stay focused on her task. "We're so close to the goal. I can't *wait* to show you how good it feels. I can't wait..."

"*I can't wait until I'm older,*" she'd said back then, sitting next to Jack on the swings. "*I'll never have to worry about stuff like this.*"

"*Like what?*" Jack had asked. "*Your dad leaving?*"

"*Men leaving,*" she'd replied, looking at him slyly, wondering if he was getting the hint. He was the man she envisioned, and she wanted him to say something in tacit agreement. "*I'd be a much better wife than Mum. I'd never give my man a reason to leave, you know?*"

Jack had kept looking ahead, seeming distracted. It was unlikely he was thinking of the grotesque ignored thing Abbie had been at that age: an invisible nothing in school, despite her size.

He was thinking about somebody else, though: somebody who wasn't Caroline.

And that was unacceptable.

"*Yeah,*" he'd said, rising to his feet. "*I guess so. Listen, I've got to go.*"

As Caroline bent over, holding the nine-inch dildo and looking over her shoulder at the webcam, she wondered who the tipping sicko was. She told herself it couldn't be Jack, even as an insane hope flared within her.

What if it was? What if he was somehow alive?

What if he was ready to choose her after all?

NINE NINE NINE

The killer winced as the tell-tale sounds started: the footsteps moving across the room, presumably to the phone.

It was the natural thing to do, ring the police, and another reason the killer regretted hiding here in panic. But there was something else happening too; paralysis was setting in, as the shock rolled and morphed and became the undeniable realisation the killer had done something impossible to take back.

It was almost tempting to just stay here, wedged into place, and pretend it wasn't happening.

But it was. Action was necessary.

The footsteps walked past the nook, giving the killer a glimpse of the person.

A click sounded; the phone lifting from the receiver in the opposite corner of the room.

Even the beep beep beep of the dialling numbers seemed perversely loud.

Three beeps.

One for each nine.

32

ABBIE

As Abbie approached Little Pint, she knew something was wrong. Usually, at this time – it was six o'clock – the entrance was quiet. It would get busy later, as the pre-drinkers came in, and after that a queue would form.

But as she got closer, she saw two strange things: her boss, Keith, was standing at the front of the door like a bouncer, and around a dozen people were crowding him, some of them holding signs.

Abbie's instinct was to dart down the closest alleyway, the same way she'd hidden in Cornwall when she spotted Caroline in public.

All that day, while she'd worked at the shop, she'd cringed each time she sold the newspaper which contained the article about her.

But nobody had said anything; she'd chatted with the regulars. She started to believe it truly might go away.

The slogans on the signs told her how naïve this was.

Fight the Feminist Killer, Now!

Justice for Women!

No Hate!

Abbie had stopped walking, without consciously deciding it. The air was cool, but she was sweating, making her uniform stick to her skin.

Keith had his hands spread, as if to stop the protestors from rushing him.

One lady turned; she was a stylish-looking woman with piercings through her septum and in unusual places in her ears. She wore a top that had frilly arms, the material slightly transparent, letting Abbie see her sleeved tattoos.

"Oh, here she is," the woman said loudly, and then they all turned.

Keith followed their collective gaze. Her boss' posture became more rigid, and then he threw his hands up, as if he wished Abbie had somehow foreseen this: as if he wished she'd gone home, quit ahead of time. She could already tell he wasn't on her side, which wasn't surprising. Keith had never wanted anything but a simple life.

Abbie knew the feeling.

The women swarmed her, a collection of trendy university types.

One strode to the front of the group, aiming her finger at Abbie. She looked like a bodybuilder, the kind of woman Jack often complimented. *You don't know the work it takes to look like that...*

Again, Abbie killed Jack's voice. She'd kill *him* if he wasn't already dead.

"So you're the one who wants me dead?"

The women behind her sniggered.

Abbie backed up, wondering how far they were going to take it. The bar, and the surrounding businesses, were right there; people and cars were passing by. Surely they weren't going to assault her.

"No," Abbie said. "That's not right."

"I know it's not right. Why do you think we're here?"

"I said something in anger—"

"What sort of excuse is that?" one woman raged; she looked like a librarian, mousy, kind. But her soft lips were warped into a hate-filled grimace. "So you can say anything, do anything, and if you're angry it's okay?"

"I didn't fucking..." Abbie trailed off, staring past her panic, really looking at the women; a couple of them were holding cameras, aiming them right at Abbie.

"I didn't mean it," she said, in the steadiest voice she could manage. "I don't want to kill anyone. I just want to live my life."

"Are you sorry?" another woman hissed.

Keith appeared at Abbie's side, giving her a stern look. But then he turned to the assembled protestors. "Let's keep this civil, ladies."

"Oh, ladies," the muscular woman said, rolling her eyes. "Here he is, the knight in *shitting* armour come to save the day."

The protestors laughed. Abbie felt sure they were one person, a single entity; it was the way their laughter came all at the same time and stopped just as uniformly. It reminded her of Caroline and the other girls in school, the ones who always seemed so distant, so cool, so not-her.

Even if they were her bullies, Abbie had wanted to be part of that laughter, to hear her voice rising with theirs.

"This is childish." Keith looked at Abbie. It was a confused expression: reluctance, but also some empathy in there, a small amount. "Come on, let's go inside."

"Fight the feminist killer!" one woman yelled, and then they all began to chant.

Abbie warned herself not to lash out. It was the bloody cameras; she knew that if she shouted, they'd clip out everything else, just as Sophia had, and the world would see nothing but a psychotic woman-hating woman.

162

The chants followed her inside, then Keith spun on them. "I'm refusing you entry to my property. That's my right. I'll call the police if you force me."

The women kept chanting, the same words, but they stopped short of the doorway.

"Fight the feminist killer, fight the feminist killer, fight the feminist killer."

Abbie looked at them, imagining them coming into her shop before this all happened: the conversations they'd have, the banter about how evil men could be, the shared pleasure in a female athlete doing well. She wanted nothing to do with them – they were bullies; they were sick in the head – but she would have happily talked to them before they hated her.

"We need to talk," Keith said gruffly, walking past her.

Abbie stayed where she was for a moment, staring at the protestors, as the chants continued. She couldn't even make out their features anymore. They were all melting together, seeming hardly human, like their faces were becoming the material of their signs, and their mouths and noses and eyes and ears and hair and wagging tongues were so much ink.

"What are you staring at?" the woman said, striding right up to the door. "Fancy your chances, do you? Come on then. Kill me. Show me what you're made of."

Abbie turned, walking up the stairs, then running, telling herself she wasn't afraid: telling herself she didn't wish Jack was there to protect her.

"You and your temper." Keith was drumming his fingers against the desk with more purpose than Abbie had ever witnessed; she sensed what was coming. "I like you. You're good at your job. Why couldn't you just keep your mouth shut?"

"Imagine when Paula was Becky's age," Abbie said, referring to Keith's daughter. "And a teacher told her that, when she grew up, she should become a prostitute. Imagine she said it after your wife passed, when you were trying to keep everything together. Would you stay calm?"

"Did she really say that?"

"Yes, she admitted it. But she deleted that part from the recording."

Keith sat back. "I don't know what to do here. I really do like you. But I've got all my other employees to think about. I've got my business. Little Pint's main customers are women just like those outside."

"Cruel bullies?"

"You get what I mean. Trendy types."

"But nobody seems to care she recorded me against my will. Nobody seems to realise how unfair this is."

"Life isn't fair. We both know that."

Abbie knew what he was going to say next.

"I'm going to have to let you go."

Rent. Bills. Chris' kickboxing fees if he wanted to start again. Money for Becky not to seem poor in front of her friends. All the big whirling mess of life.

She shook her head, gripping the desk. "Please."

"There's nothing I can do. They won't stop until I fire you. It's as simple as that."

"Don't put it on them. You could have a bloody backbone."

"Suppose so. But then I wouldn't have a business."

Abbie didn't have a union; her contract was zero-hours. She didn't have a salary. There was nothing she could do, and she knew Keith well enough to understand he wasn't going to budge on this. He was behaving the exact way he had when she'd asked for a raise.

"I've got no savings," she said. "I need this job. What you're doing, it could make me and the kids homeless."

"You'll find something else." He shifted in his chair. "You're a smart girl."

"I've worked every shift you've ever asked me to do. Christmases, holidays, the kids' birthdays. Everything. And after this, one incident–"

"It's not one incident," Keith interrupted. "If you're here tomorrow, they will be too. Next week, there will be a hundred of them. They'll start spreading nasty rumours about Little Pint. The bar won't last long, not with the sort of customers we serve. I'm sorry, Abbie. I really am. Look..."

He reached into his pocket and took out his wallet. It was packed with twenty- and fifty-pound notes, so many the clasp had come undone. He unfolded it and took out five fifty-pound notes, placed them on the desk, and slid them over.

In her mind, she said, *"I don't need your charity, you coward."* And then she grabbed the notes and bunched them up, throwing them in his face. She walked out with her chin raised, dignity making her posture rigid.

But of course, that wasn't an option. She took the cash and quickly pocketed it.

"Thank you," she said, tone heavy with sarcasm. "You're a really good man. I hope you have a wonderful sleep tonight. Maybe I'll take Ms Lancaster up on her offer, put Becky on the game. Maybe I'll do it myself too. Maybe even Chris, a whole family of hookers. I bet you'd love that."

"Abbie..."

She made for the door, pausing only when Keith said her name again, sharper this time.

"What?" she said, pulling on the door handle, feeling it strain against the wood. It would be satisfying to wrench it loose, throw it across the room, but Keith would only charge her for it.

"You might want to use the back entrance."

Abbie opened the door roughly, marching down the stairs, determined to walk out the front.

She wouldn't let them bully her.

But when she reached the hallway, she saw more protestors had gathered.

There looked to be about twenty, standing in a loose circle, talking, some of them smoking. They were like an inactive muscle, but she knew it would blitz into action the second she stepped outside.

Turning, she hurried through the bar, out the back door, and down the alleyway.

33

BECKY

Becky stood at the window, staring out at the street. The neighbour's car alarm had been blaring for a couple of minutes, but nobody had gone out there to shut it up. She didn't want the added stress; running the long way from the school bus had exhausted her enough without that screeching noise punching her right in the brain.

Finally, the owner came out and shut the alarm up.

Becky dropped onto the bed.

She was checking her social media constantly, even more than usual, waiting for Freddie's video to appear. She thought about all the things she'd said: the names she'd called Mum, the lies she'd told.

But what should she have done, let Freddie take advantage of her?

Dad would understand. If he was there with her, he'd clap her on the shoulder, giving her that just-Dad smile. And he'd say, *"Next time, do it harder. Leave the little prick on the ground."*

Her phone rang, a number she didn't recognise. A tremor of

dread told her not to answer. It could've been a bully. Somebody taking the piss. But *not* knowing was worse.

"Hello, lovely."

It was him. Freddie. His voice chilled her.

"Come to the window. I want to wave hello."

"Just leave me alone."

"Come to the window, or you know what happens."

"How did you get my number?"

"It's a small world, hot stuff. Don't make me threaten you again."

As she returned to the window, she felt like her legs could fall away any second. There was too much glee in his sick voice. He was enjoying this too much.

Freddie stared up and all his goons did the same, and Becky realised how stupid it was, being there alone. The doors were locked, but they weren't thick; glass windows broke easily.

They could rush up there, do anything, and nobody could stop them.

She wished she had a gun. Right then, she would've mown the fuckers down, just to stop that sick sneer spreading across his face. She could feel the gun metal in her hands, imagine pulling the trigger, the vibration as the bullets tore through their heads.

She refused to believe all five of Freddie's friends were as evil as him. The tracksuits, the tattoos, the heavy jewellery weren't signs. Chris used to dress like that, and she'd seen photos of Dad in his youth, wearing similar. Lots of her friends looked the same too.

But it was the eyes, the way they glinted in the streetlight. The weird hunger in them.

"You've got one week." His voice was cheerful. "Seven days to give us what we want. Or the video goes online. Got it?"

"What do you want?"

Freddie laughed; his friends joined in, a couple of them exchanging glances. Becky thought there was some compassion there, but then it was gone.

"I promise..." He beamed up at her. "We'll be gentle."

"But what do you want?" Becky said, her voice getting louder, tears stinging her eyes. "What sort of man are you?"

"Relax, darling. We're going to be real nice with you. I don't want to hurt you. But the fact is, you owe me. You assaulted me, and that's not okay, is it? Not even a little bit."

"I..."

Becky couldn't produce words. Tears slid down her cheeks, sobs cracking in her throat. She felt like an ant-sized thing, so insignificant, as if she'd never mattered and never would.

"I'll even sweeten the deal," Freddie went on. "You give us a little something, I'll *delete* the video."

She shook her head, even as she longed for it. It would be so much better, knowing it was gone. But she couldn't trust him. Ever.

"Liar," she said. And then she erupted. "You're a *fucking* liar!"

"I swear. I've got it all worked out. Before we meet, you can take a naked photo of me, save it on your phone, upload it to the cloud. Then after we're done, we'll both delete what we've got, wipe the slate clean, move on. It's a fair deal."

Freddie hung up, then strolled away, his pack of wolves following.

Becky told herself she *wouldn't* give it any thought, but it made sense, on some level. She'd have something on him too. And would it be that bad, really? She was getting good at detaching her mind from her body when it came to that sort of stuff.

But then she thought of Dad, and she wanted to scrub herself with harsh chemicals to wash it all away.

She detached herself with *boys*, one on one – mostly – her own age; mostly. That was different to letting a bunch of sad loser grown-ups do whatever they wanted, all because she'd done the right thing and defended herself.

As she walked across the landing, she heard the front door open, and guessed that was the reason Freddie and his friends had left.

It must've been Chris, since Mum was at work.

But when she went downstairs, it *was* Mum. And she was crying.

34

BECKY

Becky had seen Mum cry enough times to know these were angry tears. Becky rushed to her quickly. She didn't even consider telling Mum about Freddie and what had happened; she was beginning to wonder if she'd imagined the whole bizarre exchange, or perhaps that was just wishful thinking.

"I can't believe he did that," Becky said when they'd sat down, and Mum had told her about Keith firing her. "That isn't fair."

Becky ignored the acidic – and true – voice inside of her, the one telling her none of this would be happening if not for her. She was the one who'd decided to stir things up, informing Mum what Ms Lancaster had said.

And she was the one who'd… but it was better not to think about that.

"Fair," Mum repeated. "No, Becks, it isn't."

"But life isn't fair? That's what you're thinking, right?"

"Right." Mum leaned forward in the armchair. "I need to find a new job before Chris finds out. This isn't going to be good for him. You know how badly he wants to work, and that was when I had two jobs."

"Maybe you should let him."

Mum looked at her sharply.

"What?" Becky went on. "If he wants to help, maybe he should. I know Dad wanted him to study–"

"This isn't about what your dad would want. This is about Chris' education."

Becky wasn't sure what to say. It was like Mum had a problem with Dad suddenly. But then Mum had gone through stages like this before, soon after Dad passed: blaming him for the cancer at one point. It was part of grieving, she said, and Becky understood; she'd hated him for leaving them, an insane thought, since he didn't *choose* it. But that was life, it seemed: feeling terrible things that could rarely be shared.

"Chris can't know," Mum said, and that's when he walked into the living room.

He came in from the kitchen, wearing a hoodie and shorts, no shoes, no socks, his hair messy.

"No college today?" Mum asked.

Chris shrugged. "Nah, it was a day off. What about my education? What's happened?" He sat on the sofa and rested his forearms on his knees. "You've been crying, Mum."

Mum bit her fingernails, something she rarely did. "I... Chris, you can't panic, all right?"

"Why would I panic?"

Mum told him.

Becky expected Chris to freak out, but he just nodded all the way through. It was like he thought it was a joke, and yet Becky could tell he believed it; it was like he thought the whole world was a joke, then.

"This is the way it goes, right? A few people kick up a fuss and then we've all got to do what they say. I've been looking into it, into other cases like this. It's mental. The world's going crazy. How many people were protesting, like twenty, maybe less? But oh no, fire this single mum. Ruin her life."

But still, his voice was calm, even as his angry words flowed. It was an eerie combination. It was like he was burying all the emotions so well Becky couldn't even spot some of them.

She wondered what would happen when he finally let them out.

"It's fine, though," Chris said. "You don't need to work. I'll handle it."

"Chris—"

"I'll handle it," he interrupted, looking steadily at her. "We're not missing rent. We're not missing bills. I'm going to sort this."

"How?" Mum said.

Chris sat back. "You don't need to worry about that."

"Chris, you need to hear this—"

"No." Chris seemed far older than usual, more mature than most adults Becky knew. "I'm done listening. No offence, but you need somebody to take charge. You've lost your job and this stuff is spinning out of control. We need money, and I'm going to get it."

Becky expected Mum to snap at him: to show him she was the boss. But she seemed somehow smaller, staring at Chris, struggling to find the words.

"You're not dropping out of your course," she said after a pause.

"I never said I was."

Mum stood, triggering relief in Becky. *This* was the old Mum, with the determination in each stride. She stood over Chris. "We're going through a hard time right now. I get it. But that doesn't mean you have the right to throw your life away."

Chris shifted, suddenly a boy under Mum's intense stare. "Who said I was going to do that?"

"I know you want to be the man of the house, but it's *my* job t–"

"You clearly need help," Chris interrupted.

"I don't want you doing anything silly."

"Mum, you need to listen–"

"No, *you* need to listen. I'm the grown-up here. I'm in charge. I don't want you doing anything stupid for money."

"So what – we can become homeless instead? Jesus, I was only thinking of some cash-in-hand work."

He walked from the room quickly, leaving Becky and Mum to look at each other.

"I'll go speak with him," Becky said, rising to her feet.

"You don't need to know," Chris said, when Becky asked about his money comments. Chris threw a tennis ball at the poster of his favourite kickboxer. He caught the ball. "What you need to do is tell me what's wrong with you."

"What–"

"You've been acting strange, Becks. Don't bullshit me. And I heard you crying."

"I didn't think you were in."

"Who were you talking to? What's happening? I can help you."

She thought back to the park, remembered the agony of Freddie's fist, and then after, the sick stuff he'd said about Dad. She couldn't take it anymore; it was like the fist was striking her again, again, right there. She pulled up her shirt to just below her bra, showing Chris her bruised side.

Chris gasped, dropping the tennis ball and walking toward her. He made to touch her, then recoiled, staring. "Who did this?"

"Take a guess," Becky whispered, trying to force the tears away.

But in the end, they won. Chris tenderly pulled her shirt back down, then wrapped his arms around her more gently than Becky could ever remember. Becky wept with force, pushing her face against his chest, as Chris softly stroked her back.

Through the sobs, she told him about the park, the forced video.

"You should've told me," he said, once she'd cried herself out.

They sat opposite each other, Chris on his computer chair, Becky on the bed.

"There's been so much going on. I didn't know how to."

"He's going to pay for this. I just need to figure out how."

"He said I've only got seven days."

"That should be enough."

"Enough for what?"

"To think of a way to hurt him," Chris said. "Badly. And get him to delete that video. It takes a real sick fuck to do what he did. He's lucky Dad isn't here."

"I keep thinking that, about Dad. He'd make all of this better, wouldn't he?"

"Yeah, but he's gone. And I've been a baby about it for too long. Mum needs help, but I'm playing the kid. Going to training still. Acting like my little course is more important than my family. That's over."

"What do you mean? Have you got a job?"

"Something like that," he said. "You can't know the details. Mum can't either. But what else am I supposed to do? Sit here, wait for the world to... to crush us, you know? Mum was never the strong parent. Let's just say it like it is."

"But she's trying her best."

"I know. She is. But it's not good enough. That's just a fact.

She can't work two jobs, raise you, grieve Dad, *and* deal with this Ms Lancaster crap all at the same time. Something has to give."

"You're being very secretive."

"I have to be." He stared at her coldly. "Don't make any decisions about the Freddie thing until I've told you what to do. In the meantime, I want you to carry this."

Chris opened his top drawer and brought out a flip knife.

Becky recoiled instinctively. "A *knife*, Chris?"

"What would you prefer?" he snapped, as he unfolded it. "I can't be with you twenty-four-seven. If you're forced to use it, tell the police it was his knife. You somehow wrestled it from him. It's easy, all right? Don't overthink it. If he comes at you, you get some distance, quickly take out the knife, and you just go for him, Becks. Aim for his eyes, and when he raises his hands to defend himself, you get him right in the gut. You open that bastard up. Got it?"

"I..."

Chris flipped the knife open, handling it deftly. "We're going to practise. You need to be ready."

35

CAROLINE

Caroline lay in the marble bath. It was one of the perks of her job, far more glamorous than the admin positions she'd held before she'd discovered webcam work. She could afford the most luxurious holiday apartments, with ornate baths, everything smelling nice, heated floors, the types of things she never could've imagined as a kid grieving her dad's departure.

She wasn't washing the shift off her, exactly, since it didn't make her feel dirty; it didn't make her feel shamed, or wrong, or any of the things society would *like* her to feel.

But she had to admit, it was nicer in the warm bubbles, without the lens of the camera staring unflinchingly at her.

And that was even as she held her phone above the water, waiting for *Jack* to respond.

She'd texted him: *Right, who are you really?*

She placed her phone on the floor and sank deeper into the bath, closing her eyes and thinking about the first time she and Jack had kissed. It was after hours, just the two of them.

Caroline had made an excuse... it had been a bit of a cheeky lie, telling him she was scared to go home because her ex-boyfriend was showing up unannounced at her house.

Sure, maybe it was wrong, but it had made him pity her, want to help her. And that had felt so sweet, the perfect prelude to the perfect kiss.

Brushing up against him, she'd apologised, then looked into his eyes. She'd kept staring, knowing her perfume smelled inviting, knowing she was attractive.

Men were *always* looking at her; it was just, their names were never Jack.

Finally, she'd leaned in, kissing him hard.

She tried not to think about how he'd seemed to want to withdraw. To stop him, she'd darted her hand out and started stroking up and down his groin. That couldn't lie, never could, with any man.

He'd groaned, and suddenly, *voila*, he'd become enthusiastic in the kissing.

Caroline sat up quickly when her phone made a text alert noise, water splashing everywhere. But she didn't have to worry about making a mess, about the water settling and causing damp, about any of that nasty stuff. She wouldn't be staying there forever.

If she had her way – and she planned to – she'd have a mansion or a penthouse one day.

She was a predator, stalking through the jungle, waiting for a chance to pounce.

It's Jack, Caroline. It's ME. Please don't make this harder than it already is.

She sat up even more, ignoring the water against her privates, the friction ache between her legs. It was a small downside, compared to most jobs.

She was lucky; she often reminded herself of that. Many women who chose her profession floundered with ten or twenty viewers for their entire careers. Caroline had chased trends, maintained focus, played the game skilfully.

Come to think of it then, could she call that luck?

Tell me something only Jack would know, she typed.

I'm not playing these games. It's taken a lot to reach out to you.

It's a fair request. She moved her thumbs quickly, telling herself there was no way this could ever be true. And yet she wanted it to be. Badly. It hurt, how achingly she needed it, him. *Just one thing. Or I'm not responding anymore.*

I only ever loved you, he replied quickly. *I only chose Abbie because she was pregnant.*

She tossed her phone to the bathmat – the screen was already cracked, but she could always buy another – and quickly rose.

Whoever this was, they were truly deranged to say something like that.

She wrapped a towel around herself and forced the window open, hungrily breathing in the cool air. Then she grabbed her phone and sat on the toilet seat.

She rang the number. It declined her immediately.

I can't talk yet.

What's wrong with you? She focused on typing the message accurately, even as her hands trembled. *If you were Jack, you'd know Abbie didn't get pregnant until AFTER she dragged him away from Cornwall. Who is this?*

It's me. The response came quickly. *And you're wrong. Abbie got pregnant before. We didn't tell anybody. But it's why we left, and it's why I chose her originally. But she had a miscarriage. By then, I knew you wouldn't take me back.*

She shuddered, sat back, and felt it coming: the panic. She despised herself when these attacks struck her.

I would've taken you back, she almost typed, but then the phone was on the floor.

And so was she, lying on her side, the tiles cool against her naked body as she drew her knees up to her chest and lay there. Just lay there. Shaking for God knew how long.

Finally, she was able to drag herself to her feet. Her eyes were sore, as though she'd been crying, but she couldn't actually remember if she had. Her chest hurt from all the heavy breathing.

"Joke," she hissed under her breath. "Get your *act* together."

She grabbed the phone, texted quickly.

You expect me to believe you're Jack, but you won't tell me something only he'd know. And now you're telling vicious lies. Plus, Jack is DEAD. I've been to his grave. What you're doing is wrong on so many levels.

She walked naked into her bedroom, relieved the curtain was shut; she didn't want anybody seeing her for free.

I can't explain it over the phone.

You expect me to meet you? Caroline texted back. *You're a freak.*

I never told you I loved you, he texted. Or *they* did, whoever they were, as Caroline dropped onto the bed. *You wanted me to. You said it to me. But I never said it back. That's all I can share over the phone.*

The tears came even as she fought them. She remembered telling him so many times, draped across his shoulder with her mouth pressed against his ear. Or just after they'd made love; it wasn't sex, it wasn't screwing, any of that. It was making love, rocking together so gently, then so suddenly hard, fast, the passion exploding.

He'd turn away, shaking his head, sighing.

She'd clung to him. She'd felt it bursting from this primal place inside of her, a pulsing: *keep him keep him keep him.*

"When will you be ready?"

And she remembered – as her phone buzzed again – one time when he'd roughly stood up from the bed. He'd kicked up the scent of the sheets, the themness; turning, he'd pulled on his T-shirt like he was trying to cause himself pain. *"Just leave it."*

"But I love you so much..."

He'd sighed, running a hand through his messy hair. She'd even loved the way he did that, all the little gestures that made him up. *"I need time..."*

Caroline grabbed her phone.

Jack had sent an address. Followed by a note.

7pm. Tomorrow. Don't be late.

It was a boat bar on the waterfront. Caroline's hands trembled as she grasped the phone.

Who are you? How do you know that? What's wrong with you?

She rang the number again. He rejected her. She texted him several more times. She paced; she got dressed, forcing the crying to stop, but he didn't text back.

She marched into the living room and found her suitcase.

Opening it, she took out the pepper spray and the taser, both of which were illegal in England, as far as she knew. One of her American fans had sent it to her in disguised packaging.

She'd never needed them, but they made her feel safe... and it wasn't as though she ever gave the police a reason to search her.

Unlike Abbie, Caroline didn't make herself a target.

She switched on the taser, giving it a practice squeeze, and then aimed the spray.

Whoever this was, they'd be sorry for dragging her memories of Jack through the filth.

36

ABBIE

Abbie stood at the counter, tapping her fingernails, wondering if this was what going mad felt like. It was a quiet day, plenty of time to imagine Jack standing in front of her. She could see him so effortlessly. His arm was resting against the wall, that casual smirk on his face.

"What's wrong, little dove?"

Abbie wasn't literally hallucinating. It was more like the tear in her heart had released something in her brain. She was able to imagine him with violent clarity and imagine what she'd say in reply.

"Don't call me that."

Not-real Jack laughed softly. *"Why not?"*

"Guess the reason I went for you, Jack. Go on. Guess." Her lips were moving slightly as she imagined these words, but she wasn't making much noise. The shop was dead; the early-morning wind rattled quietly at the door. *"No? All right. Because I didn't want to feel like the fat girl anymore. I got with you because I wanted to use you. That's all you were. A way to inflate my self-esteem. Thank God you gave me the kids, but I never needed you."*

Abbie was digging her thumbnail into the tip of her forefinger, pressing as hard as she could.

"The only reason?" Jack smirked, cocky as could be. *"You're lying to yourself. You love me."*

"If you weren't already dead, I'd wish it."

A little noise escaped her. She heard it as a yelp, then shook herself alert. She was so tired, even more than usual.

The door creaked. She turned.

It was Lucky, with two big stacks of papers under his arms. Everybody called him Lucky because he'd miraculously survived a car accident a few years prior. Normally, he and Abbie bantered as he dropped off the papers.

But he was shifting awkwardly, not meeting her eye. He stared at the colourful vape pen collection as he spoke. "You all right, Abbie?"

"It's okay," she said quietly. "I'm in one of them, aren't I?"

Lucky looked at her, nodded shortly.

"What does it say?"

Lucky leaned down, took one from the bundle, and laid it on the counter. As Abbie unfolded it, wind blew rain against the glass of the door; she read the words and felt them rattling around her skull.

The page five headline read: *"Kill All Feminists!" Parent Proudly Declares.*

"Proudly," Abbie muttered.

"I'll get the rest," Lucky said, leaving her.

It was one of the tabloid newspapers. They'd gotten a photo from the internet, Abbie guessed. It was of her with her arms raised, an angry look on her face.

At first, she wasn't sure where exactly it had been taken.

And then she remembered. It was from Chris' sixth birthday, when she'd joked she was going to help him blow out the candles. She'd held her breath, making him laugh, and somebody had snapped a photo. She couldn't remember who.

The newspaper had stolen it. Blown it up. Put it next to those words.

Abbie tore at the pages.

And then Lucky was yelling at her, his hands out.

She blinked; she was on the other side of the counter.

Her hands were sore. She'd snapped two fingernails. Shredded newspaper lay all around her, with Lucky talking to her like she was a wild horse.

The glass to the fridge was smashed, three panes of it. Abbie's knuckles pulsed with blood.

She dropped the newspapers, stumbling back.

"Relax, petal," Lucky said, walking closer.

"I'm sorry," Abbie whispered, leaning against the counter. "I'm so sorry."

"We'll get this cleaned up. Don't you worry."

"But the fridge..."

Lucky winced, then went on. "Just relax–"

The door opened.

It was the owner, Mr Anand. He was a tall man, with sharp features and wire-framed glasses. He took them off, cleaning them, staring across at Abbie.

"Are you stressed? Do you need time off?"

Mr Anand spoke in quick bursts. They were sitting behind the counter, with the *closed* sign facing the street. Lucky had left, keen to get on with his other deliveries once he saw there was nothing else he could do.

"No," Abbie said quickly.

Mr Anand interlaced his long fingers. "Does this have

anything to do with today's news?"

Ten points to the brainbox, Jack tried to joke in her mind. But she ignored his voice, even as she needed it.

Mr Anand leaned forward. "You know business is hard for me. You know, in this time, how hard it is for a man to make a living. I cannot have my employees smashing up the shop, ruining our equipment. Do you see?"

"Yeah." Abbie stared down at her hands; Mr Anand had cleaned and bandaged them, though she hadn't been bleeding much. "I think I get it."

"So you tell me what I can do to help."

Abbie narrowed her eyes. "Help?"

"I have read this little article, and I have done some looking with the Google. This thing, it is not right."

"This thing?"

"To record a person, and now everybody knows your name? It's not right. I don't like it. I don't think it's fair." His heavy accent made his words seem angrier somehow. "I cannot do much. But what do you need? Some time off, Abbie?"

"I... I can't." She rubbed her sore hands together, thinking of what Chris had said the previous night, his vague hints toward money; she didn't know what he meant, still, and that was wrong. She should have. "Not to be rude, but I–"

"I will handle the money." Mr Anand pushed his glasses up his nose. "For two weeks, yes? Paid? For your regular... what, thirty hours?"

"I... y-yes." Abbie was almost weeping. "Are you sure?"

Abbie had a contract which stated zero hours were obligated, no steady work guaranteed, and there was no such thing as paid holiday.

"Yes," Mr Anand said. "I will work for a little while. You rest. Spend time with your family. And then, when you are back, no more breaking or crying or anything ugly like that, yes?"

"Yes," Abbie replied, ignoring the tightness around his eyes, the unspoken glare that said: *Why did you have to bring this here?*

But she told herself that was paranoia. He was helping her. He wouldn't do that if he was judging her. Or perhaps it was both.

"Thank you so much," she said. "You don't know how much it means to me."

"It will all blow over, I'm sure." Mr Anand reached into his pocket, taking out his wallet; Abbie ignored the déjà vu, putting Keith in place of Mr Anand. "Try to stay out of the newspaper, yes?"

"Yes," Abbie said, as Mr Anand pulled out a wad of cash and began counting.

If she wasn't out of the press in two weeks, then there would be no job for her. She was beginning to understand the scope of this, but still, this was more than she could've hoped for.

It would have been simpler for Mr Anand to kick her out the door.

Abbie drove home with a tight fist in her gut, squeezing tension through her. As she pulled up outside the house, she looked down the street.

That man was there, the one in the overcoat. It looked dirtier than last time. Abbie's heart thudded as she threw the car door open.

He was leaning against a lamp post, hands stuffed in his pockets.

This couldn't be a coincidence.

Confronting her in some random street in the city, fine, but waiting on her *street?*

"What do you want?" Abbie yelled, walking quickly over to

him, her breath coming fast. She couldn't give herself time to think about what she was doing.

The man turned, head ducked, hurrying down the street.

"Why are you following me?" Abbie shouted.

She stopped at the lamp post where he'd been leaning. She wasn't going to chase him through the city.

Should she call the police?

What would she say?

He was already gone, turning the corner, leaving her street.

37

SOPHIA

The whirlpool was spinning, catching them all; it was on the table, taking up an entire page of a tabloid newspaper. It wasn't the *front* page, but it dominated page five, Abbie's image blown up and livid.

She looked enraged, her cheeks red as if she was preparing to breathe fire. Sophia knew that wasn't far off the truth; she knew there was a deep hatred in Abbie. But she also felt, for a moment, something else.

Then Lyndsey appeared on the laptop screen. Sophia was sitting in her living room, curtains open, the early afternoon grey and bleak as the rain hammered.

Lyndsey was grinning from sunny New York, looking alert. "This is so good for us."

Sophia beamed, ignoring niggling thoughts of the whirlpool, the situation, the blackout and the confession and everything which had led to this point; she would focus on the future. Her dreams. They weren't fragile. She felt certain.

"Is it?"

Lyndsey tilted her head, wordlessly saying *oh, please*. "You got your whole country talking about this issue. And many people in mine too. People are reading those words, those sickening unacceptable words, and they're asking themselves, *Do I agree with this?* That's what it's all about, starting conversations that become movements, that then become realities. Somewhere down the line, this action will save untold numbers of women and girls."

"Really?"

"Who am I, Sophia?"

"Lyndsey La Rossa."

"That's right. Lyndsey La motherfucking Rossa." She grinned, and Sophia found herself smiling too, letting go of the whirlpool. "I wouldn't be here, talking with you, if I didn't believe this. Your one action will save lives. CEOs, politicians, they will read this. They'll be forced to respond. This honestly could be the start of a movement."

"A movement," Sophia repeated.

"With you as the figurehead," Lyndsey said, and Sophia almost gasped.

She was sitting up, feeling like she had to jump to her feet, do something. She was ready to do it, whatever it was, right then; it was thinking, wondering if she'd done the right thing, doubting, internally debating... it was all that, tearing her up, twisting her.

But she had a purpose, and it was this.

"Don't look so surprised. This is your chance. I didn't arrange this call just for the fun of it. I've got some big news."

"Yeah?"

"I'm coming to England."

"Why?"

"To help *you*, silly." Lyndsey sat back. "I've got a contact in British television. Do you know Morgan MacDermott?"

Sophia knew him as the boisterous, seemingly perpetually drunk host of a late-night show where minor celebrities and disgraced politicians ranted at each other for the amusement of a gladiatorially minded audience. "He's a friend of yours?"

It was hard to imagine the glamorous Lyndsey La Rossa hanging out with the brash blunt TV presenter.

"His show is one of the highest-rated things on British TV right now. It's hotter than all the morning shows. It's hotter than the news. But what's better... it's *edgy*. Morgan will let us really explore the issue, no nonsense, and he won't let Abbie run from us either."

Sophia forced her mind to catch up. "Wait, so me and you and Abbie are going on *The Morgan MacDermott Show*?"

"If you're ready to take your opportunity. This is it. Maybe, if your little eye-roll was any indication, you don't think Morgan's show is all that special. That's fine. We're talking about awareness here, about reaching untold numbers of people. It will be me, you, Abbie and Morgan. She won't stand a chance."

Sophia thought of Becky in class, and how similar Abbie had seemed during their interactions, fights, whatever one wanted to call them: a similar narrowing of the eyes, something in the smirk. Sophia wondered how Abbie had reacted to seeing herself prominently displayed in a newspaper.

"Is something wrong?" Lyndsey asked.

"No," Sophia said quickly. "I was just thinking... if we gang up on her, won't people side with her? She'll be able to pretend she's the victim. We don't want our message to get lost if the show gets wild, like it often does. Morgan MacDermott is in the news every other week for some scandal."

"Hmm, that's a fair point. We'll ask Morgan to treat it more like a friendly debate. But it doesn't matter. She'll be forced to repeat what she said, reminding the world that people – worse, *women*, specifically – hold such abhorrent views. Without feminism, the world would be a much worse place. Who could argue with that simple truth?"

"Nobody," Sophia said. "But..."

"Don't be shy. We're comrades now."

"I'll need help. I've never done anything like this before. And my boss, the head teacher at the school, she keeps ringing. I haven't done anything with the school yet. About my job, I mean."

"Your *job*?" Lyndsey slowly shook her head, as though Sophia was speaking an unknown language. "This is your job now. You'll help a million times more women doing this than you ever would have teaching at some school. I'll be in Bristol tomorrow. I'm messaging with Morgan as we speak. Exciting times ahead."

"Will you help me?" Sophia asked. "Coach me, I guess? A live audience is going to be way different to the podcast or TikTok."

"Morgan doesn't have a live audience," Lyndsey pointed out.

"A show, I mean. A studio. Life, not live. Real life." It was all coming out wrong. "Will you help me, Lyndsey? Please?"

Though Sophia was older, she felt like a little kid when Lyndsey shone that understanding smile. "Of course I will. You don't even have to ask."

38

CHRIS

"You all right, Chris?"

Jimmy was all jittery, doing that annoying druggy side-to-side dance as he approached. This council estate was a true shitheap. Chris had been to places like these enough times, and he never liked them. They reeked of weed and piss and depression and, he swore, it was always raining or grey.

"Ready to meet the boss?"

"I met him," Chris said. "He's the bloke from the underpass, right?"

Jimmy's nod was way too energetic. It was like the idiot was trying to snap his own neck.

"Will the one I kicked be there?"

"No, I asked like you told me."

Years melted, and Jimmy became a boy: nervous, acne across his neck, terrified of his dad, creeping through life. And then a friendship, Jimmy passing a note in science. *Need help with that?*

This kid, this man, so enthusiastic about school. People used to tease him. But Chris never did. He even bloodied his knuckles a few times defending Jimmy.

He wasn't sure he would have if he'd known how far Jimmy would fall.

"Uh." Jimmy shifted. "Shall we go up?"

"Do you like places like these?" Chris asked.

Jimmy became the kid embarrassed by his Lego set. He'd been so shocked when Chris agreed to build something with him. *"Smart lad, him,"* Dad said once. *"He's going places."*

"Jimmy, old friend, old buddy, old pal?"

"It's all right."

"It's grim, mate."

"I've got friends here. You know it hasn't been easy for me."

"Yeah," Chris said. "I know. Let's go up."

He couldn't afford to care about Jimmy, or any of this. Just Mum and Becks.

"Mike Tyson himself graces us with his presence," the man from the underpass said. His name was Tone, Chris knew, *Tone*. Not Tony. Even his name pissed Chris off. Being there, interacting with men like this: wrong.

Tone waved his hands as he paced in front of the dirty window, as if addressing an audience. Really, it was just Chris and Jimmy and a man leaning against the wall, tall and lean and with an air of violence about him; Chris bet he could fight.

"A flurrying fighter. A fiend in the ring. Or the underpass. Am I right, lad?"

"Well, I kicked him," Chris said.

Jimmy made a prey noise. A signal to bullies everywhere he would scare extremely easily. Chris just stared at Tone, his dark hair scraped back over his head, his tracksuit and trainers the only shiny things in this place.

"Fair enough," Tone said. "So, you want a job?"

"Yes."

"And you reckon yourself a, shall we say, connoisseur of violence?"

"I'm not as clever as you, but yeah."

"I was an Oxford man once."

Chris shrugged. The man seemed like he was on something. Drugs, coke maybe, talking crap like cokeheads always did. Junkies all over this place. There was one standing next to Chris, flinching every couple of seconds.

"The job's simple. Stand there and look tough. If violence happens, respond accordingly."

"And the pay?"

"Generous," Tone said.

"Define 'generous'."

Tone grinned at Jimmy. "Your friend sure likes his questions, don't he?"

"Sorry, Tone," Jimmy said.

Why was he apologising? He needed to stand up for himself.

"One thousand Great British Pounds for a night's work. How does that sound?"

It sounded like this could either be easy or end in blood and violence.

"That should be fine. Except, I'd like to take a hundred pounds less."

Tone clapped his hands together. "What an interesting bargaining strategy. I accept your kind offer."

"I need something in return."

"One hundred pounds' worth of something?"

"I'm guessing you know all the..." Words flashed through Chris' mind: *lowlives, scum, losers, saddos.* "Street people around here."

"The street people. Yes, the hobos and the whores. The rats like little Jimmy here."

"He's not a rat," Chris said, and something in his voice made the other man stand to his full height, stare at Chris.

Chris didn't need another fight, and it wasn't his job to defend Jimmy.

"Go on. Make your request," Tone said.

"Do you know a bloke called Freddie? Real mouthy. Tribal tattoo. Has a habit of perving on girls younger than him."

"How slanderous. You're lucky he's not one of my men."

"You know him?"

"My dear boy," the annoying prick said, with an annoying-prick flair of his hands, as if drawing attention to his flashy, ugly rings. "I know everybody. Freddie Watson has a little gang, runs a few schemes here and there. What do you want with him?"

"I'm going to scare him into doing what I want. If that doesn't work, I'll hurt him, maybe quite badly."

"And what *do* you want?"

Chris thought of Becks. "That doesn't matter."

Tone shrugged. "A hundred quid for that little turd? Why not? He has a flat. Or, rather, his mum does."

"Is this an act? The way you're speaking?"

Tone laughed, looking, at the same time, like he'd happily snap Chris' neck. "I didn't lie. I'm university educated. I'm going to write a book about my experiences one day."

"Right. Where does he live?"

"Jimmy knows. He can take you there. Jimmy will reach out when it's time, too."

"All right."

Tone offered his hand. Chris stared at it for what felt like a long time. It was gross, the idea of touching this man. Of being connected to him at all.

Chris took his hand, shook it quickly, then Jimmy led them outside.

"He's on the second floor," Jimmy said, as music blasted from several flats, and, above them, somebody screamed, words muffled. "We see his mum sometimes."

"What do you mean by 'see'?"

Jimmy gave him a look. Ah, obviously. They sold her drugs.

Downstairs, Jimmy gestured down the hallway. It was long and narrow, the carpet worn. It was like the edges at home in the living room, except the frayed, dirty parts were spread all over the uneven floorboards.

"What did he do, Chris?"

"Something bad to Becks."

"Jesus. I'm so sorry."

"Go knock on the door. Tell Freddie you've got some tasters for him. You can lead him outside and I'll jum–"

Jump the prick, Chris was about to say, but Jimmy started shaking his head fast. "No, no, Chris. Please don't make me. I've got to live round here. I was only supposed to show you where. Even that's risky. Please, Chris…"

"Stop begging. Fine. Fuck off then."

Jimmy flinched. Chris closed off the soft part of himself, the part that wanted to tell Jimmy he was sorry.

Finally, Jimmy hurried toward the stairs, stopping to look over his shoulder. There was pain in his eyes, but it was his fault, living there, doing this shit. Chris knew Jimmy had had it hard. His dad was a monster, a real bully.

Chris walked down the hallway and knocked heavily on the door.

"Who is it?" a woman yelled, her voice hoarse.

"I'm here to see Freddie. I've got a package for him."

"Freddie!" the woman screamed. "Door!"

Chris slid to the side of the doorway, breathing slowly. He felt like he could watch himself, pressed against the wall, a surreal feeling coming over him.

The door opened.

Chris sprung around the corner.

A flash: Freddie in grey shorts and a bright-red hoodie, unzipped to show his chest, a sleepy look on his face. Then Chris slammed him against the wall, quickly shoving his hand over Freddie's mouth.

He fought. He tried. But Chris handled him easily.

"You're going to delete that video now," Chris said, keeping his voice level. "Or I'm going to mess you up. Badly."

Freddie struggled, shouting something against Chris' hand, his breath disgusting and hot.

Chris drove him harder against the wall, then brought his knee up in a blunt motion, slamming against Freddie's groin. His eyes turned red, as Chris pressed down on his face and forced the back of his head into the wall.

"I will fucking end you, mate," Chris said. "You're going to delete it. Nod if you understand."

Freddie nodded. The groin strike had caused tears to slide down his cheeks. He looked pathetic. He looked like a scared rat when faced with real violence, with somebody who could fight back.

"All right. Do it now." Chris let him go slowly, but kept his hands raised, ready to hit him if it came to it. "Turn so I can see the screen. And shove your face into the wall if you forget what a pussy you are."

Freddie turned halfway, holding his phone up. "Look, all right? Here."

Chris grabbed the phone when Freddie scrolled to the video.

Chris clicked play, and then immediately ended it. He couldn't watch it; he'd end up wringing this asshole's neck.

He deleted it, then gave Freddie a stiff shove in the back. "Did you send this to anyone?"

"Nah, mate."

"Tell the truth. I'm going to check."

"I was saving it."

"Freddie, what's taking so long?" his mum yelled.

"Talking to a mate," he yelled back.

"Yeah, I'm your best friend," Chris said gruffly, clicking the 'recently deleted' file.

"Smile for the camera," Chris said, holding the phone up when it told him he needed face ID.

Freddie turned, still with those pathetic tears in his eyes.

Chris went to Facebook, clicked through the top five chats, clicked images and videos. There was some sick stuff, sadistic porn clips, pictures of women, girls really. But there was nothing about Becky.

"Explain why you were saving it," Chris said.

"For the, you know, mate."

"For the deal you made. You and your mates could gang rape my sister."

"Nah, that was just a joke."

"Yeah, real funny."

Chris went to WhatsApp, and then to the OneDrive application, but Freddie had never set up an account.

"Let's say I find out you've got this video saved," Chris said, dropping the phone on the floor. "Do you think I'll be happy?"

"It's o-over," Freddie said.

His voice was shivering, this brave bastard.

"It better be," Chris said. "Or I swear, I'll kill you. I'll do life to put you in the ground where you belong."

Chris shoved Freddie toward the doorway. He stumbled,

tripped, fell, his head hitting the door handle. He grunted and stood, rubbing his head, standing there powerlessly.

A true coward.

Chris walked down the hallway, kicked the door open.

He couldn't leave this place fast enough.

HELP

"P-police," the voice said, making the killer wince. "No – an ambulance. Both. Please. Oh, God. Yes, no, I can't... I'm not sure. How do I check? Please send somebody. I need help. All right. Yes."

The person walked by the nook again, returning to the corpse, presumably to check if the dead thing was still breathing. But the life had bled from the lifeless lump with far too much ease, as though people were made of paper and could be torn apart, as if nothing was ever fixed and certain.

The killer moved slowly, quietly.

"I don't think so," the voice said, a shiver of pure terror in it. "Please hurry. No, no movement. No, it wasn't an accident! Because I can tell! Nothing. I don't know who did it. Wait... you think they could still be in here?"

The killer emerged from the nook.

39

BECKY

"Why are you home early?" Chris said when he barged into the living room.

Becky had the knife in her hand, the chunky one he'd given her the previous night. But it seemed like a different world: a place Becky was thinking of as *before*. She gestured with the knife, to the armchair, where she'd thrown the newspaper.

"Because of that."

Becky hadn't gone into school, but one of her friends had told her about the newspaper. She'd almost run to the corner shop, on the lookout for Freddie.

The afternoon sun made motes of light dance in the air. Becky paced through them. She was holding the hilt of the knife so tightly, squeezing until her hand and her forearm hurt. She had been practising, slicing at imaginary Freddie's eyes, his groin, his throat.

Chris stared at the newspaper cover as Becky paced.

"Relax, Becks," he said. "I've visited our little friend. The video's gone."

"What?" Becky rushed over to him. "Are you serious?"

He gently took the knife from her and placed it on the

display cabinet. "Yeah, I made sure. He's got nothing on you now. And if he bothers you again, I'll kill him."

Chris' words chilled her.

"Still take that with you, when you go out." He nodded to the knife. "Just in case."

Becky shivered. "But the video's gone?"

"Definitely."

She threw her arms around him. "Thanks so much. Really. You're the best big brother ever."

"Yeah, I already know that."

She squeezed him again, and then they examined the newspaper together.

"These animals," he whispered. "You know where this photo's from, don't you?"

"No. Did they make it up?"

"What do you mean, make it up?"

"Like Photoshop it. Mum gets angry, but she looks crazy there."

"It was from my birthday. She was holding her breath."

"Oh."

"Is your Facebook public?"

"I don't know. What's the usual?"

"That means they got it from your Facebook, then."

"Look at her. She doesn't even look like Mum," Becky said. "The whole world's going to hate her. And it's all my fault."

Chris came and sat next to her. He must've sensed something in her voice. He wrapped his arm around her, how he often had in the days right after Dad's death. "What is it, Becks?"

She didn't want to tell him, but it was hurting even more than the fading bruises. "I was the one to post Mum's name on Ms Lancaster's video. And then other people saw it, and they started commenting. It was that night, remember, when you kicked Freddie out..."

"I remember," Chris said softly.

"I was so angry. I thought she'd ruined my chance with him. I was an idiot."

Chris rubbed her shoulder. "You're not an idiot. You made a mistake. It's all right."

Becky opened her mouth to speak, but she sobbed. She pushed the words past it. "I'm a terrible daughter."

She hadn't meant to break down, but then she was, her face pressed against Chris' chest. He hugged her, his hand circling on her back. "It's not your fault. You didn't make the video. Mum's name would've got out there eventually."

"You can't know that..."

"Things are how they are. I can't afford to care about how or why or what led here. There's a chessboard, all right, and there's a certain number of moves we can make..."

Becky laughed through the tears, looking up at him. "A chessboard?"

He grinned, but his eyes were watery too. Becky wondered why. Was he angry with her? Or just sad she wasn't the sister he'd thought she was?

"You don't remember me and Dad playing chess?"

"No." Becky laughed again, even as the tears flowed. "You're lying."

"Nah, we used to play for hours and hours... I guess it was before that pebble head of yours started making memories."

Becky shoved him, grinning somehow. "You're not a completely terrible brother."

Chris looked at her seriously. "It's not your fault. You need to accept that. None of it. You were angry. You did something you regret. Move on."

"Do you think I should tell Mum?"

"Maybe one day," Chris said. "But not now. She's got enough to deal with."

Chris ended the embrace and took out his phone. Becky wiped her cheeks as he rang Mum. She answered, and Becky sat there, remembering how justified she'd felt with each letter of Mum's name, the loathing she'd felt for that woman, the sadistic idea of *this* happening...

The newspaper covers, the headlines, the hate.

At one point, however briefly, Becky had wanted it more than anything.

"She's on her way home," Chris said, pocketing his mobile. "Mr Anand has told her to take a couple of weeks off. Paid, but... yeah, definitely keep that to yourself, all right?"

"I will," Becky told him. "I don't want to make things worse."

But Becky knew the truth.

Things were always going to keep getting worse.

40

CAROLINE

Caroline waited outside the bar, her breath fogging in front of her. The night was cold, despite her thick coat and jeans and hoodie. She had the taser up her sleeve; she'd practised taking it out. The pepper spray was in her pocket. The front of the bar was lit up, but she was in the dark, watching, waiting.

Her phone vibrated.

I can see you, beautiful.

Caroline looked up and down; the bars further up were dark, many of them only recently open or opening, with alleyways here and there.

You're sick. Disgusting.

I don't know why you'd say that. I loved you. I was never brave enough to say it. But I did, so much.

She wouldn't allow herself to come close to tears; she was ready for this. There was a little girl crying deep inside of her, but she kept her surface ice.

She itched to grab the taser, to make the motherfucker hurt.

If you've got something to say, come say it to my face. This is pathetic.

She turned at the sound of footsteps.

A man was walking at her, moving out of the shadows like he wanted to cause pain. He walked into the streetlights, and Caroline moved forward cautiously.

He was around forty, with a patchy black beard and a sizeable belly, making him lean back as he walked, like he was supporting it. He sucked on a vape pen, the smoke shrouding his face.

"Jack?" Caroline said, her tone purposefully cutting.

The man took another suck on his vape, then, as he blew the smoke out, "Yep."

"That was a pretty sick game."

"Well..." He blew more smoke. "You're a pretty sick woman."

Caroline mentally rehearsed the taser movement; she doubted she'd need it. They were in the open. Sure, it was getting dark, but they were still in public. Nothing bad would happen.

"How's that?" she said, keeping her voice calm.

"You know what I'm talking about. That shit you do online. That filth."

"So let me guess, you fat, pathetic little man. Let's see. You can't get your dick hard anymore because I'm too sexy and everything else is boring? No? Or maybe it's that your ugly pig of a girlfriend caught you stroking your bacon over me..."

Caroline giggled. He bristled, all manly, but she didn't care. "That's it, isn't it?"

"You don't know what you're talking about. Little whore. Falling for all that Jack shit. Look at you. You're a joke. You're not even a human at this point. You look like a doll."

"Buyer's remorse, you limp-dicked loser? Your true feelings came out – and I mean that literally – when you were watching me."

"Jack used to laugh at you down the pub," the man went on, his hand wrapped tightly around his vape pen; his knuckles were pressing sharply, like he was getting ready. "Clingy Carol, we used to call you."

Deep within, the little girl wailed and kicked at the walls, trying to be set free, or at least for somebody to fall into the prison with her. But there was no way she was letting this man see even a glimpse of it.

"So you were one of the losers Jack used to keep around because you paid for the drinks? He used to laugh about you saddos all the time."

"You've got no shame," the man said, as Caroline tried to place him. And failed; Jack had never made her a firm part of his life. "My wife, she found me... and I told her I was addicted. It was a problem. But the payments, she said. That was too far. All the gifts. You twist it up. You mess it all up. You make it impossible for a man to *think*."

He shouted the last word, as though he was picturing his wife in Caroline's place. She even felt sorry for him, but she wouldn't let him see that either. "It's not my fault you can't control yourself."

"All the stuff I've bought you. I probably paid for those." He aimed the vape pen at her chest. "And I bet you don't even remember my username. I'm just another idiot."

"If you had a wife who asked you not to engage in adult entertainment, and then you were too stupid to delete your internet history and make sure she's out of the house before you have a wank..." Caroline raised her hands in utter confusion. "Then maybe you should just throw yourself off a bridge. You're clearly a complete waste of oxygen."

"So funny," the man said darkly. "So clever. I've seen you doing things that'd make most women feel like dirt. They'd hate themselves for the sick stuff you've done, on camera, night after night. The stuff you say, if they pay you enough. Half the time, you're pretending to be somebody's daughter, sister, mum. Do you know how wrong that is?"

"I don't kink-shame my clients."

"Kink-shame," the man muttered. "Since when did shame become a bad thing?"

"What did you expect to get from this?"

"I don't know..." He stared at her. "You're nothing like I remember. You used to be a scared little thing, walking around town, remember?"

He moved closer; he was invading her personal space.

The bar was *right there,* but nobody was standing out front. The street wasn't remote, but it was oddly quiet. Suddenly, Caroline realised just how dark it was.

He reached for her.

Caroline took out the taser as she'd practised, but it clipped her thumb. She had to adjust her grip. She was gasping, trying to scream, but no noise would come out. It was like she needed all her attention for the taser, but her breath was making her throat tight.

She finally got it loose, then his hand was on her arm, his grip solid through her coat.

"What's that, aye?"

He wrenched it from her hand, then she felt it at her throat, the metal prongs touching her. His laugh was boyish delight, but there was a harsh edge to it. "Is this a stun gun? A bloody taser? You silly whore..."

A jolt.

Caroline's body began to tremble; any notion of screaming left her.

They were in an alleyway; it was dark and it reeked of piss and she wondered if she'd blacked out. He was clawing at her clothes, and she was shaking all over as he zapped her again and again.

"Bitch," he told her at one point, and she knew she was losing consciousness, because her body was experiencing different things each time she awoke.

Some piece of her – as he did what he was intent on doing – was aware enough to control her hand; she willed it toward her coat pocket. She still had her coat on, but he'd pulled her jeans down to her ankles.

The position into which he'd contorted her was unthinkable for regular sex. The angle was horrific; she noted all of this with a cold detachment.

The pain was somewhere, in the deep-within room.

She could feel his belly against hers. The deranged copy of intimacy, the intrusive closeness, it was almost sicker than the fact of his body invading hers.

Her hand was still moving. It was in her pocket.

He kept prodding her with the taser, but not activating it. He was just hitting her.

Every time he did it, he called her a vicious name: whore, slut, all the rest of it. Caroline thought she felt him getting soft, but it was difficult to be sure.

"Bitch?" It was almost a question as he jabbed her in the side. "Slut? Whore? Go on. Moan. Like your videos."

Caroline grabbed the pepper spray. She carefully popped the lid off with her thumb.

He was slowing down, and then he even sat back. Caroline leaned up and stared at him, sitting there with his limp cock out, the tip smeared a colour Caroline could not acknowledge; her only goal was *get out*.

"You're really a horny bitch, aren't you?" the man said. "You loved it." He lowered his voice, muttering under his breath as if to convince himself. "You... you loved it."

He glanced behind him, then stood up, his penis exposed. He still had the taser in his hand. He pressed down on it, making it spark blue, as he waddled toward her; his trousers and boxers were around his knees.

"Get up. Come on. You need to finish the job. Suck... suck..." He paused, then he grinned sickly. "Suck your blood off my dick."

Caroline sat up slowly, ignoring the cramping.

She smiled and she made herself pretty; she made herself as inviting as she could with the terror crushing her spine. "I want it. But let me stand up. I want to bend all the way over. That way you can look at my ass while I do it."

He was a moron; his hope to... to *rape* her – and she was getting ready, war drums pounding in her mind – was overpowering everything else.

He gestured with the taser, and Caroline stood.

Leaning forward, she quickly took out the spray and let loose.

She screamed as best she could with her tight vocal cords, and she sprayed, and she kept doing both, screaming and spraying, until the man had collapsed against the wall with his hands covering his face.

He'd dropped the taser.

Caroline moved fast. Her body yelled at her; her privates felt like something vital was being compressed, violently, over and over. She tripped on her jeans, then sprawled, grabbing the taser and leaping atop of him.

She drove it into his neck and squeezed, screaming in his face, as she felt ugly liquids flowing down her thighs.

She tased him and she spat in his face. She was about to dig her fingernails into his swollen eyes when she heard a woman shouting for help, and then more voices.

Caroline rolled aside, gasping, staring up at the small pocket of sky visible between the buildings.

She felt like she'd always been there, at the bottom of something very deep, only briefly glimpsing clouds and rain and sun and the things other people took for granted.

She'd always been a little too different, wanting more, never tasting it.

"It's all right, love." A woman's hand was in hers, and Caroline tightened her grip a little. "That's it. It's all going to be okay."

"I didn't..."

It was *his* voice; Caroline couldn't see, her vision bursting with stars, like the small piece of sky was infecting the walls. But there were no stars: light pollution. She was drifting.

"Don't let him," she whimpered.

"Will you get him away from her?" the woman yelled.

"I didn't..."

"Shut up, mate. Don't make us hurt you."

Caroline gripped the hand tighter, glad it was a woman's. She knew this person wouldn't hurt her. She didn't have the tool. The evil demanding tool, the sick assumption of it: *I can do what I want when I want to anybody I want just because I feel like it.*

But then she stopped thinking about any of this nasty crap.

There was a new thought. She wondered if this meant she was more than a little insane.

It was deranged, to be thinking of things like this in her state.

But she'd had an idea.

She'd never tell anybody it had occurred to her in that moment, as her body and soul twisted in agony. But she couldn't deny it.

It was a very, very good idea.

41

ABBIE

Abbie sat up in bed, staring down at her phone. It felt strange to not be at work at this time of day, despite it being the weekend.

She'd made the mistake of logging into her email account, which she rarely used. But it was like she wanted the punishment, for some bizarre reason.

Her inbox held one hundred and fifty-two messages, from people who'd managed to acquire her address. Perhaps it had leaked on some forum somewhere; that was what Chris had suggested, the night previously, when she told him.

Die you fucking dumb slut

You are disgusting!!!!!!!!1111

Ur kids are fuked

Others were requests for interviews, and then there was one from a man called Douglas Walker. The subject heading read: *I can help you.*

Abbie opened the email, knowing it was going to probably be more spit in her face.

But as she read, she dared to let herself hope. It was a silly thing to do. She was aware, after everything the world had thrown at her – fate or God or whatever else – that it was the *last* thing she should do.

Hello, Abbie,

You probably haven't heard of me, but I'm a writer and a journalist. I'm currently working on a book about cancel culture and, in particular, its effects on the 'regular person'; I hope you won't mind me branding you with such words, as I consider them a compliment.

You probably won't be surprised to hear I'm very eager to speak with you and, if possible, shadow you through whatever happens next. I may even be able to offer some words of advice here and there, as I've appeared on a number of television programmes, and I'm not unfamiliar with the media world in general.

I'm waffling. I tend to do that. Luckily, my editor is an executioner.

I want to propose a deal. Let me meet with you for my book, and I will offer you my media expertise, including help with any PR strategies you're working on. (That was a statement of authority to make you trust me; I'm aware you're incredibly unlikely to have a 'PR strategy'.)

With your best interests at heart, and I mean that sincerely...
Douglas

Abbie googled him. He was a smart-looking man, around Abbie's age – maybe a couple of years older: he might be forty-something – with thick black hair combed to the side and a smile that said: *I know things.*

The first-page results showed a number of his articles, as well as articles about him. A couple of them asked if Douglas Walker was a friend to bigots; more voiced the concern that his writing was dangerous and phobic in many ways, but Abbie trusted none of them.

Not a single bloody one.

She'd trusted newspapers, once, generally speaking. She'd never had any reason not to. Jack had often complained about them all being rubbish, and Abbie knew about some of the scandals involving the tabloids, but after seeing her face in print...

She didn't care what they said about Douglas.

It was the *fact* they hated him which made her think about replying. He was an outsider, like her, whereas all the other journalists who had contacted her had seemed fake. At least the ones whose emails she'd read.

Should she read more, see if there was somebody better?

She studied his image, his easy smile, his playful eyes. There was no world in which Abbie felt attraction to a man who wasn't Jack, was there?

She replied, hearing Becky walking loudly around her bedroom. Her music blasted through the walls. Abbie hoped she was dancing, even if it meant messing her room up.

Or that she was tearing apart a pillow to let out some of her grief. Anything to stop her hanging around with the Freddies of the world.

Hello Douglas,
I would like your help. How do we arrange it?
Abbie

She clicked send, then tossed her phone to the other side of the bed. She could act out like an angry teenager, finding a vaguely handsome man, seeing the desire in his eyes, if she was capable of producing such a thing.

You're beautiful, little dove. You always were.

Abbie forced the memory away.

"Mum." Chris' voice was loud, even over Becky's music. "Have you seen the others?"

"The others?" Abbie said, wishing she was asleep and hating herself for it.

"Can I come in?"

"Yes."

Chris pushed the door open, walking to the end of the bed. He had his phone in his hand. Abbie imagined crushing the device under her shoe: all of them, every blinking screen, stamping until the glass shattered into a million pieces.

"I've got images," Chris said. "Of the print ones. But there are more online. No front pages, thank God."

Despite the circumstances, and despite the tragedy it provoked in her, it was somehow heartening to see Chris behaving like this, ready to take control. It was good to know Becky would be okay if anything ever happened to Abbie.

"I don't need to see them," Abbie said, when he made to turn his phone.

"You haven't looked on Twitter or anything, have you?"

Abbie groaned. "I don't have Twitter. And I've logged out of my Facebook."

Chris gestured at her phone on the bed. It had landed face up; the screen was blinking brightly. "Then what are those notifications?"

"Emails. I told you last night, I logged into my account."

"And I told you to log back out. You've got notifications turned on too. Are you trying to torture yourself? Who's Douglas Walker?"

Abbie snatched her phone. "None of your business."

Chris' expression fell, and Abbie knew what she'd done right away. She'd made it sound – in her tone, in the sharpness – like she and Douglas were romantically involved. It was instant, Chris' misunderstanding and Abbie's perception of it, a mother-son gift that couldn't be faked.

"It's not that," she told him quickly, even as she secretly wondered if Douglas' easy smile was giving her silly thoughts. "He's a journalist. A writer. He wants to help us."

"Help how? He probably wants the inside scoop."

"He's writing a book. He wants to shadow me, he said, and offer media advice."

"Media advice?"

They shared a bemused smile.

"Apparently that's something I might need," Abbie said. "You know, in between pulling pints and stacking shelves. Fucking hell."

She winced; she'd sworn in front of her son. But Chris laughed quietly. "Don't worry. I doubt Becks heard."

"I will worry, thank you very much."

Chris shrugged. "I've heard much worse. I've said much–"

"I don't want to hear it." She pictured him as a boy, on Jack's shoulders. Then Chris fell to the ground as Jack disappeared. Abbie couldn't remember him like that anymore. "Let me read this in peace."

Chris waited at the end of the bed. Abbie thought about telling him to leave, but she wondered if he'd listen. It would be yet another sign she was failing. Feeling cowardly, she opened the email.

I'm actually in Bristol now. Coincidence, I swear... nothing to do with being able to work remotely; I definitely didn't drive from London on the off-chance you'd say yes, reasoning I could get a decent amount of work done anyway. I'm happy to meet, if you like.

"This sounds dodgy," Chris said once Abbie had explained.

"I'm not in the position to turn down help. I've got no way to fight back against all these newspapers. You saw what they did with my photo."

"My birthday party. That memory. They took it."

"Exactly. So let's say I agree to an interview with somebody, how do I know what to do, what to say?"

"You sound like you really want to meet him." Chris was looking at her far too closely. "Is this just about the shitstorm?"

Another swear word, and Abbie let it pass. "What else would it be about?"

"I don't know. About Dad."

"About *Dad*?"

"Maybe you're thinking... and if you are, Mum, it's all right. I won't judge you. I wouldn't be pleased, but it's not my business. I mean, it is. But what I'm saying is, you can't meet with this bloke just because you fancy him."

"Fancy him?" Abbie said, as if the idea was unreasonable.

"I found the photo, Mum."

She didn't have to ask which one: the one of Jack, which she'd shredded and stuffed into a drawer. Abbie stood, feeling tiny and fragile as she approached her giant son, the baby she'd once cradled.

"Why are you snooping around my room? You've got no right to do that. You need to remember who the parent is–"

"Somebody had to do the laundry around here. It was overflowing. I was putting some T-shirts away – trying to *help* – and I found it."

"I'm perfectly capable of doing the laundry."

Chris looked at the bed, the crumpled quilt, with accusation in his young eyes. "Right."

"I will be doing the laundry from now on," she told him. "As for the photo, it isn't what you think. I..."

"What?"

219

She almost told him. There was a vicious instinct instructing her to. It would tear him right down the middle; it would smash Becky in the teeth too. It would spread this ruin further.

But she couldn't. Would never dare.

"We all grieve in our own ways. It's been almost a year now, but it feels so fresh."

Chris' features softened. Abbie had fooled her son. What a victory.

He opened his arms. She gratefully hugged him, still in awe – she never wouldn't be – by how much bigger than her he was.

"If you want to meet this bloke, fine. But I'm going to be there. And it has to be somewhere public."

42

SOPHIA

Sophia was in the presence of a goddess. Lyndsey talked, sitting a bare few feet from Sophia.

Lyndsey waved her manicured hand as though to take in the entire bar. They were in the lobby of Lyndsey's hotel, the most expensive in the city, with Lyndsey's security man sitting at the opposite end, casually sipping his water as he stared over at the TV.

Lyndsey La Rossa, with a personal security guard, her perfume wafting over to Sophia, words coming fast and passionate, far more so than in any podcast.

"I've spoken to Morgan. He's going to reach out to Abbie. He's a good man. He'll make it worth her while. Not that she deserves it."

Sophia picked up her glass at the same time as Lyndsey, both of them drinking together. Sophia wasn't sure what to say to that, about Abbie; she tried to recall with vivid frightfulness the encounters they'd had, the stand-offs, how tiny and defenceless Abbie had made her feel.

But the whirlpool...

It was spinning too urgently, grabbing her, sending her with undeniable momentum any direction it wanted. She wasn't so arrogant to think she could somehow stop this.

And what was the alternative?

Tell Lyndsey no, ruin this stage of her life before it even began? All with no job to which she could return; Wake-not-woke had left a stern voicemail the previous evening, explaining she was already seeking a replacement. *"If you have an issue with that, contact the union. But since you're not replying to my phone calls, I'll have to assume you have more important things to do."*

Lyndsey frowned, bringing Sophia back to the bar. "Are you sure you're up to this? We need to be one hundred per cent sure, both of us, right? Don't forget why we're doing this."

Sophia sat up straighter. "I haven't forgotten anything."

"That's what I want to hear. Our cause is too important to let nerves rule us." Lyndsey was getting louder, more confident, as though sleeving into her public persona; it was a wonder to behold. "I've been reading up about your little country. Did you know, for example, that only thirty-five per cent of local counsellors are women? At this rate, equality won't be achieved until 2077. And that's just a *single* example. The gender pay gap, of course, is in full effect. Imagine that. Imagine feeling so entrenched in your perverted patriarchal power you're able to look a woman in the face and tell her, *I'm going to give you less for doing the same job as a man."*

Sophia could do nothing but sit, listen. Perhaps she'd somehow share in Lyndsey's confidence by sitting there in homage.

"There's lots more," Lyndsey went on. "It's worse for those women born on the lower end of your country's great hierarchy. It would be worse for me, obviously, than it would for you, given, well... your complexion."

Sophia knew that, without question. She raised her glass. "I'll happily acknowledge my privilege."

Lyndsey laughed softly, flashing two rows of shiny straight teeth. "Don't be silly. You don't have to do that. Would you like another drink?"

Sophia tipped her glass, finishing the cocktail, and then placed it down. "Yes, thank you."

"I remember," Lyndsey said as they waited for the bartender to mix their drinks, "a certain somebody telling me they wanted help for their first big mainstream PR experience."

Sophia shuffled in her seat. The bar wasn't busy; it was early afternoon, though it seemed earlier because of the sunlight bouncing off all the sleek surfaces.

Lyndsey's touch was warm on Sophia's forearm. "You've already spoken to millions of people on my – screw it; I'm saying it – *incredibly successful* podcast."

"I wish I had that skill," Sophia murmured. "I noticed on your podcast. The way you switch between... between modes like that. Of speaking, I mean."

These cocktails were hitting her harder than she'd anticipated.

"It's a useful skill to have. That's what I'm trying to say. You *do* have it."

"There's a big difference between a Zoom call and sitting in a TV studio."

Lyndsey suddenly withdrew her hand with a huff. "Let me ask you this. Do you think it's acceptable that women in your country have to watch their drinks every time they set foot into a nightclub? Or that, if they decide to walk home, they should fear for their lives – their *lives*, Sophia – because some men are too uneducated and, yes, evil to keep themselves in check?"

Sophia tugged at her sleeve, the place Lyndsey's hand had been. "You know I don't."

"So keep that in your mind. And don't look so heartbroken. I'm helping you. Everybody needs tough love sometimes. We're going to be up there *together*. You have to be ready..." Lyndsey took her drink from the waiter, without looking at him; it was as though the drink glided into place. "So pretend I'm Morgan MacDermott. Just imagine a big red face and an ugly bald head and a slippery – oh God, let's be real – a *wet* smile."

Sophia laughed as she took her drink. "Thank you," she told the barman, and he gave her a short nod. "That's quite an accurate description."

Lyndsey took a sip from her glass, holding it in a civilised manner. "So, darling – he does love that word..."

They chuckled together, the alcohol whirling like the pool, but it didn't seem so bad right then. Sophia wondered if she had some mental quirk which shifted her too easily between moods.

She uncrossed then crossed her legs, imagining herself in a confident shirt and dress combo, something stylish like Lyndsey, instead of her jeans and jumper. "Ask me anything."

Lyndsey adopted the role like a skilled actor, down to the way Morgan MacDermott constantly swayed in his seat: the implication being either he was drunk or he was going to attack his guests. She even deepened her voice. "So you want to act all high and mighty, Sophia, but *you're* the one who recorded her."

"I was scared for my–"

"Scared?" Lyndsey cut in. "Of talking with a parent? That's your job."

"I know–"

"No," Lyndsey said, in her own voice. "That's not how you play the game."

"You interrupted me."

"Have you watched Morgan's show?"

Perhaps it was the cocktail, but she didn't like Lyndsey's tone. "I know he interrupts people. Tell me what I did wrong."

"You agreed with him, essentially, when you said 'I know'. A conversation is a power battle, and when you agree with a hostile opponent, you are granting them miles and miles of land for free. You've allowed them to instantly – and seamlessly – reframe the conversation."

"Let me try again."

Lyndsey nodded, then changed demeanour. "You're a teacher. How can you be *scared* of talking to–"

"I'm not."

"But you said on Lyndsey La Rossa's podcast you were."

"No, I mean... yes, but I was speaking about–"

"We're speaking about your status as a teacher and how it supposedly makes you scared. I don't know what's so complicated."

Sophia looked around for another drink; the bartender moved into action without her needing to say anything. "The same?" he asked.

"Yes, please." Sophia turned back to Lyndsey. "I'm sorry. You're really good at this. What did I do wrong that time?"

"The same thing. Allowing him to reframe the conversation."

"So what do I do?"

"*You* frame it by clearly stating your position. You can't let him draw you into his game. If he asks you a question like that, you sit back, take a moment – a very *short* one – and look at him like he's the lowest of the low. You don't say it. You have to be careful with your words. But you make him and the audience *know* he's done something underhanded and morally disgusting. And then you say, confidently, 'Abbie had made me feel threatened countless times. I felt like I had no other choice than to record her for my own safety'. It's not *just another parent*. It's a possibly violent, intimidating sexist."

"That's the truth," Sophia said, eyeing the bartender, willing him to hurry up with the mixing. "Abbie had been awful to me on several occasions. She'd... she'd kicked one of the chairs over in my classroom, yelled at me, made me feel – honestly – scared for my life."

"Yes!" Lyndsey beamed. "See? It's not so hard, is it? Just don't let him back you into a corner."

———

Sophia climbed out of the taxi, thinking of what she'd said. Abbie had never kicked over a chair. But Sophia was in a tricky position. She couldn't explain how fearful Abbie had forced her to feel without recourse to a few exaggerations: enhancements of Sophia's truth which would make it clearer.

Some people might call them *lies*.

Caroline was waiting outside her flat, leaning against the wall. She looked smaller, younger under the huge puffy coat. It was a mild day, and yet Caroline had chosen to cover herself from ankle to neck, only her bright dyed hair showing, with her expression instantly vulnerable as she turned to Sophia.

"Are you okay?"

Caroline began to cry as though Sophia's words had triggered something.

Sophia rushed forward and wrapped her arms around her, softly whispering it would all be all right. She must've said that fifty times before Caroline leaned back, her eyes red, making Sophia almost cry with her.

Something was terribly wrong.

"What happened?" Sophia asked. "Oh God, Caroline..."

"I'm sorry." Caroline's upper neck, the part visible above her coat, was violently red from sobbing. Her voice was hoarse. "I've got nobody else. I'm pathetic."

"No, no, *no*." Sophia took her hand. "You're not pathetic.

Whatever this is... I'm here. You helped me. I'll help you. You're coming inside. You don't have to explain anything if you don't want to, but I'm not leaving you alone."

"Are you sure?"

Sophia's answer was to guide her to the door, as she reached into her pocket for her keys.

It was absolutely unthinkable that Sophia would leave another person helpless in this state.

SHUDDERING BREATHS

Seconds stretched as the killer moved as quietly as possible, trying not to listen to the shuddering breaths of the person hunched over the corpse, trying not to think about the future: if it would ever be possible to think, *I'm a good person. I've made some mistakes, but deep down, I'm a good person.*

The person was still talking on the phone.

The killer realised the fundamental mistake.

No planning had gone into this, no thought of what would come after.

Only the need to inflict pain.

But it was never meant to be like this.

Step by step, the killer crept away.

43

CAROLINE

"And that's it really," Sophia said. "I'm not sure when we'll be on the show, but I think it's going to be soon."

Caroline had asked Sophia what she'd been up to; she'd phrased it in a low, frantic voice, knowing Sophia would take this to mean Caroline had sunk too far into her pain to speak for the time being. This wasn't untrue, but Caroline was also a smart person.

A person who wouldn't quit.

Despite the near-constant flashbacks – the pain of it, the gore – she was harnessing this opportunity as effectively as she could. The world might look at her and laugh, like that deranged assaulter did, but there was nothing funny about what Caroline was going to do.

She was going to show them all, every cruel arsehole who'd ever criticised or doubted her. She was going to transcend the cam-girl world.

Her future was right there, begging to be taken. She wouldn't be too squeamish to seize the chance.

"I didn't mean to go on and on." Sophia tugged her sleeves,

her arms folded, staring with genuine kindness across the coffee table.

Caroline remembered outside, crying in Sophia's arms; there had been nothing false about the tears. Or her words, about having nobody. But she'd take what could be a weakness – her loneliness – and smash the world over the head with it.

Her isolation was her strength.

"We don't have to talk," Sophia said.

"I... it's difficult to say." She shuddered, her body cramping, her inner thighs aching; the physical sensation swarmed her with flashes of what had happened. "I was assaulted. In one of the worst ways a person can be. Not that it's a competition."

She tried for a dark laugh, but sobs swallowed any attempt at gallows humour.

Sophia rushed around the coffee table, wrapping her arm over Caroline. "Oh, God. Caroline. I can't even... I'm– When?"

"Last night." Caroline huddled closer to her. "He was one of my fans. Or he pretended to be. A real fan would never do what he did. Apparently, his marriage fell apart because he was watching my stream. I got angry with him. I shouldn't have but..."

"No, Caroline." Sophia's arm tightened around her. "This isn't your fault. *He's* the scumbag. He's the monster."

"He's in police custody," Caroline said, sitting back and wiping her cheek with her hand.

Sophia stood, strode into the kitchen, returning with some tissues.

Caroline took the box, dried her tears, told herself this was all part of her plan: told herself the memory of it, the act, his *thing*, the angle, all of it, his words, none of it was stabbing into her mind over and over.

"Luckily, people heard, or saw. There are witnesses."

"Shouldn't you still be in the hospital?" Sophia said softly.

"The damage is..." Caroline shivered, clutching her knees. "It's not..."

That bad, she was going to say, though it wasn't the phrase the doctor had used; he'd said much the same with some added medical jargon. The point was – he seemed to be implying – she had gotten away lucky. It could've been worse.

"It's okay," Sophia whispered, rubbing her back gently.

Caroline was thankful for the comfort, warmth spreading, Sophia whispering softly, "You're strong. You can survive this."

But she was going to do more than survive; it was a shame she had to hurt Sophia to make it happen.

And yet, with the mention of *The Morgan MacDermott Show*, Caroline knew she'd be insane not to take advantage. Her original plan – as she'd lain crippled with shock on the unforgiving concrete – had sprouted a new head. A new angle.

"How were the police?" Sophia asked.

"In what way?"

"Did you tell them what you do for a living?"

"Yes. They were actually lovely about it. It was two female officers and they didn't give me any of that judgemental crap. I was honestly expecting it. I put myself out there. But there was nothing like that."

"That's something," Sophia said.

"I know it might seem weird, me coming here."

"You don't need to justify yourself." Sophia's hand kept moving in those warm comforting circles. "You needed somebody. I'm here. I don't care if we've only known each other a little while. If you think of me as a friend, as somebody who can help you, then I consider myself lucky."

More tears slid down Caroline's cheeks, but she managed to contain the sobbing. She couldn't let herself think of backing out.

There was nothing else, only this pursuit, her end goal of ultimate success.

Who could blame her for wanting to make something good of this situation?

The world ran on shock. Caroline knew that better than most; it was the reason she had risen to such prominence as a webcam performer.

She knew how to ramp things up, to make people stop, to *have* to look.

"I hate to ask…"

"You can stay here. You can have the bed. I'll take the sofa."

"No," Caroline said, though she made the word purposefully weak. Logistically, this would make everything easier. "I couldn't possibly…"

"You can. And you will. Unless you'd prefer the sofa?"

"The bed would feel safer," Caroline murmured. "The place I've rented, I don't know, it makes me sort of sick thinking of going back there tonight. But the sofa would be better than that."

"You're taking the bed. You don't need to be polite." Sophia's voice wavered as though she'd been drinking. Maybe she had. That might put her into a deeper sleep. "What do you want to do in the meantime?"

Caroline wondered if this made her selfish in the most depraved way, considering what was to come. What she said was true. "I want to sit here with you and think about nothing. Will you do that? Just sit with me? Please?"

"I'm not going anywhere."

44

BECKY

Becky walked home the long way.

It was around eight; she'd been at her friend's house, since being alone all the time was beyond depressing. But she also felt like a different species from her friend, finding it difficult to join in as she'd blabbed about boys and school and university and goals and life.

Becky turned the corner onto their street, then leapt back when he appeared. It was like that saying: speak of the Devil. And he appeared; Freddie swaggered out from the shadows, weaving in his stride, uglier than Becky could believe.

She'd wanted this boy, this man, at some point.

Because he got you high. It was Dad's voice. *He used you.*

He was alone on a patch of green, the street sign on one side, a garden fence on the other. He walked over to her, his hands stuffed in his pockets, his eyes wide and red.

"I've been here for hours."

Becky looked across the street; a man was walking past with a big dog. Surely Freddie wouldn't do anything right there.

"That's not my problem," Becky said, feeling the knife pressing against her belly through her hoodie pocket.

It wasn't fair that he was allowed to make her feel so small and useless, that he was allowed to appear in her life like a demented demon anytime he wanted.

"You know it's day..." He paused, rubbing the pube-like hair on his chin. "Day three, I think. Or four. You haven't got long left."

"The deal's off. You haven't got the video anymore."

"Is that what he told you? I've got a whole library of backups, darling."

"Prove it," she said bluntly.

He just laughed, and Becky told herself that meant he was bluffing. It didn't help her immediate situation though.

"You're drunk," she said. "Leave me alone."

He grinned, moving even closer; the man and his dog had passed, and the street was quiet. "I've been asking around about you. I don't know why you're acting so stuck-up all of a sudden. We both know you're a prime cut of slut meat."

Becky's hand twitched toward her hoodie pocket; she'd practised taking the knife out several times. The memory of the park made her body hurt. But the sharp need to do something, to act, to not let him bully her was stronger.

"You're disgusting. Absolutely sick in the head. You're wrong on every level."

Freddie put his shoulders back. "Be caref–"

"*You* be fucking careful," she yelled. "I don't care what I did before. I don't care if I thought it was cool or if I was high or any of it. I just want it all to stop."

Her words came out choked.

But Freddie was relentless. "You're so sexy when you cry."

"Did you really think I was going to have sex with you and all your loser friends?" Becky hissed. She ignored Chris' voice in her head, telling her to run: to play him, make him believe, until she could get to safety. "You're living in a dream world. The only reason I ever looked twice at a loser like you is because you got me stoned off my head."

"You little *bitch*."

He lunged at her. Becky grabbed the knife, slid it out of the holster, just like she'd practised. She didn't let herself think; she was distantly aware of her voice raised, shouting something, as more sobs made the words shaky.

Freddie gasped when Becky sliced the blade across his palms. She cut him again, gashing his forearm as he raised it to defend himself.

Freddie stumbled back when she stopped, blood dripping from his hands, his bare arms. "You..." He was trembling all over, cut but not beaten. "You really have fucked yourself."

He lunged at her again.

Becky dropped the knife and ran.

She pumped her legs, her breath loud in her ears, struggling to believe what she'd just done.

Freddie was right behind her. She was sure of it.

She pushed the door open, rushed inside, then turned and looked through the peephole.

Freddie stood at the end of the lane, holding the knife. He eyed the door like he was going to rush it.

Instead, he stared meaningfully before walking away.

Becky collapsed against the wall, sliding to the floor, unable to breathe. She stayed there for what felt like a long time, her fingers clawing at the old rug: the rug which had been there long before Dad died, the rug she remembered from when she was far younger.

She stared down at her hands. There were flecks of blood on them, as well as on the sleeve of her hoodie. She tore her hoodie off, rubbed at her hands, her arms, kept going until she felt her skin hurting from the friction.

The hallway door opened.

Becky threw her hoodie into the corner. It landed in a heap. In shadow.

Mum looked small and tense and not at all like the woman Becky was used to. She knelt and took Becky's hands. "What's wrong? Oh, Becky, what is it?"

She almost told all of it right then: the video, the fact she'd been the one to leak Mum's name, the constant paranoia and... and the *hell* of it. But Mum was going through so much already, with the newspaper articles and everything.

"Just people being bitches." She let out a shuddering sob. "Why can't the world just be fair, Mum? Why?"

"Come on." Mum helped Becky to her feet. "Let's get you a nice warm drink. Then you can tell me all about it."

Mum was speaking like this was any other issue. Like it was something completely within her ability to handle.

She was acting like herself for the first time in days, and Becky didn't want to ruin that. Once the crying had passed, she told Mum she'd fallen out with a friend. It was easier that way.

45

CHRIS

Jimmy led the way into his flat. It was a short drive from where Tone's job had been. It had all been surprisingly easy: standing in the background as a deal took place, staring at the men on the other side of the car park, ready to spring into action if things went badly.

One of Tone's men had given them a lift. Chris had wanted to go straight home, but Jimmy had almost begged him to visit the flat. *"It's my own place. You could even sleep over one day."*

The hallway was narrow and the whole place had a cheap feel. Chris knew he'd be able to punch a hole in one of the walls by accident, barely brushing his knuckles against it.

Jimmy led him into a small living room. Everything was clean and surprisingly neat, but it still saddened Chris. The DVD case with the stickers still on, the small old-school television with the big back; the floor sofa, holes in the fabric showing the cushion underneath.

Jimmy turned, smiling shakily. There was a faint smell of weed in the flat, but mostly it reeked of cleaning chemicals.

Jimmy's eyes were red; they'd been red all night. "What do you think?"

There was something so tragic in Jimmy's voice. And it was his face too: the pride there, the expectation. Chris remembered the same look when Jimmy showed him one of his collage books, that wide grin... and before that, when they were even younger, Jimmy beaming after solving a Rubik's Cube.

"It's amazing, mate," Chris told him. "Honestly. You should be so proud."

Jimmy did that junkie arm-scratching thing which made Chris want to shout at him. "I'm pretty happy with it. It's better than living with Dad. He's..." Jimmy spun at the sound of people passing by the window, their loud boisterous voices audible through the paper walls. Once they were gone, he turned back. "He's an old-fashioned bastard."

"Are you all right? You've been jittery all evening."

"My dad rang the other night. He was pissed off his head. Do you know what he said to me?"

Chris walked over, hands in his pockets. But he wouldn't sit. He'd done his job. His place was at home, where he could take care of his family.

And yet leaving Jimmy felt difficult.

"What?" Chris asked.

"I can't repeat it," Jimmy said after a pause. "But it was something like... he hopes the next man I, you know, he hopes he kills me while we're... you know."

"Are you seeing anyone? Or was your old man saying that just to be a prick?"

"A prick, I guess." Jimmy's shoulders fell. "Mum wanted us to try and talk a little. She doesn't care he basically threw me out, but maybe she thinks if we have a relationship... but he just can't help himself. He can't accept it."

Chris said nothing. He knew when Jimmy needed to vent. The drugs and the crime and all that stuff couldn't take that part of their friendship away.

"I'm not seeing anyone, no... Can you imagine the shit from Tone and that?"

"I wish I could help you. I wish there was something I could say. Except... get away from them, then. If they're like that. If they make you this miserable. Get as far away from them as you can and never look back."

Jimmy looked up, lips tremoring. "It's that easy, is it? What am I supposed to do? Where am I supposed to go? Just rock up one day at a job interview. Hello, miss, yes, I'd love a job... Here's my CV. No, no GCSEs. No qualifications. No experience except dealing."

"We're not old men. You're talking like you haven't got any time."

"I'm talking abo–"

"You're making excuses. Because you want to keep getting high. Let's be honest about it. There *is* a way out of this. I'd help you. If I thought you weren't going to ruin any chance you got. But when you're smoking and snorting and whatever else you're doing, I don't know what to say."

"It's not that simple." Jimmy wrapped his hands around his knees. "Imagine your entire world had turned to shit. Imagine nothing you ever did was good enough. What would you do?"

Chris laughed gruffly, and then Jimmy looked at him; his eyes narrowed, and he smiled with a sadness Chris recognised. He'd seen it countless times in his friend.

"I guess that was a stupid thing to say," Jimmy muttered. "What with your dad... and your mum, all that stuff. I'm sorry."

Chris finally sat, though he still had to fight a nasty notion telling him Jimmy didn't deserve it; it was his own fault. He placed his hand on his old friend's shoulder. "I meant what I said. I'd help you get off the drugs. Even if it involved locking you in my bedroom until it was all out of your system. It's changing you, mate. We both know it is."

Jimmy's red wide-pupilled eyes glimmered as he stared. But then he frowned, shrugged Chris' hand away. "You're making it sound like all my problems are down to what I decide to put into my body. I could stop smoking a little weed here and there–"

"It's more than a little weed. If you're going to make excuses, at least be honest about it."

"I could stop it *all*. It wouldn't change the way my dad feels about me. It wouldn't stop Mum from siding with him."

"It would help you find a better way to live. You'd be able to get a real job. You'd be able to find a partner without being so paranoid about it all the time. The whole world isn't like Tone and his pathetic little friends."

Jimmy sat back, stretching his legs, staring at the old depressing TV. "Maybe. Do you want to watch a film?"

Chris stood. There was no use trying. "Nah. I've got to go."

Chris walked into the house, pausing in the hall to take off his shoes. He needed a moment to compose himself. What got him through – what made it possible to calmly kneel and untie his laces – was thinking of Dad, of how *he* would've behaved.

Dad wouldn't cry, panic; Dad wouldn't become intimidated when all the problems stacked up in his head. Mum, money, Becky.

Chris walked into the living room. Mum was sat on the armchair, her phone in her hand. She didn't notice him, just kept scrolling, staring like a zombie.

"What are you looking at?" Chris asked.

"Things I shouldn't be." Mum sat up, placing her phone screen-down on the cushions. "Comments. On a Facebook post about me."

"And?"

Mum looked so small, her hoodie emphasising the effect. "Some people support me. They think it's unfair to judge me based on a secret recording. Others... they hate me, Chris. They think *I* hate women, all women, everywhere."

Chris almost mentioned going to the police again, but he didn't want an argument about it. "I've got something for you."

When Chris placed the money on the arm of the chair, Mum opened the envelope, looked inside, then stood slowly. She was moving as though she was trying to hold back the full force of her feelings.

"Where did you get it?" She walked up to Chris, her gaze hard. "That's a *lot* of money. I thought you were going to do some cash-in-hand labouring or something. Where, Chris?"

"You don't need to know."

"I'm your mother. I don't just need to know. It's your responsibility to tell me."

"I'll tell you this. I'm not dealing drugs. I haven't hurt anybody. I got the money fairly."

"Doing *what?*"

There was no way Chris could tell her. She would try to make him stop.

"Are you going to turn down the money?"

"Tell me where–"

"Mum, you could ask me a hundred times and my answer won't change."

Chris knew he was going against what he'd thought a few minutes previously: about behaving as Dad would. Dad would never turn Mum's expression so vulnerable. But then Dad would also never allow Mum to become homeless.

"If you don't tell me, you're leaving my house." Chris almost laughed, but Mum grabbed his arm, looking sternly at him. "I mean it. I don't know who you think I am, or *what* you think I am, but I'm your mother and I always will be. So that's it. Tell me. Or leave."

"If I left, you'd have nothing."

"At least I'll be able to look at myself in the mirror."

Chris shrugged her hand away. "Christ. Relax. I sold the watch."

"Sold the... your *grandfather's* watch?"

He nodded. "It wasn't as valuable as we thought, but–"

"It *was* valuable," Mum hissed. "Oh, Chris. What have you done? You've told me yourself. That's your most cherished memory of your dad."

"Taking care of you and Becks is more important, all right? Don't make a big deal out of it. I need a shower."

He went upstairs before she could reply, pausing in the hallway when he heard the crying. Becky's sobs were quiet, but so was the evening. Chris pressed his ear against the door.

"Becks?" he called softly. "Can I come in?"

"I..." She sniffled. "All right."

Becky was sitting on her bed, one of her hoodies in her hands. She held it like she was debating tearing it apart. Chris took in her puffy eyes, her red cheeks... and the blood on the hoodie.

"What happened?"

He sat beside her, holding her as she tearfully explained. By the end, Chris was trembling, hating himself, hating Freddie more. The idiot wouldn't learn.

This was going to come to blood.

"The sick bastard. Text him now, Becks. Say you're sorry and you want to go through with the deal. You'll give him and his friends what they want."

"What if he goes to the police?" she said, as if not listening.

"He attacked you. You defended yourself."

"Knives are illegal, Chris."

"I don't care. Text him. I'll show up instead, force him to see sense."

"But all his friends will be there."

"I'll find a way. Just text him."

Becky did as he asked.

"That was quick," she said, when her phone made a sound.

"What did he say?"

Becky looked down at the message, stifled another sob, then showed Chris her phone.

Deal's off. Sleep well, you useless bitch. Maybe you'll see me in your nightmares.

"Chris," Becky said. "I don't know what to do. I don't know how to make him stop."

Chris didn't want to admit that he didn't know either.

Later, he went to his bedroom, reached into the back of his drawer and took out his grandfather's watch. He didn't enjoy lying to Mum, but it was necessary. She wouldn't understand if he explained where he'd really gotten the cash.

Somebody had to take care of this family.

46

CAROLINE

Caroline told Sophia she wanted to keep the door open that night. She would feel much safer, she'd said; she wouldn't have to worry about the man sneaking into her room, with all that hate between his legs, that sadistic glint in his eyes.

Caroline didn't mention it would make it easier to listen to Sophia sleep.

At around two in the morning, she began to snore. They'd spent the evening sitting together, saying little, except for when Caroline had condoned – or perhaps encouraged – Sophia to have a glass of wine, then another, and another...

The floor was cold against Caroline's feet.

Each movement hurt her, sent nasty sensations through her body. Her inner thighs were screaming each moment, but she hardened herself.

She wasn't going to fail. She wasn't going to hesitate.

Walking to the door, she opened it gently, wincing when it creaked.

Suddenly, her body froze, as though the man was tasing her again. She almost slipped into the memory, almost allowed him to wrench her back there.

But her life was at stake.

She kept going.

Across the room, she stood over Sophia. The one-time teacher slept on her side, pale arm poking out of her blanket and hanging to the floor... toward her phone; she must've been using it right up until she went to sleep.

Caroline picked it up, moving in a measured fashion. Panic would make her jerky, obvious.

She swiped to the unlock screen, then turned the white glare onto Sophia's face. The phone vibrated in Caroline's hand as the facial recognition unlocked it.

Moving to the nearby chair, she sat and began her work.

If Sophia woke, Caroline would hide the phone and say she'd had a nightmare and didn't want to be alone. She'd tell Sophia her phone was mysteriously missing, nothing to do with Caroline.

But Sophia didn't wake.

Caroline did what she had to.

Jack had left her, had never truly cared. He'd been everything: a future husband, a pathway to a loving family, to love-filled Christmases and children's happy laughter.

Sophia was nothing compared to that; hurting her, Caroline told herself firmly, did not matter.

Once it was done, Caroline deleted all evidence and returned the phone to its original place.

47

ABBIE

It was strange being in public. Abbie kept expecting people to recognise her. The café was quiet; she and Chris sat in the corner. But she still cringed each time somebody walked by the table, or toward it as if they were going to march right up to her.

"Relax, Mum," Chris said quietly.

Abbie could hardly look at her son. It wasn't because she thought he'd done anything evil for the money; it was because he reflected her weakness back at her. Because of her, he'd had to give away a piece of his father. And just because Chris didn't know the whole truth, it didn't mean that was a small thing.

Becky had seemed better that morning, compared to the previous night when she'd had an argument with her friend. It was almost a relief to deal with a regular problem, to be able to help her daughter.

"Who said I wasn't relaxed? Anyway, I told you. We should've met him at home."

"You want to invite a strange man into our house?"

Abbie said nothing, glancing toward the entrance. They

were waiting for Douglas Walker, the writer who'd said he might be able to help.

She'd done some more research about him that morning, learning that his wife had died almost a decade previously.

Sleeping with a man she didn't know, only a year after her husband's death, wasn't something Abbie had ever considered. She wasn't seriously considering it even then; it was more like a whispering at the back of her head.

Could it be called attraction?

Abbie wasn't sure.

More like escape: more like hiding from herself.

The door opened, letting in the sound of rushing wind.

Douglas closed the door, quieting the noise, and then looked around the café. He was dressed more casually than his online photos, and he looked thinner, fitter, his jawline defined and his black hair messy.

He approached the table, glancing at Chris, then looked fully at Abbie. "Hello."

Abbie stood. Her heartbeat had picked up a little for no reason she could acknowledge. "Hi, Douglas. This is my son, Chris."

Douglas offered his hand to Chris, and they shook. "It's nice to meet you."

"And you," Chris said shortly. "Mum said you want to help. But I'm wondering if you just want to use her for another book."

Douglas shrugged. "I want to mine this situation for my book, it's true, but that doesn't mean I can't help. They're not mutually exclusive, in my view. Would either of you like a drink?"

"Got one," Chris said.

"I'll take another coffee, if it's not too much trouble."

"If it's not too much trouble?" Chris said when Douglas was at the counter.

"What's wrong with that?" Abbie asked.

"He wants to leech off your whole life. Nothing should be too much trouble."

Douglas returned, placing the coffees down.

"Is Becky busy?" Douglas asked.

"Why do you care where my sister is?" Chris obviously disapproved of this, but his tone was angrier than Abbie had expected. "You want to write about her in your little book too, do you? Leave my sister alone."

"Stop being rude," Abbie told him.

"It's my fault," Douglas said, tapping his spoon against his saucer gently. "I'm terrible at small talk, you see. It's a curse of sorts. Or a blessing. I hope she's well; that's what I meant to say."

"It's fine," Abbie replied.

"How are you keeping, both of you?" Douglas asked.

Abbie picked up her mug, decided it was too hot, placed it down. "As well as can be expected."

"Have you looked online?"

"Not a lot."

Chris shifted beside her, but he didn't say anything; she knew he was thinking about the previous night, finding her scrolling, the comments addictive in a weird way. Like she thought she deserved the pain.

"Why did I have to say it? I've always done that, snapped. Not stopping for two bloody seconds to think about what I'm going to say."

"It's not your fault," Douglas and Chris said at the same time, then looked at each other. Douglas smiled and, without looking, Abbie sensed Chris did too.

"She had no right to record you, anyway," Douglas went on. "A person, in my view – in my humble view; I always add that bit... A human being should be allowed to make a mistake.

What's more, a person should be allowed to say what you said, even publicly, unless one can make a plausible claim for the statement having any strict bearing on reality."

"What do you mean, bearing on reality?" Chris said. "You know how many times I've been hit on the head?"

They laughed together again. Abbie found herself smiling. There was something about the way he talked. It was like he was content to hear himself speak, and they had the privilege to listen. But somehow it didn't come across as arrogance.

"Abbie, if you'd actually been making an effort to execute some kind of ideologically based genocidal scheme... If you'd *planned* to kill all feminists, then I'd agree. You should be held accountable."

"But I never would."

"Obviously," Chris added.

"That's not what a lot of the commenters have a problem with, though."

Douglas tilted his head. "No?"

"They're saying I shouldn't even think something like that–"

"They're saying that a person capable of even entertaining such evil thoughts must have something wrong with them. They're saying it's an example of your undeniable sexism?"

"Pretty much."

"I'm tempted to quote Orwell, but it's an unforgivable sin. A person is allowed to think anything they want. Putting aside the fact that you don't believe it – you said it in anger – you should be allowed... no, not *allowed*. You have the right to think anything you damn well please."

"Yeah, but some stuff's too far," Chris said.

"An example?"

"Stamping on babies' heads. I don't know."

"Jesus, Chris," Abbie said.

"It's a fair example." Douglas sat up, animated. "It's the sort of thought that could lead to violence: the sort of sick fantasising that could become true horror. And that is why each and every case has to be studied so... so *specifically*. A person's actions should be evaluated, with humility and honesty.

"And anyway," he went on. "We're talking about thoughts, not speech. A person's thoughts are thankfully impossible for us to know."

"But that's the point, isn't it?" Chris said. "People are saying Mum really *thinks* it."

"That's exactly why I'm writing my book. Partly due to the internet, partly due to plain old human nature and a whole host of other factors, the benefit of the doubt, as a concept, has been crushed. And the one thing capable of combating this decline – freedom of speech – is itself in decline."

Abbie felt mentally tired, but it was interesting to hear him speak. She imagined Jack saying, *He's like one of those fancy blokes on the telly.*

"A person can't say *anything* though," Chris said.

Douglas leaned in, staring at Chris. "Can't they? Excepting speech which is linked *directly* to violence – and I use that word intentionally, young man – why can't a person say anything they want?"

"I don't know. Loads of reasons. All right, so what if I've got a gay mate and he's getting bullied, even by his own parents... and they're calling him the worst names you can think of?"

"What do *you* think should happen? Should the bullies be carted off by the police? Should they spend time in prison? If so, how much time? Are these particular words illegal only if spoken aloud, in person, or are they illegal over the phone and online and if written in letters too?"

"I'm not saying I want people to be arrested. But there has to be... all right, we can all agree you shouldn't say the N-word."

"I agree you shouldn't say it," Douglas said. "But I don't

think it should be illegal. I don't think the government should have the right to cut out a person's tongue."

"But the N-word," Chris said. "Come *on*."

"I know." Douglas sighed. "Chris, if I trusted the people in charge, I might agree to some kind of penalty for using that word and others in a certain context. But the problem is, I don't trust them. It has been in the interests of governments since they've existed to control the speech and thoughts of their populations. They will push as far as we'll let them. They have. And look at the result; a grieving mother-of-two is turned into a hate icon because of something she didn't even mean."

"What does that have to do with freedom of speech?" Abbie said. "I was allowed to say it..."

"Freedom of speech, it's the bedrock. In eras past, we could have calmly discussed hashtag kill-all-feminists without the furore. But the modern mind has been so sadly degraded in endless ways that reasonable discourse is beyond most people. Regular people, to government, are nothing but a muscle whose flexing must be constantly adjusted."

"All right, mate," Chris said. "You're taking the piss now. A muscle? What does that even mean? And how is any of this going to help my mum?"

Abbie picked up her coffee. It was cooler now. She took a sip.

"I get carried away. But I'm sure you can see why most mainstream outlets despise me. It's difficult to argue that freedom of speech extends to something as sickening as the N-word without being accused of wanting to *use* it."

"It's just a weird thing to want," Chris muttered. "It makes people wonder why you care so much."

"It's because *people* are staring at the surface, not bothering to study the underbelly. But, Chris... the underbelly is where everything happens."

Chris turned to her. "If this bloke has been accused of saying the N-word and stuff like that... should we even be here? It won't look good for you, will it?"

"How can you help me?" Abbie asked.

Chris sighed.

Douglas smiled. "First, by saying I've got it on good authority you're going to be invited onto *The Morgan MacDermott Show*."

"That dickhead?" Chris said.

"Yes, that dickhead."

"On the telly?" Abbie felt like a girl again, walking uncomfortably through school. "I'm not sure I could do that."

"Is that really a good idea?" Chris said.

"I think so. If you let me coach you a little, you'll be able to make a case for yourself many people will be able to empathise with. *And* his show pays."

Abbie sat forward. His speech had been intellectual babble; *this* was her language. "How much?"

"It varies. He's a stingy bugger. But, if you allow me to shadow you, to help you, and to put you in my book, I will negotiate on your behalf and take nothing for myself."

"But how much *could* it be?" Abbie pressed.

"Like I said, he's stingy. He's paid as little as a couple of hundred. For you, with all the publicity, I think you'll get five at least. Maybe as much as ten."

"Ten... thousand?"

Douglas nodded eagerly. "You could find a talent agent, perhaps, and ask them to negotiate for you. But it would take time. And they'd take a cut. I'll take nothing. And I'll give everything."

"You're laying it on thick now, mate," Chris said, then turned to Abbie. "You don't have to do this."

It was an insane statement coming from her son; she *did*

have to do it. The reason was looking at her with his little boy's eyebrows knit in concern.

She would do it for her family.

"I want your help," she said, meeting eyes with Douglas. "And thank you."

48

SOPHIA

"You seriously have nothing to worry about," Lyndsey said, talking as though the make-up artist wasn't there; it was a casual I-belong-here way to speak. "I'm just glad Abbie agreed. I wonder how much he paid her. I'd bet it wasn't more than five."

Sophia studied herself in the mirror as the make-up artist worked. She could hardly feel the brush against her face, the chair beneath her, anything except for the anticipation of being in a studio, on those loud lime-green armchairs, recording a show that would air to millions and would be seen by even more online.

"Are you sure you're okay?" Lyndsey asked.

Sophia thought of Caroline, so brave in facing what had happened to her; she had moved back into her flat after that first night. But they'd been texting every day.

If Caroline could circumvent her misery, Sophia could do the same for this silly fear of cameras.

"I'm ready."

Lyndsey beamed. "That's what I like to hear."

It was almost time to go on.

Sophia paced the green room, catching snippets of herself in the mirror, not wanting to look there. She'd avoided alcohol for the most part, except for the complimentary glass of champagne, but this was too much; the pressure was too oppressive.

Lyndsey wasn't even acknowledging it. She hummed as she texted.

Sophia went to the refreshments table, took another plastic glass of champagne.

She stared down at the bubbles, wondering if it would help. The confidence would be welcome, but what if she said something she didn't mean, or panicked, or puked all over those ugly green chairs?

"Babe." Lyndsey was at her side, her perfume glamorously wafting around her, her hair styled gorgeously. "If you feel like you need that, don't beat yourself up about it. But decide soon. Morgan will be here to kiss our butts in a minute. It's one of his so-called disarming techniques."

Sophia remembered the morning she'd woken up to discover her TikTok video; the blacked-out version of her had never doubted, never concerned herself with studio lights or the feelings of a woman who proudly proclaimed all feminists should die.

It wasn't the booze; it was inside of her.

But the booze helped. She drank it quickly.

A few minutes later, Morgan swept into the room without warning. He was wearing a crumpled blue suit, looking almost artfully dishevelled. Even the gleaming sweat on his face seemed designed to provoke disgust, then regret and overcorrection, then a dropping of the defences.

Sophia's head was woozy. Her belly cramped. Champagne had never been her drink of choice.

Morgan and Lyndsey chatted for what felt like a long time. Sophia stood aside as they traded names she'd never heard of, referencing parties Sophia had never attended and mutual friends who had done hilarious things Sophia would only ever partly know.

"And *you* must be Sophia." Morgan swept a hand dramatically, as if taking in her presence. "I absolutely loved your TikTok video. And your interview with the lovely La Rossa here... it was so utterly convincing. I'd never have guessed... But I'll leave that for the show."

"Never have guessed?" Sophia asked sharply. He'd moved far too quickly from complimenting to unwanted insinuation.

"He's teasing," Lyndsey said. "He loves that. Leave her alone, Morgan."

Morgan grinned, but he didn't take his eyes off Sophia. There was hunger. But also glee. He was going to feed soon. This wasn't anxiety looping – whirling, like the pool – and making her more anxious.

She was certain something strange was happening.

"I suppose I'm not in the mood for joking," Sophia said.

"Don't worry." Morgan leered as he patted her on the arm. "I know how to get you in the mood."

"Such a pig," Lyndsey muttered, as she texted.

Morgan kept his hand there, warm and moist through Sophia's blouse. "Not like that." Speaking to Lyndsey, he continued to stare at Sophia. "Get your mind out of the gutter, La Rossa."

Sophia laughed, wanting to go along with it, though she wished Morgan would take his hand off her arm and she wished Lyndsey would look up from her phone, take note, care.

Sophia hadn't asked to be touched.

Finally, she was forced to step away.

"Oh, one more thing..." Morgan lowered his voice. Was he on coke? He was jumpy, as though he couldn't contain it, whatever *it* was. "Caroline says good luck."

Before Sophia could reply, there was a loud knock at the door.

It was showtime.

49

ABBIE

The area behind the cameras was dark and oddly depressing. Abbie tried to find solace in the sight of Douglas standing with Becky and Chris. She hadn't been sure she wanted the children at the taping, but Chris had insisted on coming. Becky had been off school all week with a cold, not leaving the house once, though Abbie wondered if she was faking.

Who could blame her? School must've been a misery.

Douglas had driven them all in his car. They were staying in his large house on the outskirts of London.

Chris' face was grim. He knew they needed the five and a half thousand pounds, but he hadn't wanted her doing this, despite Douglas' support. Becky offered a tight smile.

Abbie was finding it difficult to sit still; she refused to look across the divide, past Morgan, at Sophia and Lyndsey.

They *had* looked at each other, of course, when they'd first sat down on these horrible chairs. There was a screen behind Douglas, ominously dark. Abbie wondered what might appear on it.

With recording time so close, Abbie wanted to calm herself.

"It's the most important thing," Douglas had told her as they'd planned. *"Whatever happens, don't panic. Try to answer quickly – Morgan will interrupt you – but don't be afraid to take a small moment to think about what you want to say."*

"I love this bit," Morgan said, grinning at Abbie then at Sophia, then finally at Lyndsey.

Abbie looked at the other women. Sophia sat upright, chin raised, as stuck-up as stuck-up could be. She had her legs folded, sitting so still she could've been a statue. It was like she thought she was above everybody and everything.

Lyndsey beamed back at Morgan. "Not as fun as live, but you'll get there one day."

"You inexcusable hussy." Morgan chuckled. "Live TV is for morons. We wouldn't be able to say 'shit' and 'fuck' and 'bollocks'. That would be a true tragedy."

Lyndsey laughed, and Abbie felt alone, sitting on one side. She'd asked Douglas to request that he appear with her, but Morgan had flatly refused. It didn't seem fair, this two-on-one – more like three-on-one since Morgan and Lyndsey were such great pals – but Abbie thought of the money.

Rent, food, bills, the kids.

A mantra: repeated in her mind, *rent food bills the kids*, as the crew moved around behind the camera and somebody called for silence.

Abbie was going to hate this. She already knew it.

But Douglas had told her she needed to complete the recording to receive her payment. She couldn't leave.

She was a prisoner under the harsh bright lights.

"This is a feminist issue," Lyndsey said, gesturing with her hands, her manicured fingernails and annoyingly elegant jewellery catching the light. "We can't separate what she said with–"

"I just think it's ridiculous," Abbie interrupted, remembering what Douglas had said about Lyndsey and Sophia. *They're educated. What people sometimes call articulate; they are skilled at masking their true meaning. Cut to the heart, Abbie.*

Lyndsey kept speaking. "What millions of women are suffering throughout the world. Sexism. The patriarchy. All those words polite society would like to ignore. But we can't. We've been ignoring them for too long."

When Lyndsey made to go on with her point, Abbie snapped, "You're saying I'm a danger to women everywhere. I'm not the one who recorded another woman without her consent."

Lyndsey tilted her head. She was so up her own arse, right down to the way her eyebrows knitted before she spoke. Sophia stared at Lyndsey like the bully's bitch in school, hanging around with the cool kids hoping she didn't get picked on.

Abbie could let it out. There, with the lights glaring; all that stuff about Jack could make her rage useful again.

"This has nothing to do with consent," Lyndsey said.

"You're wrong." Her cheeks were burning, but that was nothing new; they had been ever since the recording began. Head swimming, armpits soaked with sweat, but screw it. It wasn't fair. "You're both big into consent, but you don't seem to care Sophia broke *my* consent. She didn't even ask for it."

"I'm sorry... *big into* consent?" Sophia folded her legs, trying to seem confident but looking small and pathetic and like she needed her eyes raking out of her skull. "That's a rather flippant way to put it."

"Don't start putting me down because I didn't swallow a bloody dictionary," Abbie yelled, even as Douglas' voice coaxed, *Calm, calm, calm is the name of the game.*

"It's the truth. What you did was wrong. And everybody knows it."

"What I *did* was show the world–"

Be brutal, little dove. Douglas' voice was mixing with Jack's. *Interrupt, little dove.*

"I had a personal issue with you. You were telling my daughter she should work as a prostitute one day."

Lyndsey tried to cut in, raising her hand. Abbie considered leaning over and swatting it away.

"That's a fact," Abbie went on. "You can say any fancy words you like, but it's a *fact* that Sophia Lancaster, the woman sitting right there..." Abbie pointed like her finger was a gun she was ready to fire. "Told my fourteen-year-old daughter she should become a prostitute."

Lyndsey leaned back, looking at Sophia, as though expecting her to answer.

Sophia laughed, and then did that cruel smirk Abbie had noticed countless times. It was like she was saying, *Do I really have to explain myself to this idiot?* Abbie wouldn't let it make her feel small.

"What's funny?"

"You," Sophia said. "How casually you're lying to try and save yourself. I have to laugh or I'd cry. Are you really suggesting I said that to a student?"

"Don't play that game. We both know you admitted it the same day–"

"The same day you threatened me and said you wanted to *kill* me." Sophia sat up, her heels making a *click* noise on the floor. "You don't have to remind me what day your tall tale supposedly happened. But it's not true. As for your consent point. We both know–"

Abbie spoke over her. "You're just *lying*–"

But Sophia didn't stop. "You threatened me many times–"

"You can't just sit there and–"

"And it was for my own protection I recorded–"

"Lie to my face. Tell the–"

"You'd made me feel unsafe many–"

"Truth."

"Times."

They both stopped, sucking in air. Abbie had moved to the edge of her seat, leaning almost all the way across the divide, ready to leap at Sophia.

Sophia was icily civilised, her skinny hands hooked around one knee. She looked like a gargoyle.

"All right, great," Morgan said. "Why don't we take a little break?"

They all turned to him. He was gesturing at somebody behind the camera, nodding off to the side. Then he stood and hurried away.

Abbie looked behind the camera, finding Douglas standing at Chris' shoulder, Becky on his other side, a row of expressions telling her how she'd done.

Douglas frowned.

Chris stared like he was proud, but also as though he hated the whole thing.

Becky's lips were trembling. Her body tremored too; she stared at Sophia Lancaster. It was like Becky was using all her brainpower to think of a way to hurt her.

Despite the adrenaline still pumping through her, Abbie smiled.

"Where's he going?" Sophia said quietly.

"Where do you think, *miss*?" Becky yelled. "To snort coke. Because this whole thing's a mess."

"Quiet on set, please," somebody called.

Becky turned and strode away. Abbie stood, as though to go after her, but then Lyndsey did this ugly little laugh. "You won't get your little pay packet if you go after her."

Like anything over one thousand pounds, or even a hundred, or even *twenty* could be called little when life was endlessly lurching along the precipice.

"She's right," Douglas said softly, his hand in his hair. "Morgan won't be long..."

"Quiet on set."

The voiced seemed to come from nowhere and everywhere, echoing.

Chris went after Becky. He caught up with her and placed his hand on her arm. Abbie knew she was doing it again: letting Chris handle it, when *she* should have.

But they needed the money.

And Becky was strong. She'd be okay, especially with Chris looking out for her.

Abbie dreaded whatever would come next.

The screen behind Morgan's chair was still dark.

THE KILLER'S MIND

The killer inched away, cringing at every noise, the sound of shoes against the floor, the drumming heartbeat between their ears, all of it threatening to shatter any resolve which might be summoned.

Thoughts of what would happen next assailed the killer's mind.

Did anybody see me? Why didn't I think this through? Am I going to be in prison for the rest of my life? Am I going to hate myself forever? Am I always going to feel this dark pit inside?

"Wait," the voice said. "Oh my God. I think they're in here."

50

SOPHIA

It was difficult to focus with the alcohol rushing around her system, but Sophia was fairly sure she was defeating her opponent. She was countering at the right times, intercepting when she needed to; and yes, fair enough, she was twisting the truth, just a tad, if it was required.

But it wasn't as though she was going to admit to speaking with Becky about women's sexual freedom. Abbie wasn't going to let Sophia explain herself.

Sure, she'd admitted to it on Lyndsey's podcast, but in broad terms. Vaguely, enough to give her wriggle room.

Sophia had to be smart. She *was* smart.

Morgan returned, fidgety in his chair, leaning forward then back. It seemed something of an open secret that he used cocaine; there had been no need for Becky to melodramatically scream about it, but at least she'd removed herself from the situation.

"Are we ready?" Morgan said, looking at the cameras.

After the board-clapping, Morgan sat back in a position they all knew from TV, his hands on his belly, drumming his shirt. He stared at Sophia with that soaked smile on his face: the one Sophia and Lyndsey had laughed about in the bar like sisters.

"Ms Lancaster, is there anything you'd like to share with the class?"

Sophia shifted in her seat, glancing over at Lyndsey.

Lyndsey wasn't looking at her. It was like she was refusing to.

"Something to do with a certain Caroline?"

Sophia stiffened; opposite, Abbie did the same. They glanced at each other, and for a second, it was like they weren't enemies. Abbie must've been able to see the shock; see that Sophia had had nothing to do with this.

"C-Caroline?" Sophia said, wondering how he'd know her name, just as she had been ever since he said it in the green room. Caroline needed space, peace, not to be dragged into this mess. "What about her?"

"Oh, Sophia, you look so gentle and sweet when you lie."

"When I *lie*?"

"Caroline is an online adult entertainer. I'm sure they used to have a word for that once..."

"Pig," Lyndsey said, and Morgan chuckled.

They were in on this together.

Sophia felt the whirlpool spinning closer to her.

She thought maybe she could ask what was happening. But then it was too late; Morgan killed any response with his suddenly loud voice. "But a couple of years ago, she made a sex tape for her own private use."

"Oh, God, no," Abbie whispered.

Sophia couldn't work out why, if Morgan was revealing this information, he was looking at *her* so intently.

The sex tape had nothing to do with her; she wasn't in it, had never referred to it anywhere online.

"I'm sorry, Abbie," Morgan said, sounding almost genuine

for a second. "But I think this will be good for you. It will be good to know what sort of woman this so-called bastion of virtue really is."

He chuckled, like Abbie wasn't almost crying across the short divide, like Sophia's head wasn't ripping apart trying to figure this out. "You can tell the truth whenever you like, Sophia. I think people would respect you a lot more if you admitted it, instead of making me say it. No? Hello?"

"I..." Sophia sat back, wishing she had a glass of water, wishing Lyndsey would say something, anything. "I really don't know what you're..."

"Please stop talking about this." Abbie sounded twenty years younger; she sounded exactly like Becky did sometimes in class. For a weird moment, Sophia was sure she could smell it, the class, the books, the familiar boredom. "We can't—"

"What she did was twisted and wrong." Morgan gestured at Sophia as he addressed Abbie; Sophia was an afterthought even when she was the subject. "Firstly, by recording you... which, for the record, I think was absolutely disgusting. But she's done far worse. Haven't you?"

He suddenly turned. Sophia had known this was going to happen, the freezing, the lights, too much booze; she looked at Lyndsey, but her idol was staring ahead.

"I don't understand," Sophia said after a pause.

"Let me set the record straight. Knowing your teaching career was over – due to your own disgusting behaviour – you decided to blackmail a sexual assault victim."

Sophia jolted in her chair. She almost went right off her feet. Abbie was gawping across at her, like even *she* was surprised.

"I would never—"

"Caroline Jenkins – more popularly known as Caroline the Kitty online – was sexually assaulted only a few days ago. But

268

even that didn't stop you from holding a certain sex tape over her..."

"I didn't hold anything–"

Morgan clapped, and the screen lit up. It was covered in screenshots taken from a Facebook conversation.

Texts too.

"Why don't I read one for you?" Morgan said. "I apologise in advance to any of you easily offended darlings out there, but this is real life; this is the *real* Sophia."

"How dare you," Sophia said. "You can't do this."

"I don't care if ten men... had their way with you... you're still going to pay up, you... bad word for a woman." Morgan laughed darkly. "Your actual language was a lot more vile, as you know. There are more. You tell her she deserved the sexual assault. You berate her for money. And each time, you tell her you'll release the sex tape if she doesn't do as you say. You're blackmailing a woman, Sophia, a woman who has recently suffered severe trauma. How can you sit there and claim any sort of moral virtue?"

Sophia had once wondered, why didn't people interrupt Morgan the same way he did others? But when he got going, it was obvious; he was worse than a whirlpool, than a tsunami.

"I did not send those messages," Sophia said, when he finally let her speak.

Morgan sneered, throwing his hands up. "Do you think people are idiots? Look at the screen. Is that your phone number?"

It was. And there was Sophia's profile photo. And there was her WhatsApp photo.

"Y-yes," she said, "but–"

Anybody could have Photoshopped that, she was going to say, but Morgan was relentless.

"But you didn't expect Caroline to have the courage to take

her destiny into her hands... I know that sounds cheesy, but it's true. That's what she's done. And she's here to talk about it."

Morgan stopped, slumping back in the chair, his face and neck bright red. "She's not ready yet, I take it?" he said loudly.

"We're connecting her now," somebody off-camera replied.

"I didn't send those messages."

Sophia looked around, at Lyndsey – who hadn't looked at her once since this started – at Morgan, who was staring down at his hands... and at Abbie, whose eyes were glistening like she might cry.

"I didn't," she repeated, louder. "Anybody could have edited them."

"Are you going to accuse a sexual assault survivor of faking photos to, what, *increase* her trauma?" Lyndsey had finally spun. "At least have the decency to confront this with some grace."

"I'm telling the truth..."

"Right," Lyndsey said.

Sophia felt sure this was an ambush, and Lyndsey had helped plan it. She and Morgan were working together.

Morgan sat up. "Abbie..."

Abbie flinched at her name. Sophia tried not to think of her as a person. It was a terrible impulse, but she had no other choice. Otherwise Abbie's tears would make Sophia wish this all away.

But there had to be something salvageable, surely.

"You don't have to stay for the interview."

"You can't let her do this," Abbie said.

"I'm not letting her do anything. And anyway... It's already done."

"What?" Abbie sat up.

"A couple of hours ago. That's why I want you to know, if you don't want to be here... you'll still get your money."

"All of it?" Abbie said.

"Yes, all of..."

Abbie had already stood. She walked briskly toward the closest exit. Douglas Walker rushed after her: the disgraced intellectual who'd argued that saying the N-word was a human right.

"Where are you going?" Douglas asked, his voice receding.

"Where else? To be with my children."

51

CHRIS

Chris leaned against the car, hands in his pockets.

Becky paced in front of him. "Ms Lancaster is such a bullshitter."

"Yep. That's why I thought this was a bad idea. They can just lie."

"She said it." Becky stopped pacing, staring at Chris with red eyes. "I swear she did. I asked her as a joke. And then she got all Miss Mental Case and told me I could become a prostitute."

"I believe you. But it doesn't matter now."

"Do you want to go back?"

Chris did, but he could tell Becky wanted to stay where they were. He shook his head. "Mum will be all right. She's tough. And she's got Douglas to help her."

Becky leaned against the car, next to Chris. She took out her phone and started scrolling. Chris stuck his hands in his pockets and looked around the car park. Past the car park, there was the street and then, past that, a small park in which a father and son were playing football.

Chris watched them, the boy's happy running, the dad's

pride somehow clear in the way he jogged. "You remember when me, you and Dad played football for three hours when his car broke down?"

Becky wasn't listening; Chris could hear her finger tap-tap-tapping against the screen.

"It was when we were coming home from Scotland. Do you remember that holiday? At the campsite? Dad's mate worked on it. You were little. Maybe you don't remember."

"No, I do. I think so. Was that when Mum had her bad ankle?"

"Yeah, she couldn't play. You were the one who got the football out. You'd never played. I don't think you did after that either. But for three hours, we had the time of our lives, Mum laughing, cheering us on. You and me going against Dad. Even with an open goal, you couldn't score."

She laughed softly. "I'm surprised you two didn't get bored. Dad was awesome at football."

"Nah, it was fun. I was almost disappointed when the car rescue people turned up, you know?"

She dropped her phone.

"Becks?"

"It can't be." She quickly picked her phone up, staring at the screen. "Chris, Chris, *Chris*."

Her voice had become just like it was on the day the car broke down, exactly how she'd childishly cried *pass, pass, pass...* Chris had to help her with whatever it was. He took her phone.

Freddie, the bastard: he must've done something.

But no.

Oh, no.

No no no no no no.

Chris read the headline on Becky's newsfeed: *Popular Webcam Performer 'Caroline the Kitty' Releases Sex Tape Amidst Blackmail Drama.*

There was an image, with large portions of it blurred out: the sexual parts, the things Chris never wanted to see, or think about, or know. And there it was, *he* was...

The angle showed Dad's chest, his tattoos: the newer ones, the ones Chris remembered him getting only a year or two before he died. And there was Caroline, with her dyed hair.

They were having sex.

"It's fake." Becky was yelling as she waved her hands at him. "Tell me it's bullshit, Chris. It's fake."

"It's Dad." Chris' voice was cold. He sounded robotic even to himself. "That's him. Right there. This would've been three years ago at the most, Becks. His tattoos..."

"He'd never cheat on Mum. Would he? He wouldn't. Dad wasn't like that."

"I don't know."

Mum and Douglas walked around the corner. Mum stopped when she spotted them. She was shaking all over and, as she got closer, Chris saw her eyes were full of tears. Douglas walked up quietly behind her, biting down, staring at the ground.

They all knew; it was in the air, clashing between them. Nobody had to guess.

"Is the interview over?" Chris asked.

"They're talking to Caroline," Mum said.

"About the sex tape?" Becky shouted. "I guess you've seen it?"

"I haven't watched it–"

"But you've seen she's released it! There's a news article about it all over my Facebook. Everyone's shared it."

"Oh, kids... I'm so sorry."

"Why aren't you in there with them still?" Chris asked, wondering if this was normal, feeling nothing, as though he could push any potential emotions away before they caused him harm.

So what if Dad cheated on Mum.

So what if everything he knew was shattering and would never be remade.

So what if nobody told the truth and nobody cared and nobody was ever who they should have been.

So what if the one person Chris had always known would do the right thing – had known it without questioning it once in his life – had turned out to be just as shitty as everybody else.

When Mum didn't answer Chris' question, Douglas said, "Morgan excused us. He wanted Abbie gone so it would help with his Caroline angle. Clearly, this whole interview has been a trap for Sophia."

"Trap Sophia?" Chris said. "How?"

"Does it matter?" Becky slapped him on the arm. "This is about Mum and Dad."

Douglas sighed, gesturing at his car. "I'll explain during the drive."

"Do you really think that's what it was?" Mum said. "Why Morgan let me go?"

"He doesn't do anything out of sheer philanthropy. He knew it would be more awkward to leverage this rather unusual situation if you, wife to the man who slept with–"

"Don't say anything about my dad!" Becky exploded.

Douglas leapt back as she went for him. Chris slid into place smoothly, made easier by the fact he was so distant, disconnected. He grabbed Becky and pulled her away.

"Stop," he told her firmly.

She brushed his hands away. "How can you be so calm?"

"Stop making it worse. You're acting like a spoilt little bitch."

"Chris." Mum gasped. "Don't talk to your–"

"You can all fuck off," Chris said, letting Becky go and turning to Douglas. "Open the car, mate. I need to sit down."

Douglas brushed down his jacket, and something sick flashed across Chris' mind: Dad taking off *his* jacket and then sweeping Caroline into his arms, kissing her, doing it all on video, with Mum waiting at home for him, with Mum loving him and supporting him.

A thousand moments of casual love, all witnessed by Chris: all of them crumbling to ash.

52

CAROLINE

As Caroline waited for the video chat to connect, she wondered if people would judge her. If they knew the truth – if they knew that this idea had materialised while lying broken on the cold concrete – would they think less of her?

It had come to her there, as she'd taken in the stars. All of it, in one burst, almost enough to make her religious.

She could use Sophia's new-found fame as a catalyst to launch herself into superstardom.

Why let a sad, pathetic, feeble man's act of sickness define her in a negative way? A man had... it hurt to think it. But a man had *raped* her, and there was a way for her to turn it into a positive.

Sophia had been kind, but she was also far more useful as a deranged lunatic who sought to blackmail an assault survivor. So that was what Caroline would make her.

As the call connected, Caroline thought of book deals, of massively increased revenue from her webcam career, of TV interviews, all of it; she'd always known she was born to be special, to be *something*.

She brushed down her outfit. She was wearing a cream

button-up and a brown wig, the hair tied back, making her look more respectable.

"Thank you so much for doing this," Morgan said. "Can you hear us okay?"

Lyndsey and Sophia sat beside him. Sophia was staring like she couldn't believe it, and Lyndsey had an annoying look on her face. It was a look that implied she and Caroline were in on some joke: worse, like the *assault* had been a joke.

"Yes," Caroline replied.

"Would you mind explaining why you're here speaking with us today? You've been very brave to agree to an interview so soon after what happened."

Morgan was being kind and patient, just as he'd promised in his emails; when Caroline had emailed *The Morgan MacDermott Show* team, the host himself had leapt on what she had, on her story.

"One of the viewers of the Caroline the Kitty stream had some marital troubles, it seems. He..." She remembered the night, the angle, the tearing, the flash of stars. Shuddering – there was no faking memories like this – she pushed on. "He took out his anger on me. He did... a terrible thing."

"He's in police custody now for – forgive me, Caroline – for rape, isn't he?"

Caroline lifted her chin. She wouldn't hide just because she was afraid. "Yes, he is. Thank God."

Lyndsey and Sophia were sitting there silently; Caroline knew Morgan had told them not to say anything until specifically addressed. Sophia fidgeted, as if finding it difficult.

"And yet you decide, just a few days later, to release a sex tape."

"Yes."

"A sex tape which involves the husband of the woman whose life Sophia tried to destroy."

As far as Caroline was concerned, Abbie deserved to have her life destroyed, but this wasn't personal.

It never had been, except when she thought of Jack.

Of her dear Jack who'd sent her a Facebook message one evening, just a smiley face, and she'd sent him one back...

And that had turned into heated exchanges through words, into him telling her he watched her stream.

Then the hotel trips, meeting halfway between them, in Exeter, so nobody would see.

The mind-blowing sex. The awkwardness when he wouldn't hold her afterward.

The secret recording, because Caroline had figured, why not have it?

To watch, yes, to relive, but also just in case she needed something from Jack one day. After his death, Caroline had kept it for herself. She'd never guessed it would come in so useful.

That was why she'd helped Sophia: to keep this fame train moving, the controversy rising, so she could wait for the right moment.

Fate had gifted her with the ideal circumstances.

"I need a moment," Caroline said after a long pause.

"I didn't try to destroy her life," Sophia said quietly, then her voice got louder. "I've stated many times that I–"

"Please make her stop," Caroline said, tone wavering like she might cry. "It's hard enough to talk about this without having *her* speak over me."

"I wasn't speaking over you. You weren't–"

"Please," Morgan said firmly. "I've made it clear that we won't interrupt Caroline. She's being incredibly brave, agreeing to an interview so soon after what happened. You'll have a chance to speak soon."

Morgan turned back to Caroline. "So why release the sex tape?"

"I've got no ill will against Abbie. It's true, her relationship with Jack started while me and Jack were together. But that's all ancient history. I never would've released this video if Sophia had never gotten hold of it."

"Gotten hold of it?"

"I contacted Sophia when I saw her TikTok video. I'd had experience with feeling threatened by Abbie, so I wanted to reach out. But when I met Sophia, she was nothing like I imagined. She was judgemental, cruel."

Sophia opened her mouth, like she might speak. But then she deflated. Caroline tried not to look at her; it was too difficult not to feel something, a memory of how Sophia had held her, cared for her.

For one night. There was no need to overblow it.

"Even so, I wanted to give her a chance. But then one evening, after a few drinks, she must've taken my phone from my bag. I'm naïve. Or an idiot, depending on how you look at it. I didn't have a password on my phone. She found the video. She sent it to herself. And she used it, or tried to use it, to blackmail me."

"That's. Not. True. You can't let her lie like this."

"I'm letting her speak her truth," Morgan said. "A phrase I despise, but it's appropriate here. If you want to speak what *you* consider the truth, Sophia, go ahead. Since you're intent on interrupting anyway."

"Caroline, why?" Sophia said. "I thought we were in this together."

"I've tried to tell you," Caroline replied. "This isn't a fight. *In this*. We're not *in* anything. Terrible things happened to me, but you don't care. All you care about is money and fame."

"I cared about you," Sophia said. "For one night, at least. I cared like you were my sister."

"Was that the night you sent me those messages, saying all those awful things?"

"We both know I didn't send those."

Caroline huffed, rolled her eyes, threw her hands up. She was telling the whole world how ridiculous she found Sophia's refusal to end the charade. "We can't have a conversation about it if you won't admit the truth."

"The truth is–"

"Do you think I *wanted* to be assaulted? Do you think I *wanted* to hurt Abbie more than you already have? I won't lie, Abbie and I haven't exactly seen eye to eye since she stole my boyfriend, but I never had a vendetta against her. I could've released this video a long time ago."

"Why *did* you keep it?" Morgan asked.

"I didn't intentionally," Caroline lied. "It was just one of those things."

"Sleeping with another woman's husband?" Sophia snapped, and that was good.

Her rising voice, her shrill tone.

"That's just *one of those things*, is it? You recorded yourself having sex with another woman's husband, Caroline. Why don't we talk about *that*?"

Sophia looked around the room, as if expecting support, but Lyndsey and Morgan only stared at her. That was another good thing; Sophia was nowhere near as strong as Caroline, nowhere near as capable. She needed people backing her up.

"I'm not proud of the affair. Neither was Jack. That was why we ended things amicably."

It hadn't even ended, not really; Jack had merely stopped returning her phone calls and texts, and Caroline had waited, trying to work up the courage to use what she had. And then Jack's cancer had come.

Caroline couldn't hurt him at such a difficult time. Even if he'd deserved it.

"I never planned on keeping the video. But you, Sophia, you saw it and you saw your chance at fame and money. It's exactly what you did when you recorded Abbie. You don't care that I was... I'm saying it, *I'm saying it*."

Caroline worked herself up to the word, pushing away the memory, the stars, the angle, the cramp.

"I was raped. You don't care if Abbie's had her life turned upside down. All you care about is yourself."

"I care about feminism," Sophia said. "It's been the biggest passion in my life."

"Feminism," Caroline repeated, shaking her head. "You should read your messages again. There's nothing feminist about the things you said. You're a user. You're using Lyndsey for fame. You used Abbie for a cheap bit of controversy. And you tried to use me. I won't let you. You can't hold the video over my head anymore, so make any pathetic threats you want."

Caroline had posted the sex tape to a website which also linked to her webcam and subscription-service pages.

"If there's a feminist between us," she went on, "it's me. I'm the one who's self-employed. I'm the one who's confidently claiming her sexuality. *I'm* the one who's suffered first-hand at the hands of men. It's one thing to talk about it. It's another to live it."

"I'm not the one sticking dildos up my ass online!" Sophia screamed.

Caroline almost smirked. She stopped herself, then sat back.

She stared at the webcam like she might cry; she stared like her world was crumbling.

Sophia's hand was rising slowly, like she was going to place it over her mouth, but then she let it drop.

Morgan said nothing. Lyndsey said nothing.

Then Caroline whispered, "Are you saying it's my fault?"

"No," Sophia said. "I wouldn't... I'd never..."

"I should be allowed to pursue any kind of work I like – as long as it's legal, which my profession *is* – without worrying about being assaulted. But I suppose you disagree? I suppose you think I was asking for it?"

"I didn't mean that."

"You've just shown who you really are," Caroline said. "You pretend to be a feminist, but when it comes down to it, you see me as a slut who deserved it. Who was asking for it."

Caroline didn't have to fake the tears. She broke down, and suddenly she was back there, lying on her back, staring up at the stars and knowing she belonged among them.

"Caroline, please, don't cry," Sophia said. "I didn't... I wouldn't... I haven't..."

53

BECKY

Becky sat as far away from Chris as she could get, pushing herself against the inner car door as the motorway rushed past. Douglas drove quietly; the radio was off.

Mum hadn't said anything in a few minutes. She kept trying to talk to Becky, but Becky was taking Chris' lead. She tried to think as little as possible, instead watching the world rush by.

She especially tried not to think about the screenshot she'd seen, with the blurry parts and Dad's face.

His face...

Expression twisted up, obsessed with what he was doing, with Caroline.

She shuddered, as if that would push it away.

It would be better if she could erase the image from her mind. She never should've seen Dad's face... like that.

And then she realised; she might see it again. Somebody could thrust their phone into her face, make her look before she'd had a chance to turn away. Or she'd glance at somebody's phone on the bus. There were screens everywhere waiting to show it to her.

She looked over at Chris. He'd become quiet ever since getting into the car. Sort of like Dad used to be after a long day of work.

But who was Dad?

What was he? He wasn't Becky's father. She'd known Jack Basset, and he was protective and honourable; the other girls sometimes used to make fun of him, but they all shut up when Becky swore at them and said at least her parents weren't divorced. Mum had told her off for that.

"Don't judge somebody for being divorced. Not every woman is as lucky as me."

Not every woman was lucky enough to meet a Jack: a man who would never give her reason for a divorce.

"Didn't you notice anything?" Becky asked.

Douglas tensed up as he drove, but he said nothing. Chris remained silent.

"No," Mum said coldly.

"He must've been acting different. I just can't believe he'd decide to do that, and... and with *her* of all people."

"Neither can I." Mum was holding back tears; Becky wished she'd shouted, slammed her hand against the dashboard. "It's not a long drive either way. They could've met when I was at work."

"It's *gross.* I thought Dad was better than that."

"So did I."

"It's not *fair.*"

"I know."

Becky shoved the back of Mum's seat. "You must've noticed something. There's no way he went from being the dad we knew to a fucking perv–"

"Language."

"A *fucking* perv," Becky yelled over her. "Who'd want to be with his old girlfriend? There's no way. Something must've happened between you two. Or something else. There has to be a reason."

"Maybe there is, Becky," Mum said tightly. "Maybe I should look back over every second of our marriage for places I could've done better. Let me think about all the things he said that could've been lies."

"I'm not saying that."

"Remember, he loved you. Both of you. He was still your dad."

Becky shoved the seat again, causing Douglas to glance back. But then he quickly stared ahead, as though wanting nothing to do with them. "You can't say he was still Dad when he did something Dad would never do. He stopped being that person when he did... what he did. It's so wrong. It's not him."

"But all the moments you shared, all the lessons," Mum said. "This doesn't change them. It was a mistake, what your father did, but–"

"He told me to never cheat on a woman," Chris said in his weirdly calm voice. "It was when I first started getting girlfriends, and I told him about my mate who'd cheated on a girl. He sat me down and explained why it was a terrible thing to do. You know what he said to me?"

"What?" Becky asked, more tears rushing; there was something awful about Chris' steady voice.

"He said if I want another girl, break up with my current girlfriend. He said the damage it does to them, to women, it's not fair. It messes with their heads. It makes it impossible for them to trust men."

"Chris..." Mum's voice wavered.

"He told me lots of things," Chris goes on. "And maybe you're right, Mum. Maybe I can still have some of those lessons.

But how can I ever know which ones to trust? He told me not to cheat. He cheated. He told me not to do drugs. Who knows what he was doing, probably *with* Caroline? He told me to get an honest job... he could've been dealing for all I know."

"Your father wasn't dealing drugs."

"Maybe not. But I can't be sure."

Chris' words stabbed at Becky. They were true. There was nothing they could rely on. There was no *Dad* who was real, because everything had the potential to be false.

"Once a cheat always a cheat." Becky hadn't planned on saying this, but she went on. "What you said, Chris, about Dad telling you not to cheat... how could you ever take that seriously? He cheated on Caroline."

"I guess I saw that differently," Chris said. "I never considered that cheating. Or it was so long ago it didn't matter. He was Dad, you know? I remember what you said, Mum..."

Mum tried to reply, but she was sobbing quietly, trying to fight the tears. Becky was doing the same. Douglas turned off the motorway, heading for the road which would lead to his big fancy house; they were staying the night, then travelling back the day after.

"About how much you regretted how you and Dad got together. But you thought fate brought you together. You saved each other. You built a life together. It wasn't something Dad did as a habit. It was a mistake that turned into a good thing. But yeah, Becky's right. Once a cheat, always a cheat. That was pretty fucking stupid, actually, me bringing that up."

Mum didn't correct him for swearing; it was as if they were long past that. And anyway, she was crying too hard, though she was trying to keep it quiet. Becky felt a strange aversion to touching her, her own mother.

But the crying was too terrible.

Leaning forward, Becky slipped her arm around the seat and clutched Mum's shoulder. Mum's hands instantly darted up and held on to Becky. They stayed like that, both crying, as Chris' voice rose and his tone became even more detached.

"I don't know anything anymore. I don't know who Dad is. I don't know who I am."

54

CHRIS

Chris swigged on the bottle, thinking of all the times Dad had told him to go easy on the booze and to never touch drugs.

Jimmy stood opposite, at the back of the flats, smoking a swollen fat joint.

Chris thought about the drive home earlier that day, the stuffiness in the car, the fact Douglas was still hanging around, what would happen once Morgan's interview aired, and the tape, the sex tape, Caroline and Dad.

"Can I have some of that?"

Jimmy flinched, letting out a big puff of smoke. It reeked. Dad always commented on the smell. *Stinks, son.*

But Dad was a papier mâché piece of shit.

"Really?" Jimmy asked.

"I wouldn't have said it otherwise."

Chris finished his beer bottle and threw it overarm at the wall. It exploded, glass shattering everywhere, joining the glistening shards from his previous bottle.

He'd drank two while out there and three more in Jimmy's flat.

Jimmy handed the joint over.

"This is your first time, isn't it?"

"Yeah."

"Go easy, Chris."

Ignoring the concern in his old friend's voice, he brought the joint to his lips. He sucked in the smoke, then kept sucking, even as the back of his throat burned and his lungs ached. In his kickboxing training, he'd become accustomed to discomfort; he could withstand the burning, the screaming in his body, telling him to stop.

Even Jimmy was yelling, "Enough, Chris, Jesus Christ, that's enough."

But Chris kept going. He closed his eyes and he saw nothing, and he felt nothing other than the smoke surging through his body, joining the beer.

Finally, he stopped, blowing it all out: laughing as he imagined he was exhaling Caroline and his dad, both of them gone, both of them meaningless.

"God*damn*," Chris said, dancing back on his toes, jabbing the air with sudden importance.

"You're one of those hyper stoners then," Jimmy commented.

Chris ignored him, striking the air. He'd always enjoyed shadow boxing, but right then it was all that mattered, all that *existed*. It was so much easier to focus on his technique. He wondered if he should pursue kickboxing; he'd only *not* pursued it because Dad had whined about head damage. But Dad's opinion didn't matter anymore.

Jimmy was kneeling.

Chris chuckled. "You're not proposing, are you?"

Standing, Jimmy laughed tightly. "You dropped the joint. Not that there's much left."

"You don't have any more?" Chris said.

"Nah."

"Fuck."

Chris could feel the thoughts creeping back in already, the stills he'd seen online, the stuff all over Facebook.

Everybody was sharing it. People were arguing in the comments, some saying it was none of their business, others addicted to the bizarre situation.

He could picture Dad's face, twisted in pleasure, and Chris hated it, hated *Dad*.

He jabbed the air some more, letting out *tsks* and bobbing and weaving around an imaginary opponent. "How much would fifty quid get us? I want more, Jimmy. I want to get so high I can't even see. I want to get so high I can't think."

Chris wasn't sure how long he'd been staring at the ceiling. It was like time was stretching at the edges, tearing apart.

He didn't have to think about Dad; he didn't have to imagine Dad and Caroline together, Caroline the slut with her webcam *business*, Caroline the whore probably sending Dad messages online, tempting him.

Looking for more beer, Chris leaned up. Jimmy's coffee table was dancing all over the room.

Chris grabbed a beer bottle, made to drink it; it was empty. Jimmy laughed and Chris spun on him, thinking of the shadow boxing. When was that? Before they went to get more weed; before they'd smoked... How many had it been?

Jimmy was staring at him for some reason. "I'm sorry."

"Sorry for what?"

"For laughing. Do you want another beer?"

Chris knew there was a problem, on some level. He couldn't remember what Jimmy had laughed about.

"Yeah."

"This is hilarious, isn't it?" Jimmy leaned forward, sorting through the empty bottles, finding one with some beer in. "Here you go."

Chris took it, then Jimmy gasped. "Chris, wait–"

But it was too late. Chris had swallowed the mouthful of piss-warm beer along with the soggy cigarette butt.

Chris keeled over, hands on his knees, and puked all over the floor. He felt the veins in his neck pressing against his skin, his cheeks inflaming, every sensation brought closer and made harsher by the weed rushing around his head.

"My carpet," Jimmy yelled, in that annoying-as-fuck voice Chris remembered from school. "Oh, *Chris*."

Chris looked up, attempting to take in what was happening. He kept forgetting, as though he was falling asleep, then waking up. The threadbare carpet was covered in big yellowy chunks, with more bile spattered.

Maybe Chris would've behaved differently if he hadn't recently learned his dad was a fake. Or if Ms Lancaster hadn't recorded Mum. Or if Freddie would leave Becky alone. Or without the booze, the weed.

But Chris hated Jimmy right then, his whining, his weakness. How every little thing had to become an atom bomb.

"Shut the fuck up," Chris snapped.

Jimmy flinched. "My carpet's ruined."

"This whole place is a shit tip."

Suddenly Chris was watching himself upturn the coffee table with his foot. Bottles spilled all over the floor, ash following; it was like he was an observer as his fist collided with the old-style TV, shattering the screen. He didn't feel the glass on his knuckles.

He could just about hear Jimmy screaming at him to stop.

"I don't give a fuck."

Was that Chris' voice? He faintly felt his vocal cords moving, but it was all disconnected.

Jimmy grabbed his shoulder.

Chris spun, darting his hand out, curling it around Jimmy's throat. It was so easy to squeeze and watch his old friend's face go red. Chris was crying just as much as Jimmy was, but he didn't stop.

"Do something," he roared in Jimmy's face, shaking him. "Fight back."

"P-p-please." Jimmy gasped. "C-Chris."

Chris finally let him go, stumbling backward, looking around the room at what he'd done. It was like collapsing back into his body, into the reality of it. He rubbed his face, but more tears came. He could normally control them.

Jimmy spoke quietly. "Sorry, but... I want you to go."

———

Chris left Jimmy's place and wandered the estate.

He knew it was stupid to use his last few quid on a four-pack of beer, but he did it anyway.

He drank more; he drained the can and crushed it, then threw it across the park, laughing without even knowing why. He felt like he was getting his second wind, a phrase he'd heard countless times. It had once made him think, *What a loser, getting proud of being able to drink more alcohol.*

"Son," Chris said aloud, kicking back and forth on the swing. He remembered Dad's voice, the deepness, the certainty. "Never drink so much you end up making a prick of yourself."

Chris wasn't sure how long he sat there. It was long enough to drink all four cans and think about nothing.

And then, suddenly, he was punching the ground. He wasn't sure when he'd blacked out, but he awoke while hammering his fist against the grass, crying and... Jesus Christ, he'd pissed himself. He could feel the hot urine spreading in his underwear.

He stopped, standing, managing to stop from tipping sideways as he put his arms out to the side. He weaved over to the swing and sat, ignoring the warm dampness in his underwear, knowing he should care but finding it easy not to.

"*Yes*, mate..."

Chris leaned forward, tilted his head, like a predator.

Could it seriously be Freddie?

It sounded like him.

"Nah, don't be a pussy."

At the end of the park, somebody was walking past. Chris swayed through the darkness, his eyes blurry with tears. He wiped at them, stared at the figure passing along the fence, the shape of his head, the swagger, every movement telegraphing that Freddie could do what he wanted, whenever he wanted.

There were never any consequences.

Assault a fourteen-year-old girl, cheat on a wife, record a sex tape, lie in the press, fire somebody because of a few protestors... nothing mattered.

Nothing ever came to anything.

Chris walked to the park's entrance.

Freddie was walking down the dark path, his phone in his hand, speaking loudly into it: speaking like nothing could ever hurt him.

Chris opened the park gate and followed, knowing something terrible was going to happen and not giving a damn.

Before he turned the corner, he took the watch from his pocket: the one his father had gifted him, the most precious belonging in his family. His legacy.

He crushed it under his shoe and carried on walking.

55

ABBIE

Abbie sat on the bed, Douglas' hand warm against her shoulder. He was sitting beside her, seeming slightly awkward as she wept. Chris was out, God knew where, doing God knew what; Becky was in her room, hopefully asleep, but probably scrolling through the endless comments online.

Everybody knew Jack had cheated on Abbie.

Douglas had returned to Bristol with Abbie and the kids, since he still wanted to shadow her for his book. Abbie had, bluntly speaking, thought about having sex with this man as petty revenge for Jack's betrayal, but there was no revenge, nothing to gain...

His hand was comforting, though. She couldn't deny that.

Abbie tried ringing Chris again, but it went to voicemail.

"What happens now?" she whispered.

Douglas sighed. "We wait to see how the public reacts to the show. It'll air in a couple of days. I personally think you'll gain lots of sympathy. You handled Sophia quite readily. And as for the sex tape thing..."

"The sex tape thing," she snapped, glaring at him. "The *thing*. The bomb that tore my life apart."

Douglas nodded slowly, like a therapist. "I'm sorry. I wish there was something I could say to make it better. But I can't, I'm afraid. But trust me, you did better in that interview than you think you did. The sex tape will garner you sympathy. Nobody likes to see a woman cheated on, publicly humiliated..."

"I just don't understand any of this." Abbie rubbed her hands up and down her face, as though that would jolt her from the tangled dream into which she'd fallen. "I can't believe Jack would go back to her, after all the years we spent together, after promising me time and time again he only wanted me. I wish I could hurt her, *really* hurt her."

"Like I said, I'm certain people will side with *you* here. Mothers and wives all over the country will stop seeing you as the Feminist Killer and imagine themselves in your position instead. That will change if you assault a woman who was recently..."

Abbie filled in the pause.

Sexually assaulted.

Douglas had filled her in about Caroline's interview, since he had a contact on set. One of Caroline's viewers had assaulted her, and Caroline had used it as a chance to publish the sex tape, putting a pro-woman spin on it.

"She's beyond deranged," Abbie said, fists clenched. "Doing that... after what happened to her. *Days* after."

"We live in a sick society. You can't blame her for being ill."

"I can. I do."

They said nothing for a time. Douglas removed his hand and they sat in quiet.

When Abbie's phone rang, she grabbed it quickly, assuming it would be Chris.

"Hello." Caroline was making her voice sound young, a babytalk that made Abbie's fist clench tighter; it was like she thought she could make Abbie feel sorry for her. "Are you there? Hello?"

"I'm here," Abbie said tightly.

"I wanted to say sorry."

Abbie laughed harshly. "How could you be sorry after what you did?"

"What I did was act before Sophia forced me to. If you've got a problem, you should take it up with her."

"Jack told me how you used to follow him, how you used to hang on to him, how you stopped at nothing until you got your grimy paws on him. No, Caroline, Sophia didn't do anything... I don't know how, but *you* made this happen."

"You think I arranged my own rape?"

"No, not that bit. But the messages Sophia apparently sent you, blackmailing you."

"You think she's above something like that?"

"What's in it for her?" Abbie said. "It makes no sense. But it doesn't matter, does it, these days? Nothing has to make sense. You've got a story, you've got your webcam career. You've played this well."

"I haven't *played* anything. I didn't want to release the tape. Sophia is twisted. You said so yourself... she told Becky to be–"

"Don't say my daughter's name!" Abbie leapt to her feet, pacing to the window, hoping to find Caroline in the street below so she could charge down there.

"Okay, I'm sorry. Really, I am. I wish it hadn't come to this. I never would've released the tape if she hadn't made me."

There was a long pause, Abbie stared out at the darkened street, imagining Jack walking up the lane with a bouquet of flowers, all of this melting away under the heat of his easy smile.

"Why did he do it?" Abbie's voice tremored as she held back tears. "How did it happen? I didn't ask before because..."

She'd wanted to bury it, even within herself, to push it so far down it didn't exist. If nobody else saw it, eventually she'd be able to erase it from her mind, their writhing bodies, Jack's expression of pure pleasure.

"Do you really want to know?" Caroline asked.

No. "Yes."

"He messaged me. He'd seen my stream..."

"Where you stick dildos in your ass."

"Please don't put down my work."

Abbie almost punched the window. "What did he say in this lover's note?"

"Nothing. Just a smiley face emoji. But we got talking from there. There was nothing personal in it. Nothing romantic. It was all..."

"Sexual."

As if that was supposed to make her feel better.

"Did he agree to be recorded?"

"Yes," she said quickly. "It was his idea. It excited him."

Abbie was just about fighting off the sobs, but tears slid hotly down her cheeks.

"I'm not saying that to hurt you," Caroline went on. "As far as I'm concerned, we're even. You stole him from me. I took him back."

"How many times?"

"Abbie..."

"How many times did you fuck my husband?"

"I'm not sure. Maybe twenty."

"Jesus Christ. And you kept the video because you could watch it and tell yourself you won. In this game we've been playing since school. You won. You proved Jack is as easily swayed as any other man. You proved I was an idiot for ever thinking different."

Caroline said nothing, which was basically a *yes*.

"What do you want?" Abbie paced the room, sensing Douglas' eyes on her. "Do you want me to tell you it's okay?"

"I *am* sorry."

"You've said that. You can tell yourself you're a good person now. Is there anything else?"

"I want..." Caroline hesitated. "To smooth things over between us. To make sure this is the end of it."

She was afraid Abbie would seek revenge. Good.

"We'll have to wait and see," Abbie said coldly.

"I've got a proposition," Caroline murmured. "I know you'll need as much financial assistance as you can get, and I despise Sophia for what she made me do."

"You want to pay me off."

"I want to help you. Things are in motion for me. Soon, I'll never have to worry about money again. It's not easy for me to make this offer, but if you'll let me, I'll make your life easier. Nobody ever needs to know where the money came from."

Abbie thought about Little Pint, when Keith offered her the wad of cash. She thought about Morgan's show, enduring the humiliation for the paycheque.

But she couldn't endure this. It was too far. It was *Caroline*.

"Go to hell," Abbie said, then hung up the phone.

She was suddenly full of energy, despite the time, pacing her bedroom as her hands moved endlessly through her hair.

"Abbie..." Douglas approached as though she was volatile, his posh voice full of concern. "It's going to be okay–"

She interrupted him with a kiss.

It was a wild thing to do, but she did it anyway. She wrapped her arms around him, feeling him respond, knowing she was doing it for the wrong reasons but not caring.

Douglas gently touched her shoulders, pushed her away. "This isn't a good idea."

"I know," she said, and she kissed him again.

He moved back slightly. "I don't want to take advantage of you."

"I'm not a child. I'm not some little flower. I'm a woman, Douglas. I want this. I'm *choosing* this."

When she kissed him a third time, he didn't fight her.

The doorbell never used to bring suspicion.

But right then, as Abbie lay in Douglas' arms and savoured the close warmth of his body, the bell sliced the moment clean in half and returned them to the old world, the one filled with doubt and danger, completely separate from what they'd just shared.

And it was late.

"I'll get it, if you like," Douglas said.

Abbie stood, feeling oddly comfortable naked, her skin tingling as Douglas' eyes roamed over her. She wasn't sure what was happening, definitely not love, but not *just* lust: something new and exciting, something that made her feel human.

She quickly pulled on some clothes and went downstairs.

Her reflex was to slam the door. The man wasn't wearing an overcoat this time, but she recognised his thin, combed-over hair, the panic in his eyes. He seemed different, his eyes no longer glassy, his lips no longer wet. He seemed sober.

He rubbed his hands together. "Hello, Abbie."

She tried not to show any fear on her face. Countless people knew her name. It was nothing special. And yet she hated it, hated that he was there, whoever he was.

"Who are you?" She kept her voice low. "What do you want?"

"I haven't gone about things in the smartest way," he replied. "First, I need to say sorry. Sorry for following you. Sorry for scaring you. I got the address of your workplace from that podcast, and then I... well, who knows what I was thinking."

Abbie positioned her hand on the door, ready to throw it shut. "Get to the point."

"I've been drunk and high for years. Until a couple of days ago, in fact. But I'm ready now."

"Ready for what?"

"To make amends. To say sorry."

"Please, no more riddles. Just tell me who you are."

As he spoke, Abbie softened. No matter what had happened – or would happen – family was always the most important thing. There was nothing more sacred. The man's name was Michael, and though Abbie didn't know him, she could see the sincerity in his eyes.

"I don't have that information," Abbie said. "But I can find out. Wait here."

Shutting the door, she went inside and found her mobile.

She rang Caroline.

56

CHRIS

Chris followed Freddie down the dark path, stalking like a predator. He stumbled a few times, but he managed to keep his footing, turning the corner as Freddie walked down a cut-through that was the perfect spot.

A voice in Chris' head told him to stop. It was Dad's, he realised, and that just made him more convinced he had to do this.

The alcohol rushed through his system. The weed made everything seem distant.

Chris thought about Becky and the terror this bastard had inflicted on her.

When Freddie hung up his phone, Chris called out, "All right, mate?"

Freddie turned, more of a silhouette than an actual person. He stepped forward. "Uh, hello?"

"What's wrong? Not happy to see me?"

That triggered something in Freddie; he must've recognised Chris' voice.

Freddie turned, started running, but Chris was flooded with

rage and intent and the need to inflict pain. The need to force some of this to make sense. The need to *do something*.

Chris sprinted, catching up to Freddie quickly.

He leapt into a kick that smashed Freddie in the lower back, sending him sprawling to the ground. Freddie yelped like a scared animal when Chris pounced on him, flurrying punches, seeing the image of Caroline and Dad; it was tattooed into his mind, and it was all he thought about as he assaulted Freddie, hitting him in the face over and over, feeling the impact reverberate up his arm.

"Please," Freddie croaked.

Chris blinked, as though waking up. He was straddling Freddie.

In the darkness, Chris could just about make out his swelling cheeks.

"Please?" Chris wept; he wasn't sure when that had started. "Are you taking the piss? *Please?* After what you did to my sister?"

Chris stood, ignoring Freddie's moaning. When the fucker tried to stand, Chris took two running steps and kicked him so hard in the side his toes throbbed in his shoe.

He kicked him again – again.

Stop stop stop, a plea rang out in his mind.

But he couldn't.

"W-wait," Freddie moaned, raising his hands to cover his face.

But Chris wouldn't wait.

He drove a vicious strike through Freddie's pitiful defence, crushing his face, then came over the top with an elbow that shattered across Freddie's jaw.

"I should kill you." Chris grabbed the back of Freddie's neck and hauled him to his feet, hating himself as he did it, knowing deep down he'd regret this. But the sick truth was, it felt good in a warped way. Righteous. "Not so tough now, are you?"

"I deleted the video," Freddie moaned when Chris shoved him against the wall. "Like you asked. I *deleted* it."

"Yeah, and then you still wouldn't leave her alone."

Chris pelted him with a liver shot, causing him to keel over. But Chris grabbed him, righted him, shoved him up against the wall.

"I swear." Freddie's voice was tangled with sobs and his injuries, speaking as if his tongue had ballooned in his mouth, making it difficult to move his lips. "I'll never speak to h–"

Hit, hit, hit, and Chris didn't have to think about anything else. It was like Freddie became a heavy bag at the gym. Chris took it all out on his soft middle, making *tsk* noises the same way he would during training.

Freddie was bawling. "I swear to God. Oh, Jesus. I think you've broken something..."

"I don't give a *fuck*."

Another kick, landing on Freddie's thigh. For a strange second, Chris felt the pain in his own leg, the blistering agony Freddie must have experienced.

Freddie wailed. "I swear, mate. I swear. I didn't want this to happen."

Chris launched himself onto the ground, coming down with a brutal strike. Time seemed to slow and a stunningly clear thought arose in Chris' mind.

This could kill Freddie.

Then the blow landed.

The back of Freddie's skull crushed against the concrete.

Chris stood, heaving in breaths, staring down at what he'd done. His eyes had adjusted somewhat to the low light. He could make out the shape of Freddie's ruined face, blood glimmering across his cheeks.

"P-p-please," Freddie wheezed, and then his eyes fell shut.

Chris stumbled away, his heart pulsing, panic writhing up and down him.

What the hell had he done?

"Come on." Chris weaved as he nudged Freddie with his foot: the same one he'd kicked him with. His foot tore with pain. "Get up. Don't be a pussy. *Get up.*"

Freddie groaned, but his eyes remained closed.

Chris turned and ran through the dark.

He woke with his eyes glued shut.

Somebody was moaning in his room. The memories stayed away for a few moments, and he wondered who was making that noise, their breath wheezing. Then he felt the rasp in his chest, remembered Jimmy's place, trashing it, remembered...

Oh, no.

He sat up, peeled his eyes open, stared around his bedroom as sunlight shafted through the window and attacked him. His head was pounding like there was dozens of little hammers in there, trying to crack his skull.

He blinked as tears scoured down his cheeks. No matter how much he angrily rubbed at them, they kept flowing.

Had he killed Freddie?

Chris knew he'd never be able to look at himself the same way again. He'd never be able to take pride in who he was as a person. He'd never be able to stand the sight of himself in the reflection. As if destroying the watch wasn't bad enough.

Freddie was a lowlife, a scumbag, a bully. But that didn't mean Chris should've done what he did.

He shivered as he relived the physical sensations of the assault, the cowardly kicks he'd aimed at Freddie as he lay on the ground. He remembered the moaning as Freddie had passed out.

He couldn't stop shaking, sitting up in bed and drawing his knees to his chest, wrapping his arms around them as it played over and over in his mind, a sickening slideshow.

He flinched at the knock at the door.

"Chris?" It was Becky. "Do you want any breakfast?"

"I... I'm okay."

He couldn't hide the pain in his voice. Maybe that was why Becky pushed the door open straightaway.

"What happened?" Becky rushed to the bed, wrapped her arm around him and squeezed tight. "Chris, what is it?"

He didn't want to tell her; he didn't want to tell anybody, ever. But he couldn't keep it inside either.

Becky sat patiently as he told the story through sobs, explaining what he'd done at Jimmy's flat, and then after... Freddie, the assault.

"I don't even know if he's alive, Becks. I just left him there."

Becky stared, unable to hide the look in her eyes; it was like she was reshaping her view of him in real time. Becky hated Freddie, obviously, but Chris could tell even she thought what he'd done was wrong.

"What if he's dead?" he said.

"I don't know. Oh, Chris. I just don't know."

She held him for a long time. At some point, Chris started to cry again. He'd always tried to be strong for his little sister, especially after Dad's death: always attempted to show her they could be good, do better, despite their circumstances.

But he wasn't that person anymore. She'd never see him as her role model again.

How could she?

"I need to call Jimmy," Chris said. "I can apologise to him, at least. And... and then wait. See if the police show up. See if we get news about Freddie. I could be a killer. I could've murdered him."

"H-he deserved it," Becky stuttered, but she couldn't mask the panic, couldn't hide the fact that Chris had made this worse.

Much worse.

"Where's my phone?"

Becky looked around the room, took it from the bedside table.

Chris had several missed calls from Jimmy.

"Let me make you some breakfast," Becky said. "I can do that, at least."

"I'm not hungry—"

"Just let me do it."

"Do you hate me?" Chris asked, when she stood and walked toward the door.

"I don't know what to think about anything anymore."

Becky left quickly, leaving Chris to call Jimmy.

As the phone rang, he looked around the room, at the posters of boxers and fighters, the trophies on the shelf. None of it felt connected to him; everything in there belonged to somebody else, a man – a boy – who would never assault a man from behind, never leave somebody for dead.

"Hello," Jimmy said, sounding uncertain.

Chris bit down, fighting off more sobs, wondering when he'd become so weak. "Jimmy, mate, I'm so, so sorry. I don't know what came over me. You didn't deserve that."

Chris almost wanted him to shout: to yell that there was no forgiving what he'd done. He wanted Jimmy to angrily tell him to never ring him again. It would've been the right thing to do.

It would've been justice.

But instead, Jimmy said in a meek voice, "It's all right. I forgive you. You've always been a good friend to me."

"How can you say that? I treated you like dirt."

"Everybody does that. At least you said you're sorry."

Chris groaned, lay back on the bed, stared up at a crack in the ceiling.

The question would cling to him every single day until he learned if Freddie had survived.

Was Chris a killer?

Or, if Freddie had survived, what sort of revenge would he take?

57

SOPHIA

Sophia skulked outside of Lyndsey's hotel and scanned everybody who entered. Her phone pressed through her coat against her side, like a dagger stabbing her; anytime she wanted – though *wanted* wasn't the correct term – she could take it out and read endless comments about what an evil person she was.

Lyndsey wasn't returning her calls.

The show had aired, the editors cutting the interview to make Sophia look even worse than she already did. She struggled to see how this had happened, struggled to accept the viciousness with which Caroline had manoeuvred her into position.

Sophia stared when she saw Lyndsey emerge from the back of a chauffeured vehicle. She looked so glamorous and put-together, so distant.

It had been six days since the recording. Lyndsey had forced Sophia to get the train back to Bristol from London, disappearing in her chauffeured vehicle without an invitation.

"Lyndsey," Sophia called, hating the shiver in her voice.

She didn't sound at all like the confident woman she'd

envisioned herself to be. She didn't sound like she was ready to charge into the world and make a difference.

She sounded like what she was: pathetic. And she hated that about herself.

Lyndsey turned, her luxurious hair catching the light, a different kind of creature to Sophia. She felt silly for ever thinking she could be the same as her icon.

Lyndsey rushed over, looking up and down the street; it was clear her biggest concern was being seen in public with the pariah.

"What are you doing here?"

"I... I wanted to see you," Sophia said. "I have to explain."

"There's nothing to explain."

A few feet behind Lyndsey, her security guard lurked, a man in a dark suit and a somehow faceless expression. Sophia knew that if Lyndsey ordered it, he'd drag Sophia away.

"I didn't do it," Sophia said.

"We can't talk here." Lyndsey softened a fraction. Maybe she detected the agony tearing through Sophia. "Come on."

She led her into the hotel, hurried her to the elevator. All the while, Lyndsey was looking around, clearly contemplating the terror of somebody recognising them.

It was like Sophia was an infection.

Lyndsey stood apart from her as they rode the elevator up, the security man standing in the middle.

"I'll let you know if I need anything," Lyndsey said, as they waited outside their adjacent rooms.

"Ma'am."

He walked into his hotel room, and Lyndsey pushed open her door, revealing a luxurious suite with a four-poster bed and a giant desk and a seating area set off to the side.

"What do you *want*?" Lyndsey hissed, standing behind the sofa and clawing into it with her manicured fingernails.

"To explain."

"Are you recording this conversation?" Lyndsey said.

"What? No. I wouldn't do that..."

She trailed off when she realised how ridiculous the declaration must've sounded.

Lyndsey scoffed. "I don't know what you want from me. I thought you were a good person. You tricked me. You tricked everybody. But now I see you for what you are–"

"But you have to listen," Sophia cut in. "I would never do what Caroline said I did. I'd die before I did something so evil. After what happened to her–"

"How can I take a single thing you say seriously?" Lyndsey interrupted. "Caroline has been through so much. She's suffered the worst pain a woman can experience. And you want me to victim blame? To believe that, at her lowest point, she'd invent this lie?"

"I know it's awful. I wouldn't be saying it if it wasn't true."

"True," Lyndsey repeated, as if the word didn't matter.

This wasn't about truth. It wasn't about what had actually *happened*. It was about how people perceived things. No matter what, Sophia would always be the woman who had capitalised on another woman's terror.

"She came to my flat after it happened and–"

Lyndsey raised her hand, her expression turning vicious. "I'm done listening to your lies. You can't just *will* your version of the narrative into existence."

"It's not a version. She sent those messages to my account and–"

"No, no, *no*." Lyndsey threw her hands up. "You can't expect me to believe that a woman, immediately after experiencing..." She shuddered. "*That*. Would do something like this. You can't force me to accept it. It's unthinkable. You call yourself a feminist? A true feminist would never do what you did."

"But I didn't–"

"You *did*." Lyndsey's voice rose, infusing with the passion Sophia had heard in countless podcasts. "There's nothing you could say that would make me accept your version. Nothing."

"You knew this was going to happen. You arranged it with Morgan."

"I have no idea what you're talking about."

"I knew something was off the second we walked in there. The way you were both acting. You planned it. He showed you the messages before the show. You knew I was walking into an ambush and you didn't care."

"What an interesting theory," Lyndsey said, never losing her civilised tone; it was like Sophia was a recalcitrant servant.

"You're going to use this in one of your podcasts. I'm sure you've already arranged an interview with Caroline."

Lyndsey said nothing, but she didn't have to. The slight widening of her eyes, the passing smirk, then the correction of her expression as she composed it into an impassive mask. It said it all.

"Even if what you said is true – which it categorically is *not* – how can you stand there, judging me?" Lyndsey walked around the sofa and stood a couple of feet from Sophia, glaring, hating. "*You* made this happen. You recorded Abbie. You tried to use her situation for fame, rather than to do some good. And then it all became too tempting. You saw your chance. You seized it."

"No," Sophia whispered. "That's not–"

"But you didn't count on Caroline having the bravery and self-possession to call your bluff. You thought you could shame her. It's sickening. *You're* sickening. You disgust me. You need to leave."

"Lyndsey, please..."

"You need to leave *now*. Or I'll call my security."

Mad thoughts fluttered into Sophia's mind: grab Lyndsey by her beautiful hair and throw her to the sofa, leap on her, inflict violence. Let out all the pain stowed inside on her idol.

But, despite what everybody believed, Sophia wasn't a bad person.

Sophia left the hotel room, hugging her arms around her middle. She walked to the elevator. When it opened, a young woman stared at her. She wore a stylish jacket, her hair patterned in an intricate weave.

The woman stepped forward, staring at Sophia. "I know you."

"You must be mistaken."

"You're that *bitch* who blackmailed Caroline Jenkins."

The woman said Caroline's full name the way people say *Leonardo DiCaprio or Robert De Niro*, all one word, as if her celebrity status was firmly cemented.

"I didn't," Sophia said, so sick of professing her innocence.

The woman spat right in Sophia's face.

Sophia was too stunned to react, standing there as the saliva slid down her cheek. The woman shoved past her and stomped down the hallway.

Sophia began to tremble, then she ran for the staircase, taking the steps two at a time.

But she knew she'd never be able to outrun this.

Her life was over.

And deep down, a vicious thought emerged, arising from the layers of righteousness and confidence and all the things she'd clung to during this whole ordeal.

She didn't want to acknowledge it, but it was impossible to avoid.

This was her fault. She'd birthed the whirlpool, and it was swallowing her.

———

At her flat, she stopped. Suddenly, nothing else mattered: not the recording, not Abbie, not Wake-not-woke, not even Lyndsey or Caroline.

Dad stood at her door, wearing a sad oversized coat, his cheeks grotesquely red. He was already crying when he took a step in her direction, his lips shuddering.

This was clearly a big moment for him.

He'd found her.

"Sophia," he whispered, his voice breaking.

Sophia closed off the little-girl part of herself. She wouldn't remember hiding in the bedroom, her knees to her chest, staring at the damp and flaky walls as music pumped, as Dad laughed, as his friends cheered. That had been the original whirlpool, the mayhem of their flat, trying to suck her in and make her like him.

"I've been looking for you," he whispered. "And... and following Abbie."

"Following... what?"

Sophia's nerves were taut, as if there was some violent notion preparing to twist its way into reality. Her dad had been – and clearly still was if the redness in his face was any indicator – a drunk.

"I got her work address from your podcast. Maybe she knew where *you* lived, I thought. So I followed her from work. I had a mate, well, sort of a mate, he drives... he took me there. Followed her car, I mean."

"I don't know what you want me to do with any of this." Sophia's voice was cold, distantly civilised, as she attempted to shut away any feeling. "So you've been stalking Abbie? Congratulations, Dad, I'm *proud* of you. Is that what you want to hear?"

"I even saw her by chance once. In the city. I didn't think it was her at first. She was walking past me. I was sitting in a doorway and... I've seen her photo online. A mate showed me. But I think I scared her."

He was almost crying again. Sophia imagined hugging him, offering what support she could: the support he'd never offered her. She wasn't interested in his stalking stories.

"I've stopped drinking," Dad said after a moment.

Sophia scoffed. "How many days?"

"Just over a week." He sighed, bowed his head. "I wanted to say sorry, Sophia. For everything. For not being the dad you deserved. For not–"

"You don't get to show up a *week* sober and make speeches. You can't just show up, Dad, and expect me to care. A week? Do you want a parade?"

Ignoring him, she took out her keys and opened the main door to her building.

"How many days?" Dad said, his voice cracking. "For you to talk to me?"

"At least a month." Sophia shoved the door open. "Anything less is a joke."

Slamming the door, she went upstairs, into her flat, and opened a bottle of wine.

NO RUNNING

This was the end.
    There was no running.
    The footsteps were too fast.
    There was no going back.

58

CAROLINE

The emails never stopped arriving; the phone didn't stop ringing.

Caroline jolted herself into obsessive activity, finding a suitable agent to represent her on a multimedia basis: book deals, her online modelling career, TV appearances.

But as she worked, she couldn't stop the niggling guilt. She'd seen the things people were saying about Sophia online.

Caroline had done her best to make things right with Abbie, but she'd refused to see reason. Caroline wasn't exactly surprised. Abbie had always led with her emotions, allowing her lust and her jealousy to spur her into stealing Jack away.

But Jack didn't matter anymore; the past didn't matter.

Caroline was going to write a memoir about her journey, bravely detailing the pain she'd experienced at the hands of an assaulter. She was going to help people by sharing the agony; she was going to let people know that they weren't alone.

As she walked through the light Bristol downpour, she tried not to look over her shoulder every few moments. She was experiencing nightmares after what had happened, waking several times pinned to the bed, staring at the ceiling but not seeing it.

She saw that patch of sky instead, the stars through the tall buildings.

Her phone vibrated as she rounded the corner to Sophia's flat.

It was an email: another request for an interview.

She pressed down on the buzzer.

"H-hello?" Sophia said, sounding as if she expected a mob to kick down her door.

"It's me," Caroline replied.

Sophia made a soft whimpering noise. Caroline almost snapped at her to get her act together.

Whatever Sophia had suffered as a result of Caroline's actions, it was nothing compared to what Caroline had endured in that alleyway. It was nothing compared to the hate she felt every time she thought of *him*, the man who believed he could take what he wanted from her without consequences.

"You haven't returned my calls," Sophia said.

"I'm here now. Can I come up?"

The door buzzed then opened. As Caroline ascended the stairs, she tried not to think about the last time she'd been here, when her nerves had sparked and burned so soon after the assault.

Sophia opened the door. She looked dreadful, her hair unwashed, her features pale, her eyes flitting as if she expected an attack any second.

"What do you want?" Sophia said, her tone defeated, no fight left in her at all.

"To talk."

A flicker of fight imbued Sophia, her posture straightening, but it left just as quickly. It was like she could barely summon the energy to speak.

She shrugged, stepping aside.

The flat was a mess, several wine bottles on the coffee table, clothes strewn all over the place. The shards of a shattered coffee mug sat in the corner of the room, gleaming as though in accusation.

Sophia dropped onto the sofa, looking tiny in her dressing gown, immediately picking at the fabric of the sofa. The material was frayed; Caroline guessed she'd been doing that ever since it happened.

"So?" Sophia said lifelessly.

"I..." Caroline looked around the room; it wasn't unreasonable to suspect Sophia of secretly recording this. "Can we go for a walk?"

"You're afraid you'll accidentally tell me the truth and I'll do what I did to Abbie."

"You don't have to feel bad about *that*," Caroline said in disgust. "You heard what she said. She was in the wrong there, not you. Just because you did something even worse, it doesn't mean she's suddenly innocent."

"I can't go for a walk," Sophia said numbly, not even bothering to defend herself. "A woman spat in my face last week. What if it happens again?"

She sat on the sofa next to Sophia.

"What you did was wrong," Caroline said, just in case she was recording.

"Yeah." Sophia laughed grimly. "So, so wrong."

"But you were kind to me that night."

"Yes." Sophia looked at her; the open gaze was too much to stand, and Caroline looked away. "I did my best to help you. You know, I thought we were going to become friends."

"I want to repay you for that kindness," Caroline said, studying the shattered coffee mug, the carpet discoloured.

"Why would you want to give me anything if what you're claiming is true?"

"People are complicated. You were kind... then you ruined it. But you were still kind."

"Sure, that's a narrative. That works."

"What are you going to do for money now?"

"No idea."

Sophia sounded like she didn't care about *anything*. Her weakness was making Caroline uncomfortable.

Caroline would never let herself disintegrate like this. It was good for her that Sophia *was* pulling herself apart – she was in no state to defend herself – but it was still pitiful.

And so tragic Caroline could've wept, if she'd allowed herself: if she hadn't sealed off that part of herself.

"I want to help you financially," Caroline said.

Sophia seemed too defeated to bother recording, but Caroline still knew these words put her at risk. If they came out in public, people would ask why Caroline would possibly offer this woman anything other than a slap across the face.

But her conscience wouldn't leave her alone.

"Why? I tried to blackmail you after you..." Sophia's voice cracked. "After you went through all that..."

She shattered, devolving into sobs, shuddering on the sofa. Caroline shuffled down the cushions and wrapped her arm around her.

She expected Sophia to push her away – it was what Caroline would have done – but instead, Sophia clung to her desperately.

"What did I do? What did I start? Why?"

"It's okay," Caroline whispered, stroking her hair gently. "Let me help you."

"Help me... while you slander me publicly, while you ruin my life."

"It's not slander. We both know that."

Sophia said nothing, just kept crying. A long time passed. Caroline was tempted to offer to help her clean her flat, to meet with her regularly so she could return to a sense of normalcy.

But this was a big enough risk. If people saw them together, the questions would start.

Caroline hadn't endured all that pain to let some sobbing stop her.

"My teaching days are done. I don't know what I'm going to do with the rest of my life."

"Don't worry about the rest of your life. Take it day by day."

Caroline disentangled herself.

"Will you take my money?" she asked bluntly.

Sophia stared with puffy red eyes. There was another flicker, a hint of rage, but it died quickly. She nodded, looking like a little girl who'd finally agreed to go to the dentist.

"You won't see me again," Caroline said, taking the envelope from her pocket and placing it on the coffee table, between two empty bottles of wine.

Sophia said nothing, staring at the envelope.

Caroline walked to the door, then paused, studying the woman... and studying herself, too, the notion that she could make this right. She could admit the truth; she could go public and save Sophia from this miserable existence.

And then what?

Caroline's life would be over.

Her agent would leave her.

No book deals, no financial stability, no interviews, nothing.

Caroline left the flat and walked down the stairs.

Once she walked onto the street, she was ready.

She'd chosen this path, and she wouldn't doubt it ever again.

59

FREDDIE

Freddie didn't tell anybody what Chris had done to him. Maybe there was some shame in this, not wanting to let people know he'd been jumped by that dickhead. But there was also something else; a darkness settled deep inside Freddie, and he knew he was going to do something to make this right.

He stayed in bed in his mum's flat. He'd moved there when he was fifteen, after stuff at his dad's had become too much to handle.

His mum wasn't much better, spending her time snorting whatever she could get her hands on, doing whatever it took for the dealers to give her a little extra. Or it was injecting, and Freddie there, seeing it all, trying to defend her when they got handsy.

And then she'd turn on *him*, throwing him out of the house, siding with the monsters who left bruises on her skin.

As he lay there, day after day, smoking joints and staring through the smoke, he slowly relived his life. His dad who used him as a punchbag for as long as he could remember, the secret early years spent alone in his room, inventing stories and writing them in clumsy block capitals.

His dad had found the notebook. *"What are you, a little queer..."*

Freddie didn't even cringe when he thought about the attack which had followed. It was much the same as the others. Each one had left its mark, it was true, but after a while he'd become too callused. His bruises and scars had become a part of him.

Maybe he'd sometimes let the pain turn him cruel. He could've done better with that. If he'd lived a second life, that was something he would address, the trigger inside of him.

Instead of thinking about the time his dad had dragged him from bed and made him dance for his friends, the leering red-faced dickheads flinging taunts at him, he could make fun of the other kids in school, on the estate. Smash somebody's teeth in and suddenly a boy had all the friends – or hangers-on, it didn't matter – he'd ever need.

Freddie closed his eyes and slept, woke, slept. Every so often, he dragged his battered body to the kitchen and ate something, but then returned to bed.

He was getting ready for what was to come, for what he had to do. It didn't matter what happened after, as long as he did it, made this right.

"Dad, can I have an ice cream?"

A simple request. In the middle of the zoo, his old man reeking of booze and annoyed at even being there. A meaty backhand had sent Freddie into the dirt, blood filling his mouth, and he stared at the ground and told himself not to cry. It would be worse if he cried.

All his life, nothing ever going his way, nothing ever *coming* his way, all the things the rest of the world seemed to take for granted.

His body was healing up. It would be time soon.

He began doing push-ups and sit-ups. His body still ached

and tightened, telling him to rest, but he had to get this over with.

Prison wouldn't be so bad, if it came to that.

Or death. He didn't want to die, obviously, but all right, if he had to. He would.

He'd barely lived anyway, and there was no sign that was going to change.

No real love, no prospects, no job, always waiting for the next fight.

It was a twisted world when a video of a crying teenage girl could've made the difference between him being someone and being no one. But there it was.

He did more and more push-ups, pressing his fists against the stained, threadbare carpet, his teeth gritted.

Freddie got dressed for the first time in over a week, walked into the living room, and kissed his mum on the forehead.

She was passed out from the night before, lying back on the recliner, ashtray balanced on her belly as it often was. She reeked of booze and sweat, but she was still his mum; she'd never hit him, only allowed her boyfriends to do it when she needed her fix.

To Freddie, that meant something. She was better than most.

"What you doing?" she slurred through her sleep.

Or *comedown*. Or *coma*.

"Giving you a kiss, Mum." He could still taste her sweat on his lips as he stood. "And I wanted to tell you…"

"What you giving me a kiss for?" Her eyes were watery and her eyelids fluttered as if it was a struggle to keep them open. "You in trouble?"

"I wanted to tell you I love you. I know you did your best."

"All right..."

"That's it. See you later."

"Get me some fags if you're going out."

Freddie left the flat, put his headphones in and blasted music. The rappers coaxed in his ears, telling him he could get the bag, get the money, make something of himself, *do* something.

"Never let a man disrespect. Catching bullets, no deflect..."

Freddie didn't have a gun. But he had his fists, and that was all he needed.

He walked from his estate to Chris' house. The street was quiet this early, the sun just rising. Freddie's nerves tried to play games with him as he walked up the street.

The beating had been bad. His body pulsed, as if screaming at him to get away.

But how could he, when the door was unlocked?

It was like he was meant to be there.

He pushed it open slowly, slipping inside, hate wrenching at him when he saw the shoes lined up on the rack, neat rows of them, Becky's sport shoes and Chris' trainers and all the rest of it, a whole happy family who had each other no matter what, a messed-up clan who spit on the likes of Freddie, who saw him as dirt, as nothing, as *worse* than nothing.

Fists clenched, he waited on the other side of the door.

This was it.

This was fucking *it*.

He walked inside, across the living room, into the kitchen.

"Hey."

Suddenly, a man was rushing around the kitchen divide.

Freddie moved toward him, hands raised. "Calm down, mate."

"You can't be here."

"Don't tell me where I can fucking *be*."

All his life, that had been the case, his dad telling him with fists he didn't deserve to be in this world, his mum telling him with the drugs and the shouting and the mayhem he didn't belong in her flat. Girls laughing at him if he ever tried to make it serious, more than cheap pleasure.

"You're not really the boyfriend type, are you, Freddie..."

He lashed out, meaning to shove him in the chest. Just a push to let the bastard know Freddie wasn't messing around. He had a posh voice, giving Freddie flashbacks to countless times men with the same type of voice had sneered at him.

But the old idiot took it poorly, stumbled back, tripped over his feet.

He fell and his head made a terrible noise against the floor.

Freddie had pushed him too hard. Who took a hit that poorly?

Goddamn it.

He stared down at the mess.

And that's when he realised, far too late, he didn't want to be a killer.

He wanted to be back in the musty living room with his mum. He wanted to kiss her sweat-cool forehead and tell her he loved her again.

Upstairs, footsteps.

He looked around, heat rising in his body, way too much of it. He was burning up from the inside. Sweat made every inch of his flesh sting.

He was panting, struggling to breathe.

Maybe that's why he chose such a terrible hiding place.

Oh, Christ, he'd made a terrible mistake.

He wished he could take it back already.

All of it, every bad thing he'd ever done.

60

ABBIE

Looking back on her romance with Douglas – if she could think of it in such fancy terms – it was clear to Abbie she'd only thrown herself at him out of warped revenge for what Jack had done. But following the fallout from Morgan's show airing, where most people had sided with Abbie, the very mob Sophia had ignited turning on her, Abbie had found something in Douglas.

They were a strange pairing, and they both knew it, often making jokes about it after they made love.

He'd squeeze her shoulder and nuzzle her hair, and say, *"Look at me, a lofty scholar, a Victorian gent, some might say, down here in the slums with little old you..."*

It was like they were teenagers when she spun on him, aiming tickling hands at his sides. He'd made the mistake of telling her he was ticklish, branding it a *shameful childhood holdover*, and they had plenty of fun with that.

The sex was incredible, but it was more than the sheer collision of their bodies. It was the fact Abbie felt like a woman again, wanted, *needed*.

Douglas was good with Becky, encouraging her to pick up

books, taking her to the library twice in the nine days since Abbie and Douglas had first kissed.

"For a posho, Mum, he's not that bad."

As the days passed, Abbie came to realise something.

Caroline had saved her by springing the trap on Sophia.

But there was something deeper, something Douglas explained one night. *"The longer I spend in this cockroach-ridden business, the more convinced I become that the best strategy to fight this madness is no strategy. Bury one's head in the sand, declare armistice even if only one-sided, and wait... Look, Abbie, people are already moving on. Caroline will make a career for herself. Sophia has sabotaged her career. But as far as the public is concerned, your name is already fading. There are new scandals, new disasters, new intrigues."*

He spoke so eloquently, her unlikely partner.

That was why Abbie had woken with a smile on her face. Even at the dreadful *thunk* noise, she'd been smiling, assuming Douglas had dropped something downstairs.

He was a very in-his-head person, meaning he was quite clumsy at times. That led Abbie to think what a good pair they might make one day. He could handle all the la-di-da stuff and she'd sort the nuts and bolts of life.

She'd walked onto the landing, glad to find Chris gone with his college bag. He seemed much better, more loving and attentive. He'd cooked for them three evenings during the past week. But even with the money from *The Morgan McDermott Show*, Chris had told her that he'd been unable to buy his grandfather's watch back; it had already been sold, apparently.

Despite the pain which still stubbornly clung to them, they were healing, moving on.

Sophia probably never could, but she'd brought that on herself.

Abbie had still been smiling as she'd walked down the stairs, expecting to find Douglas standing in the centre of a dishware disaster, a sheepish grin on his face.

But what she'd found was Douglas looking like a mannequin, his features pale, blood pooling on the kitchen floor around him.

He stared with lifeless eyes, and Abbie stared back from halfway down the stairs, through the balustrade.

———

She hurried toward the sound of footsteps, leaving the kitchen and almost tripping as she moved into the living room.

She'd already called the police, but the bastard was still in there. She could hear him.

Freddie.

He spun, one cheek swollen like he had ball lodged in there, a nasty cut across his eye that was just starting to heal. Abbie's slow mind tried to figure out how Douglas had inflicted so many injuries in such a short time, but no, it wasn't Douglas. The cut looked too old.

Freddie stared like a ghoul. A big teardrop slid down his swollen cheek.

"What did you do?" Abbie screamed.

"I'm..."

"Why? *Why would you do this?*"

"Just take it easy..."

When Freddie approached, Abbie quickly returned to the kitchen. She knew he must be right behind her, imagined his hand looped around her waist any second.

She grabbed a knife from the block and spun, waving it wildly.

The 999 operator was shouting down the phone, just about audible.

Abbie stalked back around the corner, keeping the knife primed, knowing the lowlife could jump out at her any second.

Hopefully, he'd done the smart thing and ran.

Not that he would get away with this. He wasn't clever enough to hide his DNA. And she'd seen him. She'd send him to jail for the rest of his miserable little life.

But he hadn't run, and he wasn't trying to attack her.

He sat against the wall, his legs splayed in front of him, his hands in his lap. His whole body shuddered, wave upon wave of tears sliding down his ruined face.

He began to tremble so badly he was throwing himself against the wall, coughing up spit and mucus, his throat hoarse as he dragged in breaths.

"No," he screamed. *"No no no no!"*

"Get out," Abbie said, waving the knife, because she didn't like what he was making her feel.

She couldn't feel *sorry* for this piece of filth.

He didn't even seem aware she was there.

"What's happening?" the emergency operator said, when Abbie returned to the phone.

She still held the knife, but she didn't think she'd have to use it.

Sirens touched the air.

"I don't know. I think he's having a mental breakdown or something."

Freddie kept screaming, trembling, ending up on the floor with his arms wrapped around himself, rocking like a baby who was waiting for his mother.

As perverse as it was, Abbie had to fight the urge to go to him, to hold him, to tell him everything would be okay.

But there were more important things to consider. She went to Douglas, knelt at his side, talked to him – told his unresponsive body it would be okay, he would make it out of this alive, life wasn't this unfair.

Each statement felt like a lie.

EPILOGUE
TWO MONTHS LATER

Sophia

Sophia plunged her hands into the earth. It felt strangely good to have dirt under her fingernails, to be out in the bracing cool morning, doing something active and making a difference.

It was a small thing, perhaps, volunteering at the local park to help with the upkeep. But it welcomed something into her heart, a fulfilment she was hesitant to brand lest it lose its power. She was listening to an audiobook about the strength of being in the present moment.

Life was moving on, fewer people recognising her, but she'd always wear the brand across her face. The consequences of the evil lie Caroline had told. As the days turned to weeks, Sophia often wished she'd thought to record the conversation in her flat, when Caroline had visited her.

But then what?

It would mean more public warring.

Closing her eyes, she looked up at the sky, letting the

sunlight rest against her face. The organisation for which she was volunteering knew about her past; they'd heard her story.

But this was a place for new beginnings. She worked mostly alongside drug addicts who were reforming their lives. She sensed judgement from a few of them, a certain distance maintained so she didn't infect them with whatever deep wrongness had caused her to manipulate an assault survivor for fame.

She would have to accept that: not controlling her own narrative.

Standing, she wiped her hands on her muddy trousers and looked down at the section she'd cleared. The weeds were piled up next to her, and just then, as if fate had a hand to play in this, the audiobook narrator spoke as if directly to her.

"If you cannot take joy in the small things, even your biggest victories will feel bland. You'll never be able to stop and smell the roses, as the saying goes..."

Sophia intentionally made herself breathe deeply, bringing the cool air into her lungs, letting the scents of nature wash through her.

She was okay for money, for a little while. Caroline had seen to that. But soon, she'd start looking for jobs.

The thought tore open a pit in her, a hole in which memories lived: smiles in the classroom, the laughter of her students. *Gross misconduct*, the word bouncing around her mind, reminding her of what she'd done.

But though it had ruined her, she knew she'd only ever wanted to make a difference. To spread awareness. To help the world.

So she made this her world, this park with the crumbling walkway and nature constantly warring to reclaim pieces of it.

She'd think about jobs later, think about the path the rest of her life would take.

For now, this was enough. It had to be.

The whirlpool had spit her out. She hadn't landed where she'd planned, but she'd landed, and she had to be grateful for that.

"Want some help?" Dad called over, looking far healthier than when he'd first appeared at her flat. His cheeks weren't as red, his eyes clearer. Lately, when he spoke about his stalking of Abbie, there was shame in his tone.

The wounds hadn't healed. The neglect. The arguments. The mess of her childhood.

But the rest of the world had thrown her away. Dad hadn't. He was stubbornly standing by her side. Whenever she'd needed him – so far – he'd been there, day or night.

Perhaps that had been the point of this all along. To bring them together. To build something good from the bad.

She returned his smile. "That would be wonderful. Thanks, Dad."

Caroline

This was the life Caroline had fought for; it made it all worth it.

She was sitting in the back of a chauffeured car, driving through New York, gazing out the window at the skyscrapers and remembering those other tall buildings, the dank alleyway, the agony.

And before that, the pain of losing Jack, the pain of never being enough.

But she was *more* than enough. Despite how she'd arrived at this position, she was here, and she was making a difference. She was on her way to record her second podcast with Lyndsey La

Rossa, discussing the prevalence of violence against women and the role toxic masculinity had to play in it.

It was a topic Caroline was extremely well-versed in.

That perverted freak who'd assaulted her – she had to sit back, fold her hands, calm her breathing; it always hurt to think about him... that *freak* had thought because he saw a certain version of her online, he had a right to her body, a right to take whatever he wanted.

It was the same all over the world, men taking what they thought they deserved from women and then discarding them. It was what Jack had done to her.

Women all over the world viewed Caroline as an icon. Her online businesses had soared in success. She would never have to worry whether she was *somebody* ever again.

The evidence was all around her. It was *on* her, the diamond rings clutching her fingers reassuringly, the fur coat so welcoming as she snuggled into it. The silk sheets, the penthouse hotel suites, the evidence of her success singing to her every morning when she woke up.

The car came to a stop.

"Sorry, miss," the driver said, lowering the partition. "Accident up ahead. Might take a while to pick our way through."

He spoke with such careful respect, as if he was afraid of upsetting her. Lots of people spoke to her like that these days.

She wasn't sure she liked it, but it was far better than the alternative: to people speaking down to her, humiliating her for the choices she'd made.

"Don't worry about it," she told him.

He let out a breath of relief. Maybe he thought she was going to be a diva about it.

Caroline rested her head against the glass, closed her eyes.

She tried not to think of Abbie, Douglas, all that nastiness.

But sometimes, it emerged in her mind like a monster ready to devour.

There were consequences, the beast told her; everything caused a ripple, and it was impossible to know how deep the wounds would go until the cut was made.

Becky

Becky stood at the edge of the lake, letting the breeze caress her face. It was peaceful out here, a secluded corner in the Somerset countryside. They'd rented a cabin, getting away from the day-to-day stress of life.

Freddie had pled guilty in the station, admitting to his crimes. Becky and Chris had expected him to mark Chris as the ultimate cause for what he'd done, but Freddie hadn't; he'd taken his punishment with a sense of warped pride. This didn't cure the guilt her brother felt. It had changed him, made him softer around the edges, less sure of himself.

"Mind some company?" Chris said, walking up beside her.

He had his hands stuffed in his pockets, his body, his general aura seeming taut.

But he smiled. Becky could tell it was for her benefit, but it didn't make any difference. A smile was a smile.

"Or am I cramping your style?"

"Not much style to cramp," Becky said, aiming a grin back at him.

"Mum said they'll be out in a minute. She wants to take a walk down the lane. Fancy it?"

The smile felt more real this time. With the sun shining

down, it was... not *easy*, exactly, but it was possible to forget about everything which had happened, about Ms Lancaster and the TV show and the sex tape.

It was possible to push the image of Caroline somewhere dark, somewhere Becky never had to think about it.

Sure, she popped up on TV from time to time, and Becky knew she'd blown up massively online, not just on her cam-girl website. She had large followings on all the social media platforms.

School had become a problem, the kids teasing Becky, but she pushed through. She couldn't think, *This is what Dad would have wanted...*

No, she had to push through for *her*, for *her* future.

She was done with drama, with causing Mum hassle. She was done with taking the wrong path.

Douglas had helped her with that. He'd encouraged her to read, had pointed her in the direction of books she'd enjoy. She'd felt silly at first, curled up in her bedroom flipping the pages.

Then, magic – a love for it, sinking into the story, everything else drifting away.

Ever since Douglas had put that first book in her hand, she'd read every night for hours. She didn't have to think about the snide comments at school, the shame, any of it when her face was pressed between the pages.

She was wondering if she could *write* books one day. That would be crazily cool.

"How are we all feeling this fine day?" Mum said, walking up behind them.

Becky turned to find her pushing Douglas in his wheelchair. Freddie's assault had left him neurologically damaged. He was recovering, slowly, but speech and mobility were still massive issues.

He sat placidly in the chair, a vacant look on his face.

But when he met her eye, his lip twitched, just a little, in the beginnings of a smile.

THE END

A NOTE FROM THE PUBLISHER

Thank you for reading this book. If you enjoyed it please do consider leaving a review on Amazon to help others find it too.

We hate typos. All of our books have been rigorously edited and proofread, but sometimes mistakes do slip through. If you have spotted a typo, please do let us know and we can get it amended within hours.

info@bloodhoundbooks.com

Made in the USA
Monee, IL
31 July 2023

40190110R00204